Ada's Children

ALSO BY LAWRENCE HOGUE

nonfiction

All the Wild and Lonely Places: Journeys in a Desert Landscape

fiction

Desert Trilogy

Daring and Decorum, a Highwayman Novel

Ada's Children

Lawrence Hogue

Glass Half Full Books
Midland, Michigan

This novel is a work of fiction. Names, characters, places, and incidents either are the products of the author's imagination or are used fictitiously, and any resemblance to actual persons, living or dead, business establishments, events, or locales is entirely coincidental.

Glass Half Full Books
Midland, Michigan

Cover face illustration by agsandrew on shutterstock

Cover design by Mari Christie

Proofreading by Abigail Provenzano

FOR DIANE

PROLOGUE

KITRAN peered into the Howling Forest, squinting through shadows between closely spaced trees. He took a deep breath, trying to slow his racing heart.

The wolves, or whatever they were, had been howling off and on all night. He'd slept within earshot of the forest, trying to bolster his courage, but the shrieks and howls had only grown worse this morning as he came to the wooded edge. Wolves were not so unusual, not with his many years trapping beaver, otter, and fox. But now he heard something else, something worse, the growls and yelps of some unimaginable beast. And screams, as if the beast was tearing a person limb from limb.

But he couldn't turn back. He would show his people Kitran was no coward. No more would they call him "Little Kit." And how much worse could the Howling Forest be, compared to the life he'd lived these past years? Even if the wolves got him, or if Lytta, the Angel of Wrath, sentenced him to die, it would be a mercy. Besides, the old stories said that those who dared break the taboo against entering the forest had two chances. Only on their third attempt did they disappear without a trace. But if he made it through, he'd learn at last what was beyond the trees, where the Goddess Ada, Mother of the Five Peoples, forbade them to go.

And if he made it back, he would be a hero. No more bowing and scraping before the great hunters of bison and bear and deer. No more begging for scraps from the women who didn't appreciate the warm furs he brought them. No more being ignored by the girls from the other villages during the annual Rendezvous. He'd have his choice of a mate. She would gather greens and berries for him, sew and mend his clothes, provide him with children. Most important, care for him in his old age, which seemed nearer every winter.

He took a deep breath and stepped into the forest. He took another step, and another. Nothing jumped out at him. The sounds seemed to recede before him and spread out on either side. He kept going, pushing his way through the undergrowth between the trees. He couldn't find a path, but continued in the direction he thought would take him straight through the forest.

He lost track of time. The forest seemed to go on and on. Sometimes the howls and screams came closer on one side or the other and he turned away from them. At last, he wasn't sure which way he was going. The oaks, maples, and cedars grew too close together to cast shadows or to give him a glimpse of the sun. He began to wish he'd never come. He'd just die here, lost in the forest.

Then he remembered his worst moment, last winter. He'd been out checking his snares when a blizzard caught him. He staggered back into the village half-frozen, falling in the snow fifty paces from his hut. His neighbors passed him by, offering no help, telling him he should have known the storm was coming. And the greatest indignity: the young huntress, Sila, the only girl accepted into the Hunt since the Wise Women were young, helped him up, speaking kind words. She supported him as he hobbled into his hut and brought him a steaming bowl of broth. The final blow to his pride. Brought so low that he needed the help of a girl, one who was a far better hunter than he could ever be. After she left, he'd turned his face to the drafty bison-hide wall and hoped the cold would take him at last.

But he hadn't died then, and he wouldn't die now.

A change in the beast noises shook him from his reverie. The sounds were behind him and getting closer. Less howling, more yips and barks, and the rustle of branches. They were hunting him! He broke into a run. He tried looking back over his shoulder, but the dogwoods and buckthorn closed behind him as he pushed through. He kept running, his neck tingling in apprehension of rending fangs and slashing claws.

He saw daylight ahead and made for it. A buzzing noise came from that direction, growing as loud as a thousand bees as he got closer. He couldn't worry about that now.

He burst into a clearing and the sight before him made him forget the wolves. Lytta, without a doubt. She shimmered like sunlight glinting off rippling water, her curved wings wafting gently, holding her aloft. She was larger than he'd expected, a giant three times the height of any person. It was hard to make out her face—hard to make out what she was. She seemed not quite corporeal, or like she was made of many small, buzzing things. But how should an angel look? He knew only that she was angry, as he should have expected. The insect whine made her seem yet more furious.

"Go back, mortal!" She had to shout to be heard over the buzzing, her voice booming across the clearing. With a shimmering, vibrating arm, she gestured back the way he'd come. "The Goddess Ada forbids any of your kind from entering the forest. You know this."

He fell to his knees. "Oh, Angel Lytta, hear me! There's nothing for me back in the Land. I must pass through and see what lies beyond. If this displeases you, then I offer my life."

"Why would you throw it away?"

"Because the people of my village treat me with contempt, and it's the same in all the other villages of the Land. No one looks twice at a lowly trapper, at least one as poor as I. And now I am growing older. The chance to take a mate has passed me by. I face many lonely years, and a lonelier death."

"Such is the fate of mortals, to grow old and die alone."

"It just doesn't seem fair. I've worked hard at my trapping, though not always with success." He hoped the angel wouldn't catch him in this lie. He was known for lacking diligence, a trait that had only grown worse as his prospects dimmed. But he bore on. "Don't I deserve someone to look after me in my old age? I thought if I could see what's beyond the Howling Forest, and bring back some proof, I would finally earn my place in the village, and live to a ripe old age."

"Foolish mortal! Go back, or you will be punished in ways far worse than death."

He looked at Lytta and weighed his chances. She hovered in the middle of the clearing. If he could only get around her! He had to try.

He got up on all fours, then launched into a sprint, angling for one side of the clearing beyond the angel.

"Stop! I command you!" She leaned toward him, outrage written across her face. Or not quite a face, but something made of many parts, all moving at once to form this ghastly visage, with two holes for its eyes, its mouth open as if to devour him. The buzzing was nearly unbearable now. He put his head down and ran for the trees.

He couldn't see Lytta once he entered the forest, but her noise was all around him, and from behind came the howls of the wolves.

A pinprick in his neck. He reached up and pulled out the dart, its shiny, thin point made from a substance far harder and sharper than any arrow point or bone needle he'd ever seen. The buzzing and howling withdrew and the forest grew quiet.

He slowed to a walk to catch his breath. Was the angel letting him go? That made no sense. Neither did waiting to discover her true intentions. He broke into an easy trot, making for what he hoped was the forest's far edge.

He lost track of time again. Lytta and the wolves returned, this time from within his own head. The angel's leering face rushed toward him, and he saw the wolves rushing at him too. And far worse, beasts out of nightmares, six-legged, eight-legged, two-headed monsters with double rows of sharp fangs dripping green slime. And always the buzzing, the incessant buzzing.

Another pinprick to the neck, but he was running too fast to bother with it. It wasn't long before his legs grew heavy. He slowed to a walk, soon falling to all fours to crawl away from his tormentors. They kept coming as he fell forward on his face, too drowsy to fight them off, not caring if he slept forever. And then he knew no more.

1
THE HUNT

SILA urged Shadow on, the horse's hooves thundering over the sloping grassland. The wounded bison was almost within bowshot, the Howling Forest just ahead. Behind her, Jun shouted for her to stop. But he was far back, and her prey was right in front of her, its massive hump looming above her as she came nearer. Only a few more strides. She let go of Shadow's mane and pulled her bowstring taut, sighting down the arrow.

Then the horse was gone from under her and she was in the air. In that frozen moment, she knew Shadow must have stumbled into a gopher hole. She hoped the horse was all right.

She tucked and rolled out of instinct, coming to a stop on all fours, her bow gripped in one hand, the arrow lost in her flight. She stood up. Nothing felt broken. She was lucky her people hadn't burned this prairie recently, the tallgrass growing thick enough to cushion her fall.

Shadow rose to her feet, seeming unhurt.

"Look out, it's coming back!" Jun shouted.

With its wide horns, the bison had found no escape in the dense forest. Now Sila stood in its only path to freedom.

Somehow, one arrow remained in her quiver after the fall. She nocked it as the beast charged, slowed somewhat by the arrow Jun had put in it, the arrow that should have killed it. She crouched, letting it come closer. Her aim and timing would have to be perfect. The bison lowered its head, its long, curving horns aimed right at her.

"Sila!" Jun shouted again, his horse racing past as he tried to distract the beast. His second arrow flew high of its mark. The bison kept coming.

Forty paces. Thirty. Twenty. There was the spot, the narrow span of chest visible between its shoulder and the massive bulk of its head. Sila let the arrow fly and leapt aside, narrowly avoiding a slashing horn. She rolled and came up in a crouch, then ran toward Shadow to retrieve her spear.

But there was no need. The bison was down and breathing its last. She walked over to it, her heartbeat gradually returning to normal. Jun, off his horse, approached from the other side, silent for now. She knew he would never interrupt such a sacred moment.

The bison's eyes still glowed with the light of life. She spoke the traditional words of thanks to the bison for giving its life that the People might live. To Artemis, Goddess of the Hunt, for keeping all the hunters safe. To Ada, Mother of the Five Peoples, for ensuring the game was plentiful. The prayer done, she ended the animal's suffering, drawing her chert-bladed knife across its windpipe. The beast's life-blood gushed onto the green summer grass, the light went out of its eyes, and it was over.

Jun came a step closer, his light brown skin glistening as his chest rose and fell, the sunlight playing across the ripples of his abdomen. She concentrated on his eyes, two wide, pale moons.

"Sila, what were you thinking?"

"I was thinking to bring food to our people. What were you thinking?"

"That I was about to see my best friend trampled or gored. You know better than to get separated from the rest of the Hunt, especially this close to the Howling Forest."

The forest wasn't living up to its name today. No wolves howling, nor any other beast out of nightmares. The horses grazed calmly nearby, not rearing and snorting and threatening to run off as they usually would.

"You're the one who's always wondering what's in there, and beyond."

He gave the trees a glance. "But what if…?" The lost look on his face was both sweet and provoking.

"What if what?" She turned away to check on Shadow. The horse seemed all right, but she had to make sure. It was a miracle the mare hadn't snapped a leg. Then there would have been two animals to butcher, and a long walk home.

"What if you hadn't jumped in time?" His voice was quieter, as if he didn't want to speak his fear.

"But I did, Artemis be praised." She took a strip of old, soft leather and began cleaning her knife, giving silent thanks to the Goddess of the Hunt.

"You might have slipped. Or jumped too late."

She tossed her head back to get the hair out of her face. "Would you ask Drin or Tio these questions?" Drin was the Chief of the Hunt, the most revered hunter among their people.

He shook his head. "Sila, you know that's different."

"Different how?"

He looked away. "Don't make me say it."

Of course he couldn't say it. It was forbidden. No young hunter could take a woman from his own village as a mate. Not that she wanted a man anyway, not Jun or any other young hunter. Yet she sometimes had to remind herself of this when Jun was nearby.

"I understand," she said, her tone softening. "But I'm fine. I know what I'm doing, little brother."

"Don't call me that!" He always protested when she used this pet name for him, and not just because at nineteen he was only a year younger and had long ago grown a hand taller. They were of different parents, though the Wise Women called all the children of the village brothers and sisters. She only called him "brother" to put him off.

He was still glaring at her when the rest of the hunting party rode up. She braced herself for the tongue-lashing from Drin. It would be a thousand times worse than anything Jun could offer.

Ever since she'd first picked up a bow, Sila's only dream was to follow Drin's path, to become Chief of the Hunt. But this was no way to do it. Hunters were supposed to work together, not dash recklessly off, no matter how valuable the prey. Yet in the moment, it hadn't seemed reckless at all, simply a challenge to match her skill. Those were the moments she lived for, and she wouldn't let Jun or Drin take them away.

She put a brave face on, gesturing at the fallen animal as her leader dismounted. "Ada provides, my chief."

"I see Ada hasn't provided you with the sense of a gopher. You're a fine hunter, Sila, but if you do that again, you'll be foraging for tubers and berries with your mother and sister full-time."

Sila felt the heat rise in her cheeks. Off to one side, Jun covered his grin.

~~*

The sun had reached its solstice a few days past, leaving the hunters plenty of daylight to dress their kills and find a camp farther from the Howling Forest. Drin insisted on the move, not daring to spend the night near that fearsome place. The forest was quiet now, but who knew what sounds might come from it after night fell? No one had slept so near it since the Heroes of Old.

The Hunting Chief's anger subsided once they were gathered around the fire. He presented Sila with one of her kill's long, curving horns, as was her due, to add to her growing collection.

Afterward, with the sun setting behind them, she and Jun lingered at the dying campfire while the others saw to their horses or found spots to bed down. Even at this distance from the Howling Forest, they were still high up, with a good view across the Land. By some trick of the last light, it seemed they could see all the way across the only home they'd ever known, a distance of many days' walk. Green grasslands alternated with stands of bur oaks and cedars and cottonwoods along the rivers, with here and there a shimmer marking a wetland. Overhead, the first stars had come out. The whole world was alive in beauty, filled with spirits. Sila just wanted to sit here and soak it in, to hear what the spirits had to tell.

But Jun didn't care for any of this. "That dark line on the horizon must be the Howling Forest on the other side, don't you think?"

"Could be, I don't know." She'd never been that far, only to her people's hunting grounds, south and west of the village, and to the summer meeting grounds in the center of the Land.

"It's not that far. We could ride there in a couple of days."

"But why?"

"To see what's over there." She knew what he really meant—to see if anything lay beyond the Howling Forest, where it was forbidden to go. She'd seen the way he kept looking at it as they dressed her kill.

"It'll be the same as here, but with the People of the Eagle or the People of the Deer. We'll see all of them at the Rendezvous."

They were silent for a time. More stars emerged as the sky turned black. It wasn't long before a traveling star rushed by on its regular course across the sky. She'd sometimes see several of these in a few hours of stargazing, as if the sky world was speaking directly to her.

It seemed the traveling star had a different message for Jun. "Why does that one move so fast when the others almost stand still?"

"Ada only knows." Everyone knew that Ada had placed the stars against the black dome of night to cheer the People and give some light when the moon didn't show its face. How Ada chose to arrange them was up to her, and not for the People to question.

Yet Jun always did, constantly asking what made the stars change from season to season, and why some moved differently from the others. And always, what was beyond the Howling Forest, if anything. Why couldn't he be content with the way things were? Sila put it down to him living alone. He'd been nearly an orphan from early on, when his father disappeared and his mother paired up with another man. Sila's parents had practically raised him from then on, but he still had a lot of time to look at the stars and ponder.

Jun was silent, his gaze following the traveling star until it disappeared near the horizon. "The sky seems so huge, yet the Land seems so small. This can't be all there is."

Not this again! "But it is, the Heroes proved it."

That got Jun's eyes glowing. "Yes, and if only we could be like them. What bravery they had!"

Shortly after the Creation, the Heroes of Old walked in a great circle for days upon days, staying within a stone's throw of the Howling Forest and the fearsome noises that came from within. Thus they showed the People the extent of the Land Ada had created for them.

"Yes," Sila said. "Every child knows this. Why doesn't it satisfy you?"

"No, the question is, why does it satisfy *you*? You're not stupid, Sila."

"How flattering." She went back to looking at the stars, wishing the conversation would end.

"I didn't mean it like that. It's just…"

"Look at all this." She gestured over the forests and meadows below them. "What more do I need? I like my life. I've found my path."

He sighed. "But there must be something left to discover. Something must exist beyond the Howling Forest, otherwise why does Ada forbid us to enter? What is she afraid we'll find?"

"Maybe you should ask Little Kit." Two weeks past, Ada's Helpers had deposited their people's poorest trapper at the edge of the village, as happened whenever someone dared venture into the Howling Forest. Most didn't try again.

"I've thought about it. But that would only make the Wise Women more suspicious." He stared into the fire for a time, pursing his lower lip the way he did whenever he was trying to puzzle out a problem. "It sounds like Lytta was trying to scare Little Kit, with those terrifying visions he kept raving about."

"But it was only his first attempt. You know what would happen on the third."

"Do I? All anyone knows is that no one ever comes back."

She had no answer.

He poked the fire with a stick. "Maybe beyond the Howling Forest there's a place where no one would treat us as brother and sister." He didn't look at her as he said it.

She had to put an end to this. She was never going to pair with a man, and besides, Ada's law kept males and females of the same village from lying together. But this wasn't enough for Jun, and his mooning around had only grown worse over the past year. Sometimes he hardly talked to her. Other times he treated her as usual, though his obvious efforts at self-control strained everything between them. She hated it. They'd been best friends since they both could walk.

"I think you should take a mate at the Rendezvous," she said. "You've proven yourself as a hunter. The Wise Women will give their blessing."

"You think I want to bind myself to a stranger? I hardly know any of those girls."

"That's because you never talk to them. Every Rendezvous, you're either hanging around with me or drinking with the other hunters. You're too busy to notice all the girls giving you the eye."

"So you want me to bring one of them back to our village? What then?"

The way he looked at her, the questioning look in his soft brown eyes—it nearly melted her resolve. Jun wasn't the tallest or the strongest hunter, but he was quick of foot, quick of wit, and quick to laugh, at least when he wasn't moping about her. The regular planes of his face, his smooth brown skin, and his thick shock of dark hair made him handsome.

But it was mostly his eyes. If she looked too long into them, her heart would beat faster, sending a warmth spreading from her center into her thighs. It was the same when one of her girlfriends rubbed balm into her sore muscles after a hunt. A safe feeling with a girl, but not with Jun. She always looked away from him, as she looked away now before speaking.

"Then you would stop feeling this way about me. We would go back to being friends, like we used to be."

"But someday you'll take a mate and move to his village." She could hear the effort it took to keep the bitterness out of his voice.

"Ha!" she scoffed. "What do I need a man for, when I've got my pick of half a dozen girls just in our own village?"

"Your followers, you mean."

Followers—he loved to tease her by calling them that. It was going a bit far, though they did look up to her, she had to admit. She was the first girl to join the hunt since Val and Luri, the oldest Wise Women, were young. She'd just turned seventeen at the time, and a year later the Wise Women had declared her a woman grown, with the right to take her own mate.

"Any one of those girls could keep me happy. I'm a hunter, I need someone to gather and sew for me, and tend to my wounds. Only the other day, Brina said she'd never look at another hunter during the Rendezvous if I pledged myself to her."

"You mean you'd become an auntie?"

"Sure. What's wrong with that? No one says a thing about Val and Luri or the other female couples. The young mothers love the extra hands to help with their babies."

"Nothing's wrong with it. Except one thing. The most important thing."

"Jun, can't you see? It's not just the law, and it's not just you. Can you imagine me foraging with the other women, and with a couple of babes in tow? Or sewing and mending for a hunter? It's bad enough my parents make me join in the foraging between hunts, but I'll put an end to that after this Rendezvous."

He shook his head. "I'd never ask that of you."

"But the babies would come, and that would be the end of my life as a hunter." No one, not Jun and not her parents, would keep her from following her path.

And then there were the Great Sleeps. Sila would never forget her first one, when she was five, and her sister, two. Ada's Helpers arrived with scented smoke, putting the entire village into a sleep filled with sweet dreams. That wasn't so bad. But afterward, the young mothers with two or perhaps three children found they could bear no more babies. And worse, her own mother had been ill and despondent for weeks after. The Wise Women said this was the way of the world, but Sila had vowed it was never going to happen to her.

"But don't you want to know why, Sila? Why does Ada put all these rules and restrictions on us? If she even exists! No one has seen her in generations. Maybe she's just a story the Wise Women tell us so we'll follow their rules."

This was madness. Of course Ada existed. Her spirit ran through everything, from the smallest blade of grass to the deer and the bison, and to the People as well. "What about Lytta? What about Ada's Helpers? People have seen them, and not only Little Kit. The Wise Women didn't just make them up."

Jun had no answer for that. They sat in silence, but the questions hung between them, as thick as the smoke of the dying fire.

2

ELECTION NIGHT

NOVEMBER 2040

"I can't believe it," Carol Marsh said. She wanted to throw her drink at the largescreen, but it belonged to her friends, Shondra and Michael. "Walker was supposed to be running away with this election."

"It's looking bad, but I'm not surprised," said Michael, returning from the kitchen with a fresh Scotch, his frame nearly filling the doorway. "Nothing in this fucking country surprises me."

Shondra, sitting next to Carol on the couch, stared at the screen, probably adding up the poll results from different states scrolling across the bottom. An analyst gestured enthusiastically at a tiny spot on the Pennsylvania map, his lips moving without sound. They'd long since turned down the volume; the talking heads had no more idea who would be the next president than they did.

"I just thought we were better than this—that we'd *become* better than this," Carol said.

Shondra mimed an explosion with her hands, adding "Kaboom!" for a sound effect. She gave Carol a sympathetic smile.

"I know," Carol said. "Another white liberal illusion up in smoke. I thought we'd stopped the fascists and white supremacists for good back in the twenties—or at least driven them into a part of the country hardly anyone cares about."

Shondra's smile turned wry. "Out of sight, out of mind, right?"

"Ha! If only," said Michael, glaring at the screen. He stroked his closely trimmed beard the way he did whenever he was worried.

For months, the country's media had been flooded with images from the Interior Northwest Semi-Autonomous Zone, the base from which Richard Cass had launched his improbable run for president. The spots were filled with shots of happy tech workers, healthy people outdoors, and the vibrant nightlife of Boise—all completely white. "No riots here!" was the message that didn't need to be said out loud. Along with the racist dog-whistles and outright bullhorns, there was plenty of Russia- and China-baiting, pledges to rebuild the nuclear arsenals, and a determination to go back to coal and oil for fuel, despite the destruction the climate crisis had already wrought.

Carol never thought the rest of the country would fall for it. She'd been too naïve. Her friends knew better, especially Michael, a former professor of Black History at the same liberal arts college in Minneapolis where Carol had once taught. They'd originally bonded over their shared activist background, his in the racial justice movement, hers in the George Floyd protests her senior year in high school and later with the Extinction Rebellion occupations.

On the screen, Florida switched from gray to red. "Shit," Michael said, coming over to sit next to Shondra on the couch. He set his drink down hard on the glass coffee table, sloshing a few drops. "Walker was supposed to carry that state."

"Too bad the whole place didn't just wash into the Gulf of Mexico," Carol said. "I'd gladly trade Orlando for New Orleans."

"Carol!" Shondra glanced back at the screen. "I didn't know enough white people still lived down there to push Cass over the top."

Carol looked from Michael to Shondra and back again.

Michael appeared to choose his words carefully. "Babe, they're letting them vote in Florida even if they've been back in New York or Michigan since Miami went under."

"Sorry. I guess I've been…busy." She looked down at her drink.

"It's all right," said Carol. "We know you don't have time to follow politics like we do."

Carol had lost her teaching post two years before, but she tried not to envy her friend's continued employment. As a leading AI researcher, Shondra was secure in her position at the University of Minnesota, the irony lost on none of them that her work had indirectly led to Michael and Carol losing their jobs to instructorbots. They'd both managed not to hold Shondra's work against her, or at least Carol thought they had. Shondra would tell them, "Whatever humans *can* do, we *will* do. So if there are going to be AIs, Black folks better help create them." A racist robot overlord was the last thing they needed, though Shondra always insisted they'd never have to deal with an AI apocalypse. Life wasn't a sci-fi movie.

AI overlords or not, Michael and Carol both wound up at the end of a long list of those made redundant by automation and artificial intelligence: assembly-line workers first, then truckers, wait staff, retail clerks, call center workers, line cooks, janitors, voice actors, personal accountants, half of all lawyers. All now eking out an existence on Universal Basic Income, which wasn't truly universal and hardly covered the basics. It was hard not to feel resentful, if not toward Shondra, then toward AI in general.

Fortunately, Michael had landed on his feet with his political podcasts, quickly earning more than the equivalent of two UBI units. This was called "shooting the donut hole," since the government took away fifty cents of UBI for every outside dollar earned. Carol, laid off a year later, had taken longer to make the adjustment. Now she scratched a living with tutoring and a few scraps of curriculum design. These side gigs would never allow her to reach the magic double UBI marker, but with her clients paying in crypto under the table, she'd managed to stay out of the donut hole.

"Let's talk about something else," Shondra said. "Carol, how's your novel coming?"

Carol shrugged. Writing fiction was her way of pursuing the self-actualization awaiting the masses once they were released from drudge work. "I try to get in a thousand words every day. I'll soon have a hundred thousand words to shove in a drawer—or post on *Writers and Readers*, same thing. It fills the time between tutoring sessions."

"Oh, come on, it's going to be great. Better than anything an AI can produce, right?"

Carol could barely remember when that statement might have seemed like a joke. Of course she could write better than an AI! But that was before AustenBot. For a fleeting time after the release of the large language models, the human novelist had struggled to hang on, becoming more AI content manager than writer. But with the advent of AustenBot, readers simply entered keywords and answered a few questions, and the service would spit out whatever number of novels they wanted, all for a low monthly subscription price. No writers needed, just coders and accountants. These days, even human self-fulfillment was outsourced to machines.

True, some writers had found followings on platforms like *Writers and Readers* and others. If you could find "a thousand true fans," then you could earn a living. But the amount of online interaction growing that kind of following would take—she just wasn't made for that.

"Better, yes. More marketable? I doubt there are many readers left who can tell the difference. Besides, who reads books anymore?" People were too busy with their MINDs—Multimedia Interactive Narrative Devices. Carol had avoided them like heroin. She'd seen the blank looks her former students wore after they'd spent too much time at a game farm, the imprints of the VR headsets still visible around their eyes.

Shondra, as always, pushed back against her pessimism. "Honey, it's like I keep telling you, bots may technically be able to do a job, but people are still going to want the human touch in certain areas."

"You betcha they will," Carol said, employing her mother's best Minnesota accent. Sometimes she just couldn't help herself.

Shondra glared sideways at her. "Professions, you know what I mean."

"Come on, babe," Michael said. "Blondie's right, that's not even true for sex anymore."

Shondra gave him a playful slap on the arm. "Carol, I can't believe you let him call you that."

"He's the only one who gets away with it," she said with a smile.

Shondra wouldn't be distracted from her point. "It won't be long until people wake up and realize they want interactions with real, conscious humans—at least until AIs become conscious themselves, which is years off. Look, just the other day I was down at the coffee shop, and you know what I saw?"

"A human serving coffee?"

Shondra looked at Carol as if she'd suggested driving herself to work. "No, of course not. A singer, a real human singer, with a guitar and everything. And she was singing a song she wrote herself."

"Maybe she can get a gig at the Smithsonian. 'Diorama with live singer-songwriter.'"

"*Human* singer-songwriter," Shondra corrected her, "but yeah. Or like that writer, Justin Tovar. Maybe you could get some billionaire to give you a gig like that."

"Maybe, but I doubt I'd do very well ensconced in a glass office, with a bunch of the billionaire's rich friends gawking at the quaint writer at work. He'd probably want me to give weekly seminars, glimpses into the life of an anachronism or something."

"Shit, there goes Virginia." Michael was still paying attention to the results while they tried to distract themselves. Shondra looked at the screen, getting that abstracted look she had whenever she ran numbers in her head. Except now, Carol thought she looked more worried.

"Michael, you don't think Cass is serious about these voluntary racial homelands, do you?" Carol asked.

"It would be suicidal to think anything else. And 'voluntary,' my ass."

"But he can't get away with it," Shondra said. "We'll still have the House."

"Oh, then no one has anything to worry about," said Carol.

Michael was leaning forward, elbows on knees, gripping his empty glass in both hands. "He'll just declare a national emergency and claim extraordinary powers. He's already said that's the first thing he's going to do after the inauguration. He'll probably include it in the inaugural address."

"But the courts…"

Michael gave a derisive snort.

Shondra glared at him. "Your activist friends at No Escape sure gave him a boost. It's probably why he's winning."

"No Escape is a tiny fringe of the Majority-Minority Power Movement," Michael said. "Cass is only using it as a pretext. If it wasn't that, he'd find something else. Besides, they didn't do that much damage to EarthXit's facilities."

"Enough to scrub flights for the rest of this Mars launch period. They put the colonists' lives at risk."

Michael got up, pacing in front of the screen. "Black and brown lives are at risk every day. Those rich white folks helped make this bed, they should have to lie in it."

Shondra shook her head. "What a way to give power to our enemies."

This was the latest round in an old argument for the couple, one that went right back to the day they'd met. Carol never got tired of hearing that story: Michael protesting outside a police technology conference, Shondra on her way in to present a paper on bias in facial recognition. When another activist got in Shondra's face, making comments about her straightened hair, Michael used his imposing presence to screen the guy out of the way. He escorted Shondra the rest of the way in. By the time he came back out, they'd exchanged numbers.

Carol couldn't imagine life without either of them. After her layoff, she'd thought for a minute or two about applying somewhere out of state, but that would have meant leaving these friends. Now that she had little reason to visit her former campus, they had become her entire social circle. At least, that's what she told herself. But really, she just didn't have a knack for keeping people in her life. She'd learned early on that she was alone in the world, which made it hard to let anyone get close. Except for Michael and Shondra—they were the two who had stuck.

On the screen, the analyst at the map gesticulated while the hosts behind the desks remained serious, even grim.

"What do you think, Ms. Human Computer," Carol asked, "is Cass going to win?"

Shondra nodded and took a long drink. "Maybe one of the western states will surprise us."

"What will you do, if…?"

"Fight like hell," said Michael.

"Michael…" Shondra said. Carol didn't like hearing the fear in her voice.

Carol stood up. "I can't take this. And I know you have to teach early tomorrow." She gave them each a long hug, then hailed an autobot. She left them standing stiffly in their apartment doorway.

The election results were playing on the taxi's TV when she got in. "Turn off the news, please."

"Would you like kittens instead?" came the cultured male voice as the vehicle pulled away from the curb, slotting itself seamlessly into a line of autobots traveling in the same direction.

"Sure, why not?" She didn't particularly like cat videos, but some people found them comforting. Maybe it would work for her this time.

She did feel more relaxed when she arrived home, but the effect was short-lived. She was ready for her door's retinal scan when her handheld spoke from its slot on the side of her purse.

"Carol."

She reflexively looked down to pull it out. Bad habit from her youth.

"Scan error," said the door.

"Yes?" Carol said.

"You wanted a notification when the presidential race was called."

She took a deep breath. "Okay."

"CNN has called the presidential election for Richard Cass. Walker leads the popular vote but has no chance of winning the Electoral College."

"Fuck." The tears surprised her.

"Scanning again," said the door.

Damn. She'd never get inside at this rate.

3
THE HERMIT

THERE it was again—the crack of a twig somewhere behind him. Jun urged his horse more quickly down the narrow forest path. He didn't want anyone from his village tracking him on this particular errand.

He turned into a little opening in the oaks and maples, screened from anyone coming behind. He waited. And waited. Not a sound.

Probably just a squirrel. But he couldn't be too careful. A tongue-lashing from the Wise Women wouldn't be too bad, but it was better not to raise their suspicions.

He rode on. The trail wound its way through the forest, sunlight dappling the understory of ferns and cedars. He hoped he was remembering the way. He hadn't been up here in years. That time, he'd been lost. This time, he'd split off from the rest of his people on their way to the summer Rendezvous, careful that no one noticed or followed. It wouldn't do to be gone too long.

And then there she was, right in front of him as he came around a bend. Sila, standing in the middle of the trail, hands on her hips, a big grin on her face. A warmth spread through his chest, as it always did when he saw her after any absence, no matter how brief. He'd kept his distance from her these past weeks, ever since that day she'd nearly gotten herself trampled, stirring up feelings he'd long tried to suppress.

Those feelings returned in full force now, seeing her this close. She wore her brown hair in braids, the forest-dappled sunlight making it glow. The glints of green in her brown eyes sparkled. Her bare arms were lean and well-muscled. Buckskin leggings hung low on her hips and clung tight around her legs. Her light summer halter was cut low and cropped short at the midriff, revealing the light brown skin of her toned belly, the deep navel at its center, and the curve below. His mouth went dry.

He tried to keep his eyes trained on hers, but it was difficult. The worst thing was, she probably had no idea what effect she was having. Woe to the hunters from the other villages who would once again face her indifference. And woe to Jun, he couldn't help thinking.

Her look turned stern. "You're going to see that crazy old hermit, aren't you?"

"How did…" he started, but the question died on his lips. Sila was among the best at tracking and circling prey. It was one way she'd earned her spot in the Hunt.

"Did you think I didn't see you slipping off?"

"You seemed too busy with your followers to notice." They'd flocked around her, Ori and the others walking beside her horse as she rode double with Brina, her favorite. Everyone expected the pair to declare for each other during the Rendezvous. He'd pretended it didn't bother him.

She ignored the barb and went on smiling. "I'm right, aren't I?"

"What if I am going to see him?"

"Oh, nothing. Except you know it's forbidden to speak with one of the Shunned. And the only thing you'll get from him is more silly ideas."

"They're not silly. The Land has to be bigger than what's inside the boundaries of the Howling Forest."

"Why?"

He tried to remember Mar Gan's reasons. "Haven't you ever looked at the moon during an eclipse?"

"Sure, hasn't everyone?"

"What do you think makes the shadow that covers the moon? It has to be big. And you can see from its curve that it has to be round."

"So?"

"So, the thing that's making the shadow is the place where the Land is, but it has to be much larger. There's got to be something else beyond the Howling Forest."

"And Mar Gan told you this."

He had to admit, he wasn't making much sense. The hermit had used a walnut, an apple, and a round gourd to show how the shadow was cast on the moon. That was years ago now, and the details were hazy.

"But besides all that, Ada wouldn't forbid us from entering if there was nothing on the other side."

Sila gave an exasperated sigh. "I have to get back with our people, or they'll think we've run off together. Come with me. Leave Mar Gan alone."

"No, Sila. He said he had something more to tell me when I was older. And now I am."

Sila shook her head. "I hope the Wise Women do catch you, if you're going to be this stubborn." She whistled for her horse and stepped aside. "You'd better be on your way."

Jun rode past her without saying a word, kicking his horse into a canter.

~~*

Jun replayed the argument with Sila over and over as he rode. Why wouldn't she listen to sense? She never saw anything wrong with Ada's rules. She'd been well rewarded for her skill as a hunter, so why question the way of things? He knew the Great Sleeps bothered her, but she had a plan to never let what happened to the mothers happen to her. A plan that didn't include him, or any other man.

Ever since his first encounter with Mar Gan at the age of fourteen, Jun had dreamed that he and Sila could dare the Howling Forest together. The meeting had been an accident. He'd gotten separated from a group of other boys during a rabbit hunt, coming across the old man while looking for a way back to the village. The hermit had been busy picking berries, but stopped what he was doing when he saw Jun. The old man asked him a lot of questions, as if testing his knowledge of the Land and his beliefs about Ada. Apparently satisfied, the hermit had revealed his ideas about eclipses, what existed outside the Land, and more, then swore Jun to secrecy before pointing him in the direction of home.

"Come back to me when you've joined the Hunt, and we'll talk more. I have much to teach you."

The old man's notions were strange, but no stranger than the idea that everything ended at the Howling Forest. Jun had never believed it, and neither had his father. Jun could remember his father talking about what must lie beyond the forest, that it couldn't just end. When he'd disappeared, everyone assumed it was to pursue this mystery, and Jun had been left with the same questions. Growing up neglected by his mother and her new mate, he had plenty of time to himself, time to ponder and wonder.

The encounter with Mar Gan only heightened his curiosity, but he'd never been able to get Sila to share his enthusiasm. Maybe it would be better to go without her. That would be easier than seeing her every day, knowing they could never be together. And maybe he'd be ready to leave the Land after this visit with Mar Gan. The hermit must have some idea how to get through the Howling Forest and past the Angel of Wrath. Jun didn't want to end up like Little Kit, half-crazed and raving.

The trail left the forest and crossed a meadow. Beyond, oaks dotted the low, grassy hills. Yes, this looked right. He dismounted, leading his horse along the base of the hills. The hermit's cave couldn't be far.

"Stop! Who's that?"

The voice came from the hillside above him. He raised his hands to show he held no weapon.

"Ah, young rabbit hunter, you've returned." Mar Gan stepped out from behind a large oak, lowering his bow.

He was ancient, a few gray wisps of hair clinging to his brown scalp, his mouth opened in a gap-toothed smile. He wouldn't be around much longer if he kept losing teeth like that.

"Bison hunter now," Jun said. "I earned my place in the Hunt last year."

"Ah, very good. Did you bring Mar Gan a fat, juicy steak?"

Jun nodded. The old man scampered down the slope. "Come, come! Let us sit and you can show me your presents!" The hermit seemed as giddy as a child with a new wooden horse. "What was your name again? Many young hunters come to visit Mar Gan, he can't keep track of them all."

This was news. Jun thought he was the only one who would risk speaking with the Shunned. The others probably came from different villages. "I am Jun, of the People of the Bison."

"Yes, yes, I know who you are, now come quickly."

Strange old man! Jun hoped the hermit hadn't forgotten everything he'd promised to teach.

They came to the camp. The cave opening was sheltered by a ramada of cottonwood limbs thatched with reeds. Great oaks shaded the cleared space in front of the cave, which had a fire pit in the center. Mar Gan took a seat on one of the upturned logs near the banked fire and waited for Jun to reveal his gifts.

First, half a dozen new apples from the trees that grew wild in the valley bottom near the village. Mar Gan laughed with delight as Jun handed them over. "Yes! Yes! It has been nearly a year since Mar Gan had an apple." He took one and sliced into it with his bone-handled knife, its blade a glossy black, and so sharp it seemed to go through the apple as if it were water. Jun had only seen one other like it in his life. Such blades were exceedingly rare, prized by all, and jealously guarded by all who had the good fortune to possess them.

"Ah, you're looking at my knife, I see." Mar Gan munched happily on a slice of apple, juice dribbling down his chin. "Have you seen its like before?"

"Only in the hands of Drin, the Chief of the Hunt. He has a spear tipped with a blade much like it. You're lucky to have one. Where did you get it?"

The old man looked at him more seriously before speaking. "That's the wrong question. What should you ask when you see a rare object like this?"

Jun pondered for a moment. "Where did it come from? Who made it?"

"Yes! And?"

"I don't know. Not from anywhere around here."

"Good. And how do you know this?"

"I've never seen this type of black, shiny rock anywhere I've ever been. And there mustn't be any in the rest of the Land, or one of the other peoples would be making tools from it."

"Yes, and earning much in trade, since these blades are much better than the usual."

"Maybe the People made these tools long ago but used up all the black rock."

"And left only a few behind? I can count on one hand the number of these blades in any of the five villages. Does that seem likely?"

"No. So the black rock must not come from here. Maybe from the Howling Forest."

"Good. Now, how old is it?"

Jun looked at the blade.

"Here, you can touch it if you want. Maybe it holds more answers for you than for me."

Jun ran his thumb across the leaf-thin blade and over the indentations along the sides. He imagined its maker chipping away at it with another rock, just as he had chipped away at countless edges and points since he was a boy. But he'd never made anything so fine, not with the gray and white rock available to him.

Jun shook his head. "I can't tell."

"Another question then. How did it get here?"

Jun looked at it again, biting his lip. How was he supposed to know that?

Mar Gan persisted. "How would such a valuable object get here?"

Ah! "Someone brought it from far away to trade." He realized what he'd said. "But how did they get through the Howling Forest?"

Mar Gan shook his head. "Silly boy. Do you think the Howling Forest has always been here?"

Jun looked up at Mar Gan. "You're saying that some other people, not of the five villages, brought this here more than a thousand years ago?" But that made no sense. Everyone knew that Ada had started with a vast lump of clay, breathing life into it to create the People and the Land at the same time. A thousand summers had passed since then.

Mar Gan clapped his hands together. "First lesson over! And you haven't shown me all my gifts yet."

With a groan of frustration, Jun turned back to his saddlebags. He pulled out a package of skunk cabbage leaves containing wild rice and millet mixed with dried blueberries. "Ah, yes, good for Mar Gan's fragile teeth." Next, a package of dried bison. "Not so easy on the teeth, but Mar Gan will soak it in water mixed with elderberries. Very tasty." And last, the bison steak, the size of Jun's forearm.

Giggling with glee, Mar Gan set the meat down and turned to stoking his fire. When he had it going, he went to fetch more wood from a large cache on one side of the clearing. The old man must spend all his time chopping firewood, Jun thought. But he'd have to, in order to survive winters on his own.

"I'm surprised you have a fire going in summer," he said.

"Tending the flame, keeping it alive, this is Mar Gan's duty."

Duty? Duty to whom?

The old man took his knife back and carved the steak into bite-sized pieces. The blade sliced through the firm meat like it was a hunk of fish. He skewered the chunks on a long shard of sharpened deer bone, setting the ends in two forked sticks on either side of the fire.

Jun waited impatiently through all this, hoping the old man would explain what he had implied. But Mar Gan said nothing, squatting on his haunches before the fire, grinning happily as he turned the sizzling meat.

Finally, Jun could take it no longer. "You mean there was something before Ada created the People?"

"All in good time, young hunter. First, tell me how much you remember of what I taught you the last time we met." Mar Gan removed the skewer from the fire, moving to sit on a log nearby. He blew on a piece of meat, then bit into it using only the molars on one side of his mouth.

Jun took a deep breath. Of course the old man would want to test him before revealing new knowledge. He should have been prepared.

He recited all he could remember: the size of the moon, the fact that it must be round like a walnut. And so must the Land, or the place where the Land was. Which meant that a man could set out in a particular direction and eventually come back to the place he began. That would be a journey to outdo the Heroes of Old.

"Very good," the hermit said, coming to the end of his meal. "Want some?" He held out the skewer with the last piece of meat.

Jun shook his head but took a seat next to the old man. "I want to know how you know these things."

"I like your curiosity, young hunter." He pulled the last bite off the skewer with his teeth, continuing with his mouth full. "You have done well. You are sharp, and curious. And I can tell you have an adventurous spirit."

He smacked his lips and set the bone skewer on a rock next to the fire. He moved to sit with his back propped against the log, stretched his legs out in front of him, and clasped his hands behind his head. "We will see what role you will play. Yes, we will see. But first, you must swear not to share this knowledge with any but one you judge worthy, as I have judged you."

"I swear."

"Good." The old man remained seated with his eyes closed and said no more. A moment passed with Jun staring at the hermit, waiting for the knowledge to be revealed. Then Mar Gan snored.

Jun couldn't believe it. He reached over and poked the old man's shoulder. "Hey! You said you had much to teach. Let's hear it!"

"What?" Mar Gan's eyes fluttered open. "Oh! Now, where to begin?" His eyes settled shut again, but he kept murmuring as if half asleep. "Ah, yes. Earth." He breathed the name like that of an old friend. But what did that mean? Earth was just another word for dirt, or soil. "That is the name of the place where the Land is. But Earth is much larger, unimaginably huge. You could not walk around it in an entire lifetime. And long ago, long before Ada, humans ruled it."

Jun sat silently for a moment, unsure if he understood, though the words were plain. Humans ruling the Land, and a place much larger than the Land—what would that even mean? "How do you know this?"

"Shh. In good time, young hunter. There were so many people that no one could count them all, more people than there are stars in the night sky. Their villages made ours look like mole hills. They lived and worked in gigantic lodges many times taller than the tallest tree. They didn't need to hunt, for animals were tame, like our horses, and easily slaughtered. The people didn't gather plant foods but had things they called machines to gather for them. They didn't ride horses but rode in different machines that were many times faster."

Jun gawked, trying to imagine all this. It was much to take in. "These…machines, you call them? What were they?"

"Hard to know. Inanimate objects, much like our knives or spears, but made to work together with some kind of power like fire. Then they could do work for the people."

Jun would have questioned him further, but the old man held up his hand.

"Wait, there is more. Still other machines let the people fly through the sky. When you look up at night and see a traveling star, that is a type of machine these people put there. If you could look at the moon close enough, you would see human footprints there, and more of their machines and huts. And know this: Ada herself is but one more of these machines."

Ada, a machine? He'd suspected she might not exist, but this was worse. All animals had a spirit—he'd seen the light go out of their eyes when they died. He could hear the spirit in the calls of the birds to each other, even in the soughing of the wind or the rumble of thunder in the distance. But if Ada was nothing more than an inanimate object, where did this spirit come from? Or was he only imagining it?

His whole being rebelled at the thought. "No! This cannot be. What proof do you have?"

Mar Gan opened his eyes. "Good. You want proof. Smart." He rose. "Wait here."

He walked on stiff legs over to the cave and disappeared within, returning in a few moments with a long object wrapped in leather. Taking his seat once more, he carefully placed the parcel on the ground before him.

"What I am about to show you, young hunter, was given by the First Hunter to the First Boy. And when that boy grew old, he passed it down to another young hunter, and so on from hunter to hunter for a thousand summers, and at last to me. And along with this relic, the knowledge I have shared with you. Of course, the Goddess and the Wise Women do not want you to know of this. It is why the First Hunter chose a boy to receive this knowledge, and to receive it in secret. And it is why I am shunned."

He began to unwrap the leather, folded many times around the relic. "Behold, the only proof we have of the time before Ada." He removed the last layer to reveal a knife.

Jun gasped. This knife made Mar Gan's black blade seem a crude thing. It had a black handle made of a material he couldn't identify, shaped to fit the hand and fingers. Its blade was of an equally strange substance that glinted silver in the sunlight, like the scales of a trout. It bore no marks of its shaping but was utterly smooth and polished to a high sheen.

Jun gave Mar Gan a questioning look. "You may hold it. But be careful of the blade."

The workmanship, if one could even call it that, was exquisite. How was the blade attached to the handle? Hard to tell. It had nothing as crude as the bark fibers and leather thongs his people used to fashion their tools. Whatever the blade was made of, it was far harder than any rock he'd ever seen. How would you work with such a substance? And it was far sharper than any blade, sharper than the blade he'd marveled over a short time before. He set it back down.

"That blade, young hunter, is made from a substance called metal, and a very particular type of metal called steel. Humans in those ancient days made many things from this and other metals—metal lodges, metal machines, metal pathways."

"But why does Ada keep such things from us?"

"No one knows. But we do know she didn't create us. No, she put the first people here when they were children. Ever since, the Wise Women have taught that the Land is all there is, and that Ada created it, and us. Only a few have held this secret knowledge."

Jun gazed at the knife, not knowing what to say.

"I can see that you want it," Mar Gan said. "Any hunter would. But it must never be used, it is that precious. Still, you now have a choice. You could become the next keeper of the knife and the secret knowledge, as I have been. It will be your task to keep the flame alive, even if the People shun you."

The prospect sounded bleak. He didn't want to become a lonely hermit like the old man. "What's my other choice?"

Mar Gan gave a sad smile. "I dared not hope you would take up my mantle and become the knowledge keeper. You are too curious and too adventurous. Your other choice is to make your way through the Howling Forest and past the Angel of Wrath to see what lies beyond. Maybe there is a place where humans still rule and make tools like these. Or you can return to your village and forget everything you learned here today, speaking of it to no one."

"But you must know a way to get through the Howling Forest."

"Me? No, Mar Gan is no adventurer."

"But what of other young hunters? You must have taught others who tried to make it through."

"In all my years as knowledge keeper, only one other. And he returned raving like the others who tried to leave the Land for more selfish reasons. He tried twice more, and never returned after the third attempt. I like to think he did make it, but reason tells me he failed and received Lytta's punishment."

"Then what hope do I have?"

Mar Gan looked Jun up and down. "You have more wits than the last young hunter. And more strength, by the look of you. Beyond that, I can give you no hope. You must decide if it is in you to do this." He folded the leather back around the knife. "It is time you returned to your people, before you are missed. It will do no good for the Wise Women to guess you've been visiting me. Take the Rendezvous to decide. And if your choice is to enter the Howling Forest, I wish you luck."

Jun rode away with more questions than he'd started with. Who were these people who once ruled this place called Earth? What had happened to them? And what was Ada, really? Why did she keep the few hundred remaining humans penned up here on the Land, ignorant of what had come before? It was much to think on.

If only Sila would come with him! She was as sharp as he was, if less curious. Her speed and strength nearly matched his own. She had a better aim and could move more quietly. Maybe working as a team, they'd have a chance. And most important, they'd be together.

The knife, that was the thing. There must be more like it out beyond the Howling Forest. A hunter like Sila couldn't pass up the chance to get one. He vowed to tell her during the Rendezvous. If this didn't convince her, nothing would.

4

RESISTANCE

APRIL 2041

When the first tear gas canister flew over the makeshift barricade, Carol wasn't bothered. She'd had plenty of experience with the different "dispersal agents" the police employed, beginning with her first Black Lives Matter protest back in 2020. George Floyd's brutal murder, when Carol was seventeen, had become one of those "do you remember where you were when?" moments, like 9/11 or Obama's election. Schools were closed due to the pandemic, and she'd been at home completing an online AP English assignment when she heard about it. Her phone buzzed with a text from Gemma, a friend from Extinction Rebellion: *did u hear abt the police shooting*. Only it wasn't a shooting. Far more barbaric, if anything.

Carol's parents, always the good liberals, accompanied her to that first BLM march in the wake of Floyd's death. But she'd insisted on staying past nightfall and returning to protest day after day, defying her parents' wishes and creating the rift she'd regret forever. They were only concerned for her safety, justifiably so. The red eyes, scratchy throat, and bruises from police batons were just some of the wounds she received during that time, and the more easily healed. But at least she'd developed a deep familiarity with tear gas, not only in those demonstrations but in the still more confrontational Extinction Rebellion occupations that came later.

Now, with the National Guard and federal agents approaching the barricades protecting the Multi-Racial Minneapolis Autonomous Zone, Carol was ready, equipped with her old gas mask, along with kneepads, work gloves, and a bike helmet. Michael had his own gear, including a newer mask. He'd grinned sheepishly as he told her of snagging nearly the last one available online, then guarding the parcel box every day to keep Shondra from discovering what the package contained.

Seeing her friends argue over Michael's involvement in the resistance had been one of the hardest parts of living under this new authoritarian regime. Activists had begun planning a response to the proposed deportations immediately after Cass's election, declaring an area of the city centered on North Minneapolis an autonomous multi-racial zone, independent of the federal government. The city had supported them where it could, banning the police from working with the Department of Homeland Security. But now that Cass was in office, the National Guard was coordinating with DHS, becoming a de facto arm of that agency.

Shondra thought they'd lost their minds, that the activists would get themselves killed. Michael said he wouldn't just go quietly when the roundups began. He had to do *something*.

Their argument came to a head the day Cass finally made the announcement in late April that deportations would begin the next week. They were all having dinner at Shondra and Michael's when their portables beeped with the news alert.

Michael swallowed. "It's really happening. It's time to go." Both he and Carol had go-bags ready for this moment.

"And what's going to happen when you're trapped in there, or something worse, and I'm out here?" Shondra demanded. "We're supposed to stick together for better or for worse, isn't that what we promised?"

Michael took her hand. "You could join us. There'll be plenty of people who aren't defending the barricades, elderly, children. I know you don't want to fight, but you could help out with logistics."

Shondra shook her head, a tear rolling down her cheek. "I don't see how this ends."

"Honey, if we push back hard enough and long enough in every city, they'll have to back down."

She shook her head again. "You're dreaming."

Carol got up. "I'd better go. We all need to make our own decisions, and you two need to talk this out on your own." As if they hadn't already. But she didn't want Shondra to think she was pushing Michael into anything. At the door, she turned back to them. "Just remember, I love you both, no matter what you each decide." She closed the door behind her, hoping this wouldn't be the last she saw of them, with those anguished looks on their faces.

When she met Michael outside the Zone the next morning, he said that Shondra finally had resigned herself to his choice. "She knew she married a fighter. She only made me promise to get back alive."

"I'll hold you to that," Carol said.

At the time, it had seemed like they were joking and Shondra was overreacting. But that night, with the drones buzzing overhead and occasionally diving on an armed resister, Carol knew this was more serious than any protest she'd ever been part of. Two men had already fallen to the bots, one of them dead where he dropped. The darts the drones fired usually tranquilized their targets, but these had been aimed for the eye with lethal precision. No one had expected the first deaths to come so soon.

An hour later, the first drone tank crashed over the barricade of derelict cars, concrete road barriers, and rusted steel beams, crushing two resisters who couldn't jump out of the way in time. The tank kept moving forward. Carol struggled to steady herself and, next to her, Michael cursed. They had been assigned to an anti-tank squad, and their leader, an AWOL National Guardsman, ordered them to drive the steel bar they were carrying into the tank's treads. Short of a shoulder-fired missile, it was the only way to stop the things. They lugged the bar toward the machine, Michael doing most of the heavy lifting and Carol guiding from the front.

Before they reached it, the tank sprayed tear gas at them. Carol had been confident before, but now she gasped. Her old mask had stopped working. Her nose and throat stung, filling with mucus. Still, she managed to aim the bar between two cogs as Michael wedged it in place. She staggered back, turning to Michael and gesturing to her malfunctioning respirator.

"Carol, are you all right?" Michael's voice was muffled by his own mask.

She shook her head, choking on her own phlegm. He grabbed her by the arm, pulling her to the sidewalk where others huddled, away from the thickest clouds of the stuff.

"Just try to relax and breathe. Do you have any spare filters for that thing?"

Carol couldn't answer, she was so preoccupied by what was happening behind him—dozens of National Guard troops climbing over the barricade in the wake of the tank. This made no sense. Their leaders, both the Guard and off-duty city police, had been certain the government would use bots, at least in the first days. Now it was as if everyone was taking a deep breath as they realized they were about to fight flesh and blood humans, some of them former brothers in arms.

The calm broke when someone on their side shouted, "Nazi motherfuckers!" There was a bang and then a whistling sound. The grenade exploded on contact with the tank, not doing much damage, but blasting the nearby guardsmen off their feet. Others opened fire toward the source of the RPG.

Carol would have screamed, but she could hardly breathe. This mask was going to suffocate her. Without stopping to think, she ripped it from her face. Her eyes stung and teared up. She could barely see.

"Carol, this way, into the alley!" She tried to stay on her feet as Michael pulled her away. "We've got to get you away from that gas!"

The screams and shots and buzzing of the drones receded as they moved away, but Carol still couldn't see where they were going.

"Stop!" came a commanding voice from behind them. "Hands in the air!"

Carol complied, trying through her tears to make out the figure coming toward them. Was that a rifle he was holding?

Michael seemed to be pleading with him, his hands stretched out.

"Calm down now. You can see we're not armed." He must have removed his mask, since his voice was no longer muffled.

"Down on your knees, asshole!"

Michael made a sudden motion as the guardsman swung whatever he was holding. Once, twice. Two loud thuds and Michael was falling into her. They went over onto the pavement, Michael partially on top of her.

"Stop it!" she screamed as she struggled to get out from under Michael's inert weight.

A crackling came across the thug's radio and he turned on his heel, walking back the way he'd come.

"Michael! Michael, wake up!" She had gotten out from under him, but he was little more than a dim shape as she knelt over him. She put a hand on his chest and felt it rise and fall, thank god. She slapped his face, but it did no good. She tried to lift his head, but her hand came away warm and sticky. "Oh, no, Michael. Come on, you've got to wake up. Think of Shondra!" She grabbed him by the arms and tried to shake him.

That woke him up, exclaiming in pain, his left hand going to cradle his right arm.

"Oh, thank god you're all right!" Carol wanted to hug him but didn't dare hurt him more.

"I don't know about all right." He sat up and raised his left hand to his head. "And you don't look so great either." He took his hand away. "Shit."

"How's your head?" Another stupid statement. She wished she could see well enough to tell what his pupils were doing, whether he looked dazed. "Do you remember what happened? Where we are?"

"Yeah, we're in the Multi-Racial Minneapolis Autonomous Zone, at least that's what it's called for the time being. That motherfucker was too fast for me. Clocked me with his baton. Got me pretty good in the arm too."

Carol didn't know if it was the tear gas or actual tears keeping her from seeing, but she tried to smile.

"Do you have any water and bandages?" Michael asked. "If not, I've got some in my pack."

"Of course." The resisters had been told to equip themselves with emergency supplies. She took her pack off and fumbled with the straps and zippers. Michael tried to help with his one good hand. Finally, Carol felt the water bottle and pulled it out.

"Good. Now flush your eyes with it."

"But your head…?"

"I've got more in my pack, but neither of us can do much until you can see what you're doing."

He was making more sense than she was. She poured half the bottle over her eyes and drank some to clear her stinging throat. That was better, at least until she looked at Michael and saw how much blood was pouring down the side of his head.

"Oh, god."

She fished in her pack, ripped open a bandage pack, and pressed it on the wound. When she thought the bleeding had stopped, she flushed the wound with water. It wasn't as bad as it had seemed with all the blood. She put a fresh bandage on.

"Do you think you can stand?" She looked in his eyes. His pupils seemed steady and equal so far.

He nodded and got shakily to his feet with her help. He let go of her and swayed, and she reached for his arm to support him.

"Here, let's go this way." Carol led them toward the other end of the alley. The street where they emerged seemed calmer. They slowly made their way toward the aid station at the center of the Zone.

The place was already crowded, and Michael's were far from the worst injuries. They sat together on a cot, Carol looking at the brown and black faces around them. So few white folks had shown up. The world's previous atrocities and genocides seemed to have taught people nothing.

Next to her, Michael chafed at the waiting. "I want to get back out there. I wonder what's going on?"

"You can see what's going on from all these wounded," said the young Latina doctor, approaching. "And some didn't make it. Now what have we got? Cracked arm and a lump on the head?"

"That's about right," said Michael.

"We've seen a lot of those. It's like they're trying to put as many as possible in the clinic, when they're not using live ammunition."

"Those weren't plastic rounds?"

She shook her head.

"I need to get back out there."

"So do I," said Carol.

"You're not going anywhere except home," the doctor told Michael. "Are you staying in the Zone?"

He shook his head. "Just here during the action."

"Look, you'll need to be monitored for brain swelling for twenty-four hours. You can do that at home or in a hospital, but not here. And let me take a look at that arm." She cut his sleeve away, then scanned his arm with her mobile ultrasound. "Mm-hmm. You've got a hairline fracture. I can give you a sling, but you'll need to see a doctor within a day or two. Tell them you fell off a ladder. Is that your dominant hand?"

Michael nodded.

"Then you won't be much good here anyway. You need to go home, and you need someone to go with you." She looked at Carol.

"I was hoping to stay and help."

"So you're not…" The doctor looked back and forth between them.

"My wife's at home," Michael said.

The doctor turned back to Carol. "You need to help him get home. With this kind of injury, he could become disoriented or unable to walk at any time. The feds haven't blocked us in yet. There's a safe way out on the north side. Once you're away from the cell jamming, you should hail an autobot."

Carol nodded.

"Do you know the signs of intracranial pressure? I've already handed out my last FAQ sheet."

Carol nodded again.

"Good. If he shows any signs over the next twenty-four hours, he'll need to go to a hospital right away."

The doctor moved on to the next patient, but Michael still sat there, staring at the pavement in front of him. "So it's over."

"For us, at least. But maybe I'll come back..."

"If we survive the tongue-lashing Shondra's going to give us."

Carol smiled at that, trying not to feel guilty over how little they'd done.

5

THE RENDEZVOUS

SILA stood with the other hunters from her village, the ones ready to claim mates. It was the opening dance marking the first night of the Rendezvous, when young men and women could announce their intentions and display their attributes. Around them, drums beat the rhythm for the dancers while onlookers from the other villages shouted out to their favorites. A great bonfire lit the figures and cast long, shifting shadows.

Six young women from their village and one of water-nature—a person whose gender flowed like a stream, not fixed in either male or female—occupied the dance circle, their synchronized steps moving sometimes with the beat and sometimes in syncopation with it. This part of the dance was meant to show how well they could work together as they sought and gathered plant foods, winnowed millet seed, or did the countless other tasks expected of gatherers. But Brina, dancing with them, didn't seemed too concerned with the group's unity, often looking up to find Sila in the crowd of hunters.

Next, the dancers broke into individual performances intended to entice particular mates. A couple of the dancers knew hunters from other villages from previous years and moved towards them; others were content to circle in front of the four other peoples.

But not Brina. She turned and moved toward her own people, eyes locked on Sila's, hips swaying seductively, arms lifted above her head to show her figure to best advantage. The crowd hooted. As she came nearer, she plucked a bright red cardinal feather from deep in the cleft created by her halter and held it toward Sila, coming so close that the hunters in front had to step aside.

Sila took the gift and nodded in thanks as Brina danced away. The crowd yipped and howled like coyotes, the taunts encouraging rather than malicious. Sila held her prize aloft and gave her own yip of victory.

Wouldn't that make her parents mad! As if they weren't angry enough already. For the first time, Sila had insisted on walking with the hunters during that morning's ceremonial procession to open the Rendezvous. No one could remember when a woman had dared such a thing. But her fellow hunters weren't going to stop her; she was one of them.

That was bad enough, but when her parents found out she was planning to dance with the men, they'd stopped speaking to her altogether. She'd never danced before, because she had never been looking for a mate. But she'd seen twenty summers and had established herself as a hunter. The Wise Women had pronounced her ready two years before. It was time.

Her parents had no trouble with her being a hunter, and no trouble with her taking a woman for a mate. But the ceremonies were sacred. There was no tradition that covered how a couple of the same sex should participate. Drin and his mate, Bar-Un, hadn't bothered with any of it, simply moving into the same lodge together. No one could remember any other same-sex couples doing differently. But neither could anyone remember a female hunter. Sila would claim all the rights that went with her status, no matter how much her parents thought it tarnished the sacred ceremonies.

She looked for her parents and sister, Ina, in the crowd massed behind them, but instead spotted Jun standing two rows back, glowering. She was surprised he was in the group of hunters ready to dance for a mate. When she'd suggested it a few weeks back, he hadn't taken her seriously. Maybe he was doing it to spite her.

She had tried to avoid him since he went off to see Mar Gan. He'd stopped her for a private talk after they arrived at the meeting grounds. Fortunately, the hunters were supposed to see to the semi-permanent lodges, replacing any broken poles and lashing on the bison hides. And they had to set up the monument of bison horns, displaying the success of their village's hunts. It was a lot to do before sunset, and she'd used this excuse to avoid talking with him in private. After that, she'd been careful to maneuver her family into a lodge separate from his. And today he'd kept his distance.

Looking at him now, she wondered if he'd ever speak to her again. Maybe it was better this way. If he was going to get himself shunned, she wanted no part of it.

The young women finished their dance and now it was the hunters' turn. The drums took on a faster, more aggressive tempo. The hunters of the Bison People moved into the dance circle as a tightly packed unit, with Sila toward the middle. Like the women's dance, this first part would show how well they worked as a team, using the different skills of tracking and bringing down prey, while also showing their strength and stamina.

At first they charged around the circle, as if chasing bison on horseback. Then they turned to stalking their prey on foot, crouching low as they moved through imaginary tallgrass. Last, they lunged at their prey one at a time, each trying to outdo the others with their spectacular leaps.

Most of them had been working together to ensure perfect timing—all except Jun, who had joined at the last minute. He was out of step through much of the group dance, inviting laughter from the gathered crowd. He made up for it when it was his turn to leap at the imaginary bison. Instead of sailing through the air, one arm thrusting an imagined spear at his prey, he rolled and came up with hands thrust forward for the kill. The thrust merged seamlessly into a somersault, as if he were vaulting over the bison, using its horns as handholds. Except there were no horns to push off from. The crowd's laughter turned to gasps of amazement, then to cheers. Even Sila was impressed.

Landing lightly on his feet, Jun posed for a moment before the next dancer took his turn. His skin glowed with sweat, bronze in the firelight. Sila's insides gave a little unwanted flip. He looked over at her, caught her looking at him, and smiled.

She looked quickly away. A woman dancing for a woman, or a man for a man, might draw yips and hoots, but dancing for a fellow villager of the opposite sex—that was forbidden.

Now it was time to impress the young women from the other villages with their individual prowess, mainly displays of the power and fortitude necessary for the hunt. Some went to dance in front of the villages where they had a favorite, while a few merely circled before the four other peoples.

Sila joined the latter. She was a proud hunter—why should she forgo her one opportunity to strut before everyone? She'd told Brina they should spend the week of the Rendezvous getting to know the youth of other villages, to be sure they really wanted to spend the rest of their lives together. And Brina had agreed.

The drums beat faster and the hunters kept time, competing to see who could raise their knees the highest or stamp the ground the hardest. When they came before the prospects of each village, Sila would stop her dancing and stand imperiously before them, the haughty hunter surveying likely mates. It was all a pose, but they didn't need to know that. Some might think she was catching her breath, but she controlled her breathing, standing so the crowd could see that her chest barely rose and fell, as a bow hunter had to do at the end of a long chase.

All was going well until they came before the People of the Deer. A woman stood among this village's hunters and dressed like them too. So Sila wasn't the only female hunter! She wondered why she'd never noticed this huntress before. Though this one must have been younger, she returned Sila's gaze with as much hauteur as Sila herself could muster, a look of challenge in her eyes.

The other hunters moved off, but Sila stood frozen before the new huntress. At last she realized she was alone, her people's portion of the dance nearly done. It was time to present her gift to Brina, announcing her claim for all to see.

She put extra effort into her steps to show Brina that she would hunt the hardest for her. But when she tried to catch Brina's eye as she approached, the girl wouldn't look at her. Sila danced up to her and stopped, holding out the gift, a bison's tail decorated with beads. The dangling tail barely quivered as Sila held it at arm's length.

A long moment went by, the drums pounding on. Finally, Brina looked up and Sila winced at the hurt in her eyes. Only when the drums changed rhythm, indicating the next village's turn in the circle, did Brina take the gift, quickly looking away. Sila resumed her place with her fellow hunters, wondering what she'd done wrong.

6

FAREWELLS

MAY 2041

Michael opened the apartment door. He looked haggard, his arm in an inflatable cast. Carol looked past him to the packed suitcases in the hall. "This is it, then?"

"Get inside before someone sees you." He checked up and down the street as she stepped through the doorway.

Shondra was in the living room. The place looked empty without their pictures and keepsakes on the shelves, their framed certificates and awards on the walls. Shondra looked empty somehow, too; thinner, but also hollowed out, a vacant look in her eyes. She'd looked that way even before the events in the Zone. The university had finally let her go the month before, unwilling to lose its federal funding.

Carol went to her and hugged her for far longer than was comfortable. "I'm not letting you go."

"What do you want us to do?" Michael demanded.

"I've got my car packed."

"And where would we go?"

"They're still resisting in Chicago."

"Girl, do you *want* to die? You know what happened in the Zone after we left. And how would we get there? It's four hundred miles. What are you going to do, put us in the trunk?"

"If I have to."

"And then you're going to just drive on down to the South Side? 'Excuse me, officer, I have to get around your barricade to join the revolution. Please don't search my car.' That's assuming the bot will take you that close."

"I've got Dan's old Prius. He couldn't afford it. He wanted me to take it off his hands when we broke up." She'd met Dan at the anti-Inauguration march. Their relationship had been brief. "And don't think I don't know how to drive it."

"So there are advantages to dating a deadbeat," said Shondra, grinning.

"How can you joke at a time like this?"

"What else can I do, hon?"

"That's just great," Michael said. "We'll probably break down outside Eau Claire, or Menomonie. Won't that be fun? I'm sure all the Casshats will help us on our way."

Carol stamped her foot. "I can't believe this. Especially you, Michael. Don't you want to keep fighting?"

"With every bone in my body."

"Literally," Shondra put in, rolling her eyes.

Michael let the comment pass. "I also know when they've got us beat."

"But the resistance is only getting started."

"It's too little, too late. We failed in the Zone. It only made it easier for the Guard to round everyone up. And your white brothers and sisters didn't show up. Where's the general strike? Where are the mass protests? Most people are content to watch this happen. Hell, half of them voted for it."

"Carol, we're done," Shondra said. "You and Michael tried to fight back, and look how that went. I won't go through that again." She'd been so relieved when they'd returned from the Zone, she'd hardly uttered a cross word.

"You're going to give up? Let me take you to Canada, at least."

"It would be the same there," Michael said. "They'd search your car, then you'd be under arrest. And any brothers or sisters who do get across the border are being deported straight to Texas or Louisiana."

"But what if it's another Holocaust down there?"

"Carol." Shondra put a hand on her arm. "We have to go. Sasha and Malia are going, and a lot of folks are willing to follow them. The payouts for those who cooperate are decent, especially since the UBI is only for 'citizens' now."

"White people, you mean."

"It could be a new start for us. The governor of Louisiana says come on down, they're going to welcome us with open arms."

"What's left of Louisiana. New Orleans…" She stopped. She still had a hard time contemplating what had happened to that city in the previous year's floods. "Where will everyone live? And the heat. Do they even have power for air conditioning anymore?"

"Haven't you heard?" Michael said. "Climate change is back to being fake news. Just balmy summer days and a little coastal erosion, perfectly natural. Everything's going to be fine."

"I can't believe you can laugh about all this. I can't believe…" Her voice caught and her eyes clouded. "I can't believe it's happening this fast."

"It's PoliSci 101, a president's got to rack up the victories in the first hundred days."

How could Michael make light of this? He must still be in shock.

"I can't believe I'm never going to see you again." She couldn't help it, no matter how ashamed she felt. She broke down completely.

Both her friends hugged her at once, Michael wrapping his good arm around her. "We'll miss you too, honey," said Shondra.

"Look at me, crying my eyes out, when you're both being so strong."

"What choice do we have?" Shondra's eyes were moist, at least. "Do you want to help us take our things to the curb? The autobot should be here any minute to take us to the bus station."

As they waited on the street, Michael said, "You know, Carol, if you want to help someone, you should think about your Jewish friends. You notice Cass hasn't set up a Jewish homeland."

That was true. Black, Latino, and Muslim homelands, yes, all across the rapidly eroding and rapidly warming southern-tier states. Citizens of Chinese descent had simply been expelled, with tensions between the US and China as the excuse. But not a word about any other Asian nationality. And nothing about the Jews. Yet.

"You don't think…"

"I think 'Jews will not replace us' was the most popular chant at Cass's rallies."

"You could use that car to get them to Canada, if it comes to it," Shondra said. "The Canadians will take them, even if they won't take us. You'll save lives, and you'll feel better."

"What do my feelings matter in all this?" Carol looked around helplessly.

"Oh, honey, they matter to me. If anyone is going to feel survivor's guilt, it's you. Promise me you won't give in to it. *Do* something to fight these bastards."

"You know I will."

"Just don't get yourself killed. I want to see you when we come back."

Michael rolled his eyes. Clearly he thought they weren't coming back, but he didn't say it.

The autobot pulled up, and it was like they were saying goodbye at the airport for a long trip, not an ethnic cleansing. The bot pulled away and Shondra and Michael were gone from her life.

7

MAKING AMENDS

SILA saw the female hunter from Deer Village the morning after the opening dance, when the young people gathered for the Forager-Hunter Relay. This was one of many events leading up to the Dance of the Full Moon. It was open to all the young people, not just those approved to take mates. Even those who had already set their eyes on a partner would sometimes team up with a stranger, so why shouldn't Sila approach this other huntress? Besides, Brina had been frosty with her this morning. Maybe they needed some time apart.

She took a breath and stepped up to the young woman, trying to calm her growing jitters. Why was she feeling nervous? Maybe it was something in the way the female hunter stood so confidently, scanning the crowd of young women for a partner while studiously ignoring those begging to race with her. She was both intimidating and alluring, though Sila guessed she wasn't more than seventeen or eighteen.

"Have you picked a partner yet?"

The female hunter turned to her, her large brown eyes showing surprise. An improvement on the challenge of the previous night, at least. "No. You?"

"Not yet." Sila hesitated. Why was the girl so stand-offish? "I'm Sila." She held out her hand for a forearm embrace, but the huntress didn't take it.

"I know. I've seen you at other Rendezvous."

"But this is the first time I've seen you."

The huntress looked away. "I earned my spot in the Hunt last fall. Before that, I was just another girl you would never notice." Something in her voice sounded bitter. Could it be she was the one who was intimidated?

"You've been a hunter for less than a year, and your Wise Women already pronounced you ready to take a mate? Impressive!"

The young woman looked back at her with half a grin. Now, if only Sila could turn it into a full-fledged smile.

"Won't you tell me your name? I was hoping we could run the relay together. We'll make a great team."

The look of surprise returned, but only for a moment before the huntress turned away again. "I'm…I'm Rea," she said at last. "And you want to run the relay with me?" Her eyes scanned the crowd of young people. "But who would run first?"

"Whatever you want, it doesn't matter to me. I'll run the long leg with the girls, if you like. I'll lap them all and you can jog the sprint."

"But we're supposed to be finding likely mates."

Sila laughed. "Let's not get ahead of ourselves. You're very attractive, but I'm not ready to pledge myself just yet."

"That's not what I meant."

"Look, there hasn't been a female hunter since the Wise Women were young, and now there are two of us. Why shouldn't we be interested in each other? We're supposed to be looking for a person who will make us happy, right?" She was certain—almost certain—that Brina was that person for her, but getting to know other people couldn't hurt. They hadn't pledged to each other yet.

"It's not going to happen." The half-smile was long gone, replaced with a look of defiance. "I'm here to find a mate. If I wanted a hunter, it would be a man, but how would that work, two hunters living together?"

"Our Chief of the Hunt manages it with his mate."

Rea didn't answer this. "No, a hunter needs to pair with a forager, a woman who will gather and cook and mend. I don't imagine the great

Sila of the Bison People would do those things." She looked away. "Besides, I don't like women that way."

Sila was appalled. Rea's only interest in a mate was to have a helpmeet? But then she remembered telling Jun nearly the same thing. Was that how she'd sounded?

"But what about love and happiness?"

"Is that what you think this is about?"

"Of course! Brina makes me happy."

"Oh, does she? Then why are you here with me?"

"I told her we should take our time at the Rendezvous, consider our options. There's no need to rush. I still think I'll end up with her and be very happy. I thought we'd agreed." She realized she was talking too much.

"It didn't look that way last night. At least I know what I want. I know the sacrifices I have to make if I'm going to follow the hunter's path. Watching you all these years, so proud and alone, I thought you knew that too."

"What can I say? I'm a human being."

"As I'm learning. Excuse me, but I have to find a partner."

Rea turned away, as did Sila, only to find her sister watching from a few paces away.

Ina arched an eyebrow at her. "What are you doing, Sila?"

"What do you mean?"

Ina nodded off to their left. There was Brina, talking to a hunter from another village.

"So?"

"Don't you think you should be guarding your interests? Or aren't you that serious about her?"

"What's it to you?"

"Just trying to see how this is done. I might be stepping up for the dance next year."

Sila felt a pang of guilt. What kind of example was she setting for her younger sister? "It's not such a big deal. It's only a race."

She went over to Brina and the male hunter, a hulking brute, telling herself she wasn't guarding her interests, only being polite.

Brina gave her a noncommittal stare as she approached. "Oh, Sila, good to see you. I decided you're right, we should get to know other people. This is Garth, of the Bear People. He's agreed to race with me."

Sila tried to smile. "Well, good luck. I'm sure you'll both do well."

She turned to find her own partner for the race. As she surveyed the crowd for any girl still available, she noticed the aunties, Val and Luri, observing the scene from a rise a little way off. Val caught her eye, the corner of her mouth turning up as she gave a little shake of her head. She turned to Luri and said something Sila couldn't hear, then both turned to look at her. Why was everyone paying so much attention to what she was doing today?

She went back to her search, but the few girls who'd had the courage to approach her at past Rendezvous had already chosen other partners. A couple of them did look at her with regret as they turned her down. Ori was hanging around as well, looking as if she wanted Sila to pick her. It was a tempting thought. She'd always liked Ori, but running the race with her would only make Brina angrier. Sila settled on one of the last girls available, a younger one from the People of the Wolf. She was too young for Sila and not ready to take a mate, so at least Brina couldn't be jealous.

The girls and young women all set off on their leg of the race, ten laps around a course through the nearby forest. It added up to ten thousand paces, demonstrating the endurance necessary for a long day of foraging. Then the hunters would take over for the second leg, showing off their explosive speed in a sprint of two hundred paces to the finish line.

By the fifth lap, Sila knew she would be among the last to receive the token from her partner.

While the hunters waited, Jun came over. After everything else last night and this morning, she was glad to see him—if only he would stop talking about Mar Gan and the Howling Forest.

"It looks like we'll both be running toward the end, but maybe one of us will beat the drum," Jun said.

Unlikely, but they could always try. "Oh well, endurance isn't the most important thing in a mate, is it?"

Jun smirked. "I thought endurance was the first thing a woman looked for, in a man at least. Or wait, is that size?"

She punched him playfully in the arm. "How would I know?" It was good to be laughing with Jun again. "I see you didn't put much effort into finding a partner."

"Did you expect me to?" He gave her a defiant look, which vanished as he went on. "Besides, this girl is pretty."

"Then there's hope for you yet."

"I saw you talking to that other huntress."

Sila nodded. "Rea. She didn't want to run the race with me."

"You asked her?"

"Sure. We would've won for sure. No girl would best me over ten thousand paces."

Jun laughed and shook his head. "It wasn't just that, was it? I saw the way you looked at her at the dance. You like her."

"Who wouldn't? Those eyes. And that haughty manner. Such confidence."

"It would be like having yourself for a mate."

"So? Don't tease me." She told herself Jun's grin was annoying. "Besides, she's taller than me. That might be nice."

"But she broke your heart."

"No, she didn't break my heart! I haven't seen anyone who would turn my heart from Brina. Besides, Rea doesn't like women."

"Wait. She's looking to take a woman for a mate. That sounds sort of…"

"Mercenary?"

"Yeah, since you said it."

Did Jun think that's what she was? Mercenary? No, Brina made her happy, she wasn't likely to find anyone who would make her happier.

The racers came into view as they completed their seventh lap. Brina was second, loping along easily as she trailed the leader by ten paces.

"Tell me again why you didn't just pick Brina this morning?"

"Because I'm a fool. I wanted to be sure. I wanted *her* to be sure."

"You'll be sure to have lots of competition if she comes in first, especially with that opening you gave the other hunters last night."

Of course he was right. Brina was a remarkable catch, and soon everyone would know it. Why hadn't she seen it earlier?

"Listen, Sila, I want you to know you have other options. Mar Gan said…"

He wanted to talk about this now? What did Mar Gan have to do with her dithering over Brina? "Stop, I don't want to hear it."

She tried to shut him out, concentrating on the race. But she couldn't help hearing something about people ruling a place called Earth before Ada existed. It was nonsense, of course. No wonder the old man was shunned. Good thing most of the hunters had moved toward the starting line, out of earshot.

And then there was something about a wondrous knife that sounded like magic, one that made Drin's shiny, black spear blade look like dull river rock. And there could be more of them? No, it was all a fever dream.

Fortunately, the timing drums started pounding in regular cadence, drowning out Jun's voice. There were three alternate prizes for the sprinters who finished in the fewest drumbeats, and the fastest was said to have beaten the drum.

The lead runner broke out of the forest. Even from this distance, Sila could tell it was Brina by the way she ran. She finished twenty paces ahead of her nearest contender, and Garth lumbered to an easy victory on the sprint course, not even trying to beat the drum.

Brina put her hands in the air in triumph, looking over to see if Sila noticed before going over to stand with Garth at the finish line. Sila gave her a hearty cheer, trying not to sound at all sarcastic. She wasn't sure Brina noticed.

"Better luck next time," Rea shouted over the drums. Her partner was approaching the finish line in a cluster of three vying for fourth place.

"A mug of berry wine says I beat you in the sprint," Sila said.

"You're on!"

Rea took the token from her partner in sixth but managed to pass the two hunters ahead of her to take fourth overall. Sila would have to work hard to win that bet.

The wait for those in last place seemed to take forever, especially with the victory celebrations for the main race already under way. Finally, the last three emerged from the trees. Jun's and Sila's partners were even, with the last-place runner slightly behind. With twenty paces to go, the laggard put in a heroic effort and passed the other two.

"By Ada, I won't be last!" Jun shouted.

"Neither will I," Sila said under her breath.

They took their tokens from their partners at the same instant, then dashed off in pursuit of the only runner left on the course. They only had two hundred paces to catch him. Jun always had an edge in foot races, but Sila vowed it wouldn't be true this day. She wouldn't be last, or even second from last.

They passed the other hunter on either side halfway down the course. Jun let up slightly, but Sila didn't, pushing ahead. She imagined her feet were wings and tried to ignore the burning in her legs and lungs. Right before the end, Jun crept up next to her and then they were both lunging for the line, collapsing next to each other in the grass.

She hadn't finished last. That was something. A moment went by while the judges conferred. At last they announced the hunter who had beaten the drum. It was neither of them. Jun got to his feet and held out a hand to her, the other hand on his knee. She ignored him and rose on her own, standing bent over as she caught her breath.

The judge announced the second-place sprinter. Again they were both out of the running. But neither had he called Rea's name.

"And tied for third, Jun and Sila, of the People of the Bison!"

Sila was too winded to raise her arms. So was Jun, or he simply didn't care about third place. He moved over and put his mouth close to her ear.

"You see, Sila, we're a team. We belong together, and you know it."

8

THE BORDER

MAY 2041

The Texas pre-dawn humidity was oppressive, like Minneapolis in July. But it was only early May, three days after Michael and Shondra had boarded their bus, and nine hours after Carol's car had broken down outside Bloomington. She'd switched to an autobot, which had dropped her here at the side of the road south of Waco, claiming no Caucasians were allowed south of that point without government authorization.

Nice of it to warn her. Happy Cab would be getting a bad review, or at least it would have if there weren't so many bigger things to worry about. Like catching Michael and Shondra's bus before it crossed the border into New Texas.

Her automatic suitcase tried to follow as she walked along the darkened frontage road. The suitcase was cheap and old, and kept falling on the rough, gravel-filled shoulder. She was bending to pick it up for what seemed like the hundredth time when headlights lit the road behind her. The lights came with a strange sound—the roar of an internal combustion engine.

The beat-up pickup—what else should she have expected?—passed her, then slowed to a stop a hundred yards down the road before backing up even with her. The passenger side window slid down, but she still couldn't make out the person behind the wheel. "I don't mean to scare you, ma'am, but what in hell are you doing out here at this time of the morning?" A man's voice, a hint of concern under the lecturing tone.

"I'm headed for the border crossing. My bot wouldn't take me any farther."

"I'm headed the same way."

She took a few steps into the road to see him better. He helpfully flipped on the dome light.

He was Black, about fifty, with gray stubble around his jaw, wearing an old Texas Rangers ballcap. She smiled. She'd liked baseball too.

"Are you going to turn yourself in?"

"Emigrating to New Texas to be with my people, yes."

How could he be so sanguine about it? Just like Michael and Shondra. It was infuriating.

He looked down the road for a moment, then back to her. "Tell you what, we could help each other out, if you know how to drive."

"As long as it's not manual."

He grinned. "I'll drive you down, then if they won't let me take my truck in, maybe you could drop it with my neighbor on your way back."

"I'm hoping not to come back."

His eyes widened. "Get in." He eyed the suitcase as it followed her around to the passenger side. "Need help with that thing?" he asked as she opened the door.

It took a moment for the suitcase to pull itself up and maneuver into the space behind the passenger seat, then she climbed in.

"I'm Carol."

"Damian." He put the pickup in gear and started down the road. After doing one-twenty the whole way from Minnesota, fifty-five felt slow.

"What are you doing at the border? Work with the government? You're not one of those protesters, are you? I can't get mixed up with no protests."

"There are protesters?"

"Yep. Never hear about them on the news, and they've blocked all the social media down here, but we get a few coming through. Friends of mine with farms down there have seen them."

"You're from around here?"

"Just the other side of Waco."

She hadn't answered his question yet. "I want to emigrate too. I'm done with this country."

He glanced at her sideways and shook his head. "Are you crazy? It won't be good for you down there. Lotta anger right now."

At least someone had the sense to be angry. "I can imagine. But I'm not giving up on the idea that we can all live together."

Damian whistled and shook his head again. "Living together ain't the problem. Me and my white neighbors, we got along just fine. Other farmers down at the feed and supply, same thing. My white customers at the farmer's markets, you'd think we were family. But who did they all vote for? I don't understand it, but we might as well try living apart."

"I don't understand it either, but I'm not giving up."

"There must be more to it than that."

She told him about Michael and Shondra. "They're my only friends, really. If I can find them…"

"Your only friends? That surprises me. You seem nice enough."

"You just need to get to know me."

He shook his head. "They're not going to let you in."

"I have to try."

"All right." At least he didn't tell her it was her funeral.

They spent the rest of the ride talking about Damian's farm, five acres of fruit trees, vegetables, and greens that he sold at farmer's markets and restaurants in the Dallas suburbs.

"You do all that on your own?"

"My wife and son used to help out, but my wife passed last year, and our son was in New Orleans back when…" Damian paused.

"Oh, I'm so sorry."

"He was at LSU. He and a couple of his frat brothers went down to help out, and that big wave came through. Least, that's what I heard." He paused again.

"Losing family is hard. Especially children. I can't even imagine."

He looked at her. "You?"

She hadn't talked about it in years. But Damian seemed an easy person to confide in—perhaps because of the likelihood they'd never see each other again. "My parents and my sister. During the pandemic back in the twenties." She told him about leaving home to spend more time at the BLM protests, staying in her friend Gemma's apartment close to downtown. About ignoring her parents' texts and calls. But she'd happened to look at one, telling her that her sister was coming home from college in Michigan the next day. Her sister had stayed in East Lansing even after the university went fully online in the midst of the COVID crisis. *Say hi to the party girl for me,* she'd texted back.

"That's the last they heard from me until it was too late." She paused, fighting down the mix of bitterness and grief that always arose whenever she thought about what had happened. "By the time I got to the hospital, they were all in isolation units, on ventilators. Our last conversations were through Zoom and text message."

"And you were alone?"

"Not entirely. My aunt helped me make it through my senior year, apply to colleges, just, you know, carry on."

"It's the carrying on that's hard."

"But she died a few years later. I've been on my own for years, except for Michael and Shondra."

They were silent for a time, Carol trying to decide if talking about it made her feel any different.

"So, what did you do on the farm, after...?" she asked. Returning to safer subjects.

"I hired Mexicans for a while, Guatemalans. Hard workers. But now they've all been deported, and I probably wouldn't be able to keep the farm going anyway." He sniffed, then grinned. "But you know, I got my tools and a lot of saved-up seed in the back. I can fix anything, grow anything. If they'll just let me bring my truck."

"Do you keep it running yourself?"

"This baby? Oh yeah. Runs on ethanol I make on the farm."

They'd navigated a series of poorly maintained state highways and county roads and could see lights up ahead, still bright despite the sun rising on their left.

Before they could get that far, they ran into a traffic jam of buses coming off the freeway. Damian slotted the truck into line and killed the ignition when traffic stopped again. A drone buzzed overhead, but Carol couldn't spot it.

After half an hour of crawling ahead one bus length at a time, a security bot mounted on a three-wheel motorcycle pulled up to the driver's side window.

"No private vehicles allowed, sir."

"Damn, that's what I was afraid of. Is there someone else I can talk to, someone human?"

"Watch Commander Hayes at the main gate, but he'll give you the same answer."

"What do I do with my truck if I can't take it through?"

"An impound lot is located outside the gate." The bot's twin light sensors, anthropomorphized to vaguely resemble human eyes, switched to Carol. "No Caucasians allowed into New Texas without special clearance."

"Let me guess, I'm supposed to talk to Watch Commander Hayes about that clearance."

"That's correct. Report to WC Hayes." The bot pulled away, but the buzzing continued overhead.

After another ten minutes Damian said, "Damn, might as well walk."

"I wouldn't mind. I've been in a car for most of the day." She craned her head out the window. "There's a wide spot off the shoulder up ahead."

"Good. Don't know if they'll let you take the truck back out of that impound lot once we park it."

While Carol waited for her suitcase to dismount from the cab, Damian pulled a rucksack from behind his seat. "Packed this in case they don't let me take the rest of my stuff." He took a look at the pickup, patting the bed cover. Carol tried to imagine all he was leaving behind—what they'd both be leaving behind if she got through as well.

The buzzing grew louder as they started down the road. Soon a drone was hovering around Carol's suitcase and Damian's backpack. It zoomed away. "Guess we passed inspection."

As they passed buses inching along the road, Carol wondered about the people inside. Were Michael and Shondra among them? On most, the newer, driverless buses, the windows were tinted too dark to see anything inside. But the Department of Homeland Security had drafted all types of vehicles, including some old Army buses with slide-down windows and no tinting. Most of the riders stared at them listlessly as they walked past, but a few opened their windows and leaned out.

"Hey, you two are heading the wrong way!"

"Yeah, especially you, lady!"

Another one hooted. "Now, now, none o' that's allowed down here."

It wasn't allowed anywhere these days. The government had split up interracial couples as if *Loving v. Virginia* had never been decided. The ACLU had sued, but their preliminary injunction had been denied by every court up to the Supremes. Children were being deported with the parent of color under the ancient "one-drop" rule.

At last they approached the gate in the border wall, where guards were inspecting the buses one at a time. The impound lot was off to one side. A hundred protesters, all white, stood around in it, waving signs. A woman with a bullhorn led the chants: "No Wall! No War! No Segregation!" Soon it would be, *"El pueblo unido, jamás será vencido!"*, though Carol guessed somewhat less than half the crowd spoke any Spanish.

She shook her head at herself. How cynical she'd become! But after what had happened in the Zone, she had little patience. A hundred protesters with no news coverage and no social media weren't going to accomplish anything. Some people didn't know when they were beat. Michael had convinced her of that.

Four or five quad copter drones zipped back and forth above the crowd, their buzzing like an insect whine. She shuddered, remembering the Zone.

They went up to the one human guard at the gate who wasn't busy going on and off the buses. He was in full police tactical gear, with a

DHS ballcap replacing the helmet. He looked at them through his mirror shades, impassive as they approached.

"The bot said I should talk to Watch Commander Hayes."

"That's me."

Damian explained about his pickup and tools.

"No personal vehicles allowed across the border."

"But how can I make a living without my tools and my truck?"

WC Hayes just looked at him.

"Isn't there a higher-up I could talk to?"

A slight, tight-lipped exhalation was the Watch Commander's only response. He turned his mirror shades on Carol, still without a word. The security bot had more personality.

"I'm going in with him."

"And who are you?"

"Carol Marsh. I have friends on one of these buses. I want to find them and stay with them, wherever they end up."

"No whites allowed, except on official government business."

"Then I'd like to speak to a superior officer as well."

WC Hayes cocked his head. Carol wondered if the roboticists had made some huge leaps while she hadn't been paying attention. This guy was very uncanny valley.

"Wait here," Hayes said. He turned and walked away, shaking his head. "Takes all kinds."

The WC was on his radio for a couple of minutes, standing out of earshot past the gate. He came back to them, thumbs hooked in the sides of his bulletproof vest. "I put in a call. It might be a while. The Agent in Charge is a busy man."

While they waited, Carol studied the protesters. They were a mixed bag. A few clergy, some college kids, some old, second-generation hippies. A few of the girls wore sandals. None of these looked like they'd come ready for a brawl with the police, though a few did have gas masks. But off to one side there was another group in combat boots and knee pads, some in helmets. Along with the gas masks, they had scarves around their necks, ready to pull over their faces in violation of the national ban on face coverings. She'd seen what a few provocateurs could do, and didn't like it. The bulk of this crowd looked like lambs being led to slaughter by their more radical companions.

She was about to go over and talk to one of the clergywomen about the danger they were in, but the WC's radio beeped. He stepped out of their hearing, returning a moment later.

"It's a no, for both of you."

"Goddamnit!" Damian said.

"Settle down now." The WC's tone remained as flat as before.

Carol should have known. Why hadn't she planned for this? Maybe she could have smuggled herself aboard one of the buses. But where? In the luggage compartment? On top? She eyed the security cams around the gate.

"I see what you're thinking. That's why we search every bus, especially the ones without automated digital manifests."

"I just want to be with my friends."

"I'm sorry, ma'am, it's not allowed." His mouth twitched. "Maybe in a while, when things settle down, they'll let you visit."

Carol looked at the buses again, blinking back tears.

"Okay, I've got to get you through, sir. But you can't walk through the gate. You'll have to get on a bus. You'll get the same orientation as everyone else."

"Whatever you say." Damian was staring at the ground, kicking the asphalt with a boot. Hayes went to find space for him on the second bus in line, one of the old ones.

"At least we tried."

He looked up at her. "Yeah, we did. Oh, before I forget." He pulled the truck keys from his pocket and handed them to her.

"Well, good luck."

He held his arms open. "Hug for a stranger?"

"You don't seem like a stranger," she said, hugging him.

They separated and she looked at him for a moment, but then the buzzing of the drones over the impound lot grew louder, and the crowd's chanting broke into scattered cries of "Here they come!" and "Gas masks on!"

"Okay, there's room for you on this bus," the WC called to Damian.

He gave her a wink. "Drive safe."

He was getting on the bus when she heard her name. "Carol? What are you doing here?"

There was Shondra, one arm reaching out of a lowered window of the bus Damian was boarding. Carol ran over and took her friend's hand.

Michael squeezed in next to Shondra to look down at her. "What in hell are you doing here?"

"I came to live with you. I thought maybe they'd let me through."

"Girl, are you crazy?"

"Maybe so." She dried her eyes with the back of her free hand. "I didn't think I'd catch you."

Shondra shook her head in disgust. "This is our third bus. All the artificial intelligence in the world at their disposal, and they can't even get a mass deportation right."

"Are they treating you well, at least?"

"Just fine. They put us up at hotels in Wichita after the second bus broke down."

"They want everything to go as smooth as possible," Michael said.

Until they get you across the border, Carol thought.

"Who's your friend?" Shondra asked.

"That's Damian. Good guy, valuable skills. You should get to know him."

Behind her, the shouts from the crowd had grown louder, the buzzing of the drones more frantic.

"Look, you're right here. It's a miracle we ran into each other. I'll take that as a sign that they have to let me on."

She reached into her pocket and pressed the call button on her luggage fob. The suitcase rolled toward the bus.

"Now, Carol, don't do anything foolish."

"I have to try." She let go of Shondra's hand and walked toward the door of the bus, the suitcase following.

WC Hayes moved to block her as she came up. "Ma'am, you know I can't let you board the bus." Again that twitching around his mouth. He took off his sunglasses. He didn't have the cold, dead eyes she'd expected from a jack-booted thug. They seemed kind, pained even. "Look, I respect what you're trying to do. Loyalty to your friends, it's admirable. But it's not going to happen. It's time for you to leave."

She looked up at him, knowing it was no use. "Can I at least say goodbye again?"

He nodded and she went back to the window where Michael and Shondra were waiting.

"I love you!"

"We love you too, Carol," said Michael.

"I'll message you when we're settled, honey," Shondra said.

Then the bus was pulling forward. At the same moment, the crowd behind her broke into chants. "Down with the drones! Down with the drones!" A larger drone circled twenty feet above them, a plume of tear gas spurting from it, descending on the protesters.

"Ma'am, you better leave now," Hayes said.

There was a loud clank, and the tear gas drone fell from the sky. The crowd cheered, and one of the kids in battle gear shook a slingshot at the remaining drones. Idiot.

The WC left her and moved toward the protesters, talking into his radio. "We need extra security at the lot. And a drone spec."

More drones were already buzzing toward the scene as the guy with the slingshot aimed it again. A single drone buzzed toward him. Here it comes, Carol thought, hoping the thing would do no worse than dart him in the arm.

The fool was trying to hit the drone hovering and dodging above him. It dove straight at his face, and he raised both hands, still holding the slingshot, to block it. But it was only a feint. The drone evaded his raised hands and went for the top of his head. He wasn't wearing a helmet. The thing clamped onto his skull and he fell like a marionette whose strings had been cut.

Someone in the crowd screamed. Others threw rocks at the drones, now numbering in the dozens, massed in an ever-shifting cloud above the protesters.

Carol had been watching, frozen, but then snapped out of it, certain of what she should do. Someone had to show the world what was happening here. That drone was new, lethal tech, and people needed to see it in action. She couldn't stream from here, but she could record it and send it out later.

She pulled out her handheld, but Hayes stepped in front of her. "Don't even think about that, if you want to see your home or your family again. Now let's get you out of here. As long as you're with me, you'll be safe."

A phalanx of drones broke off from the main pack and swooped down on the crowd. Screams. One fastened itself to an older protester's head and his friends tried to swat it off, encouraging more drones to swoop in.

"Damned things!" Hayes grabbed her arm. "Come on, we've got to move!"

Carol didn't argue, knowing there was nothing she could do. They ran back along the line of buses, which were moving now. Her suitcase tried to follow, but it soon hit a rock and fell over.

"Leave it!" Hayes pushed her farther along ahead of him.

She looked back. The crowd was swarming out of the lot and into the road vacated by the buses.

Hayes spoke into his body mic again. "Command, I'm escorting a civilian away from the action. We need more human security at the gate. And the drone specs have those things dialed to eleven. They need to get them under control."

They kept running and soon a security bot approached, heading toward the chaos. The WC flagged it down. "Stop what you're doing and escort this woman to her vehicle. See that she gets in it and drives away." The robot scanned her, giving her an unpleasant feeling.

"Stick with the bot and you'll be safe. And don't try any goddamned heroics."

He turned and jogged back the way they'd come. She was so shocked, she'd forgotten to thank him. When she got to the truck, she started it, turned it around, and didn't look back.

9

DANCE OF THE FULL MOON

SILA took another gulp of the berry wine, hoping it would drown her humiliation. It was what, her fifth cup of the night? The first being the ceremonial cup the courting dancers passed to each other before the Dance of the Full Moon. Drinking from it, Sila had seen her future with Brina shining before her, as bright as the light of the rising moon, full of delight and possibility. Now the moon rode high in the sky above her, just past its zenith, mocking her and all her folly, revealing in its harsh light the wreckage of her hopes and dreams.

She gave a bitter laugh. Hadn't she grown maudlin! Maybe it was the wine. Brina was only one girl, after all. There were others. Hadn't she told Jun she had the pick of them?

She looked at the other hunters gathered around her, those who had been rejected and those who had never tried. Between them sat a pot of wine they'd carried up to this hillside overlooking the meeting grounds. What did they have to feel upset about? They might not have found a mate this year, but at least they hadn't caused a scandal.

The worst part was, she really thought she'd regained Brina's trust over the past five days, bringing her gifts and doing every activity with her. Sure, other suitors were hanging around Brina too—older, more established hunters with great stores of bison hides and sturdy, roomy lodges already built for their new mates. But love was more important to Brina, Sila was sure of it.

Sila had been quietly confident right up to the day before, when she ran across one of the aunties from her village.

"Hello, Sila, how are you faring?"

"Well, Auntie Val." She lowered her eyes in respect. "And you?"

"Well, very well, though my bones are creaking. We've sampled the berry wine and it is coming along nicely. The chokecherries from up north were especially bountiful this year, Ada be praised. It should have quite a kick." Auntie Val's eyes twinkled. "And the dance looks to be auspicious. Many happy couples will be bound tomorrow night. But one couple is giving us concern."

"Who is that, Auntie?" The old woman simply looked at her. "You don't mean Brina and me?" How could this be? Auntie Val had also paired with another woman, although, come to think of it, Auntie Luri was a person of water-nature, though many had forgotten it. But even so, how could Val object to her choosing Brina? "It's because I marched with the hunters and danced with them, isn't it? That's why my parents are angry with me, because no one's ever done that before. It goes against tradition, they say."

"No, that's not it. It was a bold, confident choice, as one expects from a hunter."

"Then what?"

"You know we Wise Women want everything settled between a couple before the hunter steps into the circle and picks their mate for the dance. We sing the Song of Names every night so they'll know their pairing will be to Ada's liking. We should never have to declare a pairing taboo because the names come close together in the song."

"But that won't be a problem for Brina and me."

"No, but it's worse if the dance ends with one partner rejecting the other. And worse still for hunters to vie to be first to ask for a girl's hand. Such indecision leads to chaos and even violence, when the night is supposed to celebrate new love and happiness."

"But I'm sure Brina will have me."

"She's said as much?"

She hadn't, Sila had to admit, not lately.

"Sila, a hunter needs to be bold and decisive..."

An auntie was telling her this? What did she know about it?

"Don't give me that look, young huntress. You're not the only female hunter in our village."

Sila's mouth fell open, but nothing came out.

"That's right. You've heard you're the first huntress since the Wise Women were young? I was that huntress. My path ended early when I was gored by a bison. Luri nursed me back to health, praise Ada."

"I didn't know."

"Of course not. It was long ago, and most have forgotten. But the point is, when I courted Luri, do you think I dithered about, wondering who else might have me? No, I pursued them like I would a fleeing bison, no turning aside. And thank Ada, they consented to have me. And Drin, do you think he showed an instant's hesitation while pursuing Bar-Un? No, he was like an arrow shot from a bow, and Bar-Un could not resist, though two hunters pairing for life is even more rare."

"And you think I lack boldness? Why was I accepted into the Hunt?"

"No, certainly not. You are the boldest, strongest young woman of your generation. No one expected the behavior we've seen from you this week. You've dallied around, toying with this girl's affections. I have to wonder why."

"Auntie, I promise you..."

The old woman held up her hand. "Life can be hard for those such as you and Drin and I. No one looks down on us, but nevertheless, there are difficulties, uncertainties. Your parents' anger over you marching with the hunters is just a small part. A large part is, who will care for us in our old age if we have no children?"

"Many will care for you and Luri, Auntie. And for Drin and Bar-Un too, when the time comes."

"We know that now, but did we know it when we started out? No. Nor do you and Brina. Can't you see what a gift it is, to find even one woman who loves you so much she's willing to share this difficult, uncertain path with you?"

"I see that now. I took Brina for granted. But I had to be sure."

"That tells me everything I need to know."

"But I'm sure now."

"Are you, I wonder?" Auntie Val's eyes bored into her, but Sila dared not look away. "Or is it that you have yet to learn the difference between pride and arrogance? Perhaps it's just that you'll be humiliated if your quarry escapes?"

"That's not fair, Auntie! A minute ago you were saying a hunter should never deviate when pursuing her prey."

Auntie Val gave a wry smile. "You'll have to forgive an old woman for mixing her parables. But here's the lesson: You must know your own heart and that of your intended by tomorrow night. See that you do."

After that conversation, Sila redoubled her efforts to win back Brina's trust, spending every available minute with her and lavishing her with attention. Then at last the Dance of the Full Moon was about to begin. She felt confident waiting for the ceremonial cup to come to her, but her certainty vanished as soon as a hunter ahead of her offered for Brina's hand in the dance. At least she refused. Then it was Sila's turn. Brina hesitated only for a moment before accepting.

The dance went well at first, with Brina responding positively to the stylized advances of the hunter's steps, first approaching, then moving slightly away, then approaching again, as was the custom in the opening moments.

Too quickly, something in Brina's demeanor changed. Sila could see it in her eyes. She was thinking over her chances with Sila, compared to one of the other hunters. Instead of turning to Sila in acceptance, as she should have by now, she was turning away, showing her shoulder as she sidled off. At last, Brina was positively fleeing her, and Sila stopped the chase. A mate wasn't a beast of prey.

The Wise Women gave the sign that the dance was done. They could have ended it a minute or two earlier to save her the humiliation.

The walk back across the dance circle seemed to take forever, with the crowd silent and the drums growing quieter as if to underscore her defeat. The worst was having to stand near Brina and the rest of their village's young people. After long moments of this torture, Sila couldn't help herself. She accosted Brina while another couple danced. The shame of what followed would stay with her for the rest of her life.

"Please," she begged, "give me until next year. You're young, you've got time."

"I don't think I can, Sila."

The look Brina gave her was so heartbroken it made her ashamed to have been the cause of it. But it also gave her hope. She threw herself down in front of the girl and wrapped her arms around her waist. "Don't do anything you'll regret. Give me another chance, please!" She couldn't help breaking out in sobs.

Brina's tone turned harder. "It's not me you're crying over, it's your own selfish pride. Now let me go and leave me alone."

Sila did as Brina commanded, slinking back to stand with the other hunters. They wouldn't look at her. For the first time, she noticed Jun wasn't among them. At least he wouldn't be asking any young woman to be his mate, and none would ask him when it came time for woman's choice. To lose her lover and her best friend on the same night would be too much.

And then the final blow. Garth, the hunter from the Forager-Hunter relay, approached their section and held his hand out to Brina. A murmur went through the crowd. She accepted before the sound could die out, eliciting gasps. When the Wise Women sang the Song of Names, Garth's came long after Brina's, and they were approved to dance.

Brina showed signs of acceptance more quickly than any girl yet. Soon she was beckoning the hunter to her. The crowd had grown almost louder than the drums. If the Wise Women didn't signal to end the dance soon, the couple would be consummating their pairing then and there.

Sila didn't stay to see the rest. She pushed her way through the crowd surrounding the dance circle and into the ring of lodges beyond, where a group of children too young to attend the dance were playing. Sila overheard one say to another, "Did you hear what happened with Sila and Brina?" The other child caught sight of Sila. She bared her teeth at them and they ran away.

One thing was certain. She and Brina would be the talk of the Five Peoples until the next Rendezvous.

After that she went in search of the wine, finding this group of like-minded hunters absconding with the largest pot they could carry. They sat on the slope, bitterly watching the festivities grow more raucous as the courting dances ended and the general celebrations began, one of the hunters occasionally making a snide comment. A couple of the men from her own village would sometimes look over at her and give a sympathetic nod.

It wasn't long before the first of the mated couples walked past them and into the forest where they would "finish the dance," as the saying went.

Sila took another gulp of wine and considered her options. What about Ori? She'd been hanging around this whole Rendezvous, looking more hopeful than the rest, as if she knew something was about to happen with Sila's first choice. Ori had a sweeter temper than Brina, and she and Sila always had a good time together. Now Sila wondered why she hadn't considered Ori more seriously in the first place.

And then she caught herself. Brina had just broken her heart, and she was already considering a replacement? She must be more confused than she'd realized—or maybe it was just the wine.

"Big steaming load of bison crap, this is," said the hunter next to her. Sila drank to that.

Another hunter stood up and raised his cup. "A drink for every fucking couple who comes by." He took a drink. "No, a *fucking* drink for every fucking couple who comes by." He took another drink. "Noooo," he said with a belch. "A *fucking* drink for every *fucking* couple who comes *fucking* by!" He tried another swig and nearly fell backwards as he sat down.

And so a new drinking game began. Four or five couples passed them—Brina and her new mate thankfully not among them—and then the wine pot was empty, eliciting groans from the men. But Sila was content. She was drunk enough.

"Gotta pee," she said, standing up.

"Need any help?" said the hunter who'd invented the game. She was surprised he could still speak at all.

"Fuck off." She wasn't prone to swearing. Maybe he'd rubbed off on her, or maybe it was just the wine.

"If you insist!" The hunter got to his feet and reached to loosen the thongs fastening his breeches.

"Sit down, Tanner, before you embarrass yourself," said a friend from her village.

She left them to it, walking up into the forest. She had trouble finding a private spot, as the forest was filled with the sounds of lovemaking. Ada preserve her! She headed one way, then another, and at last found a quiet spot, all without tripping over any of the couples. She'd already had enough embarrassment for one night.

She was starting to squat when she heard someone climbing the hill toward her. Whoever it was, they certainly weren't trying to disguise their presence, not with the racket they were making. A loud belch gave her follower's identity away. She spotted him a few yards to her right— Tanner, the rude fellow from the drinking game.

"Where are you, bison huntress? Tanner's got something for you!"

Would he spot her? She didn't much care. He was too drunk to overpower her, and she thought she could take him anyway. Her hand went to the hilt of her dagger, but she doubted she'd need it. He was such a big lunk, he was probably as slow sober as he was drunk. Besides, the way she felt, she could use a good fight.

She didn't get the chance. He turned around, trying to get a glimpse of her, swayed a couple of times, then toppled like a felled tree.

She continued up the hill and found another private spot. She dropped her buckskin breeches and squatted, the wine gushing out of her with a sound far too merry for her current mood.

She stood up with little difficulty when she was done. Clearly she needed more wine. She headed downhill past Tanner's snoring body, then past the sounds of lovemaking—past the 'fucking couples'; she'd heard those words and now she couldn't unhear them—and ran into someone coming around a tree. Whoever he was, he was the drunker, because he stumbled backward while she kept her feet.

"Sila! What are you doing here?" It was Jun.

"Peeing," she replied. "You?"

He grinned sheepishly. "Same."

"Where've you been? Did you go to the dance?"

The pitying look he gave her made her want to scream. "I was there, in the crowd. I saw." He held his arms wide. "Friendly hug?"

She couldn't help it. She accepted his embrace and broke into tears. He patted her back and shushed in her ear. His arms felt good around her. It took several moments to recover enough to speak. "Lytta strike me down, that's twice in one day. I haven't cried since I was a little girl."

"I know. Sila the Stoic."

A moan of pleasure broke out nearby and Jun looked away, embarrassed.

Sila grabbed his hand and pulled him back up the hill. "Come on."

"Where are we going?"

"I don't know. Away. Anywhere but here."

They moved quickly up the hill and down the other side, striking the Bear River. She paused at the bank and splashed water on her face. That felt better. They continued upstream.

"Sila, what are we doing?"

"I'm not sure. Let me think." She couldn't tell him what was going through her mind.

They walked in silence for a long time. "How far are we going? We'll be at the Howling Forest soon."

"You're exaggerating, but wouldn't you like that?"

"No, really, how long are we going to keep this up?"

"Until I don't feel drunk anymore." If she was going to do this, she didn't want to have any excuses or regrets.

They came to a meadow after a time, the grass silver in the light of the westering moon. This would do perfectly. It was a lovely night, with only a hint of chill in the valley bottom.

Her head felt clearer. Back at the Rendezvous grounds, surrounded by clamor, with the wine coursing through her veins, she'd felt afloat in the world but disconnected from it. Now her senses had returned, and she could listen for what the spirits had to tell. Were they with her or against her?

She closed her eyes. The call of a whip-poor-will from the forest nearby, and farther off, the low howl of a wolf. Howling at the moon. Yes.

She grabbed Jun's hand again and nodded toward the pale orb. "It's beautiful, isn't it?"

"Mm-hmm," he agreed, looking up at it. She knew, because she was looking at him, not at the sky. The moon was overrated, anyway. But she liked the way its light played over the planes of his face. She put a hand on his shoulder, willing him to turn to her.

"You know," he said, but hesitated, still looking at the moon.

She waited for him to complete the thought: *I've been waiting all my life for a night like this?...All this walking is tiring, let's lie down?* No such luck.

"Mar Gan says..."

"You think I want to hear about that crazy old man right now?" She gave his shoulder a push to make him turn to her. Once he noticed the look in her eyes, he'd realize what was going on.

He seemed confused for a moment. What was he going to say? *Sila, the moonlight when it hits your eyes...*Or maybe, *Why look at the moon when I can look at you?*

No. He pointed up at the silvery disk. "Do you know there are footprints up there..."

Footprints on the moon, that was a new one. Maybe he'd gone mad, but she didn't care at the moment. "Shut your mouth."

"...human footprints..."

He still wouldn't shut his mouth, so she shut it for him, with her own.

He hesitated for a moment, then started kissing her back, his arms going around her. That went on for a moment. It was nice. But not enough. She reached behind him and pulled him closer, grinding against him.

He pulled away, panting. "Sila, what are you doing? I know you're disappointed, but this won't help. It's forbidden."

"I don't care." She gave a laugh. "I don't *fucking* care!"

His eyes opened wider. "What's gotten into you?"

She'd have to explain it to him. "Look, Auntie Val was right. I hesitated with Brina when I shouldn't have, and why? Because I had doubts. And that's because I've never been with a man, even though I'm attracted to men as well as women. How can I commit to a woman if I don't know what a man is like? What a man feels like?" She slipped her hands under his buckskin tunic and ran them along his bare, muscular back. "What a man tastes like?" She tipped her head and placed wet kisses on his neck and down his chest. He tasted salty and good.

Jun groaned. His body was ready, even if his heart and mind weren't, not quite. "Sila, you know I want to. I've been dreaming of you every night since my thirteenth summer. But we should wait. Maybe there's a place where it's not forbidden."

"Shh! I don't want to hear it. You're my best friend. Who better to do this for me? Only this once." She pulled him closer. "Please?"

He looked at her, the internal struggle plain on his face. She was using him, and she knew he knew it. But she also knew there was only one real question for him: could he make her love him in just one night? He didn't seem certain.

"But Ada's rules…" It was merely a whisper.

"Fuck Ada's rules. And fuck me."

He hesitated a moment more, then his jaw untensed and turned into a smile. "All right, then." He pushed her down into the grass.

Now this is more like it, she thought as she tugged at his breeches.

~~*

She awoke with her head cradled on Jun's bare chest. She was naked against him, his tunic thrown over them both for a bit of warmth. The moon was still up; not much time had passed since she'd nestled against him after their exertions.

She gave a contented sigh, thinking back over everything they'd just done and felt. It hadn't been awkward at all, as she might have expected with her best friend. She'd heard there could be pain the first time with a man, but there was none of that either, only pleasure. And a pleasure that none of her girlfriends had managed to give her; not better, but different. One she would hate to give up.

Jun opened his eyes and smiled at her, the light of the moon glinting off his teeth and striking sparks in his eyes. He gazed at her as if he couldn't get enough of her. It was the most complete look of love she'd ever known. And she found herself returning it.

The first doubts didn't creep in until later, as the moon touched the horizon and she realized what deceptions they'd have to employ if they wanted to return to the meeting grounds without being discovered. *By the Goddess, what have I done?*

10

CLIMATE CRISIS

JANUARY 2043

Carol tramped through the snow, sinking to her calves, exhilarated to be outside after a morning at home working on her laptop. Ten or twelve inches had already fallen, with more coming down in dense flurries. She felt like she used to when she was a kid, as if she were one of those tiny figures in a snow globe. There was something comforting in the image. The peacefulness of falling snow. The carefree hours of a day off of school. Making snow angels and snow people with the neighbor kids. All contained in a protective sphere where everything was safe, predictable.

At least that's what a good winter storm used to mean. But no more. It was January, and this was the first solid snow of the season. The winter storms came irregularly, and when they did, they dumped snow by the foot. Heavy, wet stuff, not like the light flakes you could barely form into a ball.

Then Cass and his cronies would claim the globe couldn't be warming if it still snowed this much. But the asshole president would have nothing to say when the predicted January thaw sent all this frozen liquid downstream to flood Davenport and St. Louis. That's why she was out in it today; she wanted to enjoy it before it turned into slush, then ice, then disappeared for good.

That, and Craig had called, asking if she wanted to come over. She'd been staring blankly at her laptop screen for half an hour, making no progress on the course outline she was updating for "Rhetoric of the Climate Crisis." The AIs might have figured out how to teach any class, but they weren't creative enough to design one yet, leaving this bit of contract work for otherwise redundant professors.

And this class was her baby. She'd first pitched it to the state university when she'd been teaching there, back in the thirties. Back when they had some chance of holding warming under anything like an acceptable level. When humanity had been headed for massive discomfort and expensive storm damage, not mass drowning and heat death.

The course started at the beginning, back in the 1970s with scientists' first too-hesitant warnings, then the oil company-funded think tanks' campaign of denial, rebranding "global warming" as "climate change," right through the environmental groups' more alarmist rhetorical strategies. The alarmists had been vindicated by events, small comfort though it was. There was the lost decade of the teens, followed by the more militant rhetorical and political strategies of Extinction Rebellion and the Sunrise Movement. But even then, most efforts were of the too little, too late variety.

Now, since Cass's election, the course had new approaches to cover. Few these days questioned the existence of the climate crisis; it was simply that nothing could be done about it anyway. And Cass had his own extra-racist spin on this argument: "If the brown people would just stop having so many babies, we wouldn't be in this mess." Never mind that birthrates everywhere in the world were at 2.1 or below—acknowledging this new reality wouldn't give the white supremacists anyone to blame. New coal-fired power plants were already coming online, not bothering with the "clean" technology that had been developed before the US banned coal outright. "It's not doing any good in the ground," Cass would say at his many rallies in Appalachia and Wyoming.

That should give her plenty of grist for this new course unit, which she'd titled "The White Right to Pollute." But the words wouldn't come. Her brain felt as frozen as the world outside.

She took a break and checked her social media feed. Even more doom than usual. A hurricane had made landfall in Miami that afternoon, the latest Category Three storm ever recorded this far into the season. The sea walls on the new beach line in what had been downtown had failed, and the water was already washing over the raised streets farther inland. Of course, a lot of the well-off in those neighborhoods had already moved to higher ground, knocking down houses and rebuilding on land vacated by the deported Black and Latino populations.

But right after that piece was a rival media company's response, claiming the flood footage was faked, all part of the climate socialists' plot to destroy capitalism. You couldn't trust video footage as evidence of anything these days, not without expensive software that could analyze its authenticity. The entire media ecosystem now comprised rival channels making claims and counterclaims about what was real and what wasn't.

Carol put her head down on her desk. What was the point of any of it? That's when Craig had called.

Craig was her mechanic. She didn't really think of him as her boyfriend; more as the guy who kept her archaic car running and with whom she occasionally slept. And she was pretty sure he didn't think of her as his girlfriend. Actually, they didn't talk much at all. The "relationship" had started when she noticed the nice curve of his jeans as he leaned into the engine compartment of her car. They'd ended up doing it that first time in the back office of his shop. He hadn't even charged her for the work he was doing. It amused her that he seemed to think he was trading repairs for sex. But he was as good in bed as he was around a car. As far as she could see, the deal was completely in her favor.

The truth was, he was a distraction from her own loneliness and the numbness that had engulfed her since the mass deportations. Since Michael and Shondra had been suddenly ripped from her life. It felt like she'd been sleepwalking for the last year and a half, as had the nation, or what was left of it.

And what good had she done? Not much, she was sad to conclude.

The expected deportation—or worse—of Jews and LGBTQ folks had never materialized. Mass shootings and hate crimes targeting both groups had risen to horrifying, but not surprising, levels. Many were leaving the country, but they didn't need her driving them to the border. She'd attended a few vigils after these events, but this was nothing. She'd volunteered and donated what she could to shelters for queer kids fleeing conversion therapy, which had become accepted public policy. That also seemed too little.

She should have fought back harder at the beginning, even if she'd gotten herself killed. But no, she'd limped back home after the debacle in Texas and spent the summer staring at the wall. Only the tutoring requests that came with the new academic year had pulled her out of her shell.

She'd tried a hundred different ways to get in touch with her friends. Their social feeds had gone dark as soon as they boarded the buses taking them to New Texas. She'd tried emailing, but everything had bounced back. Calls had gotten a disconnected number message. And she'd received no messages from them at her physical address. She tried sending a letter to "Michael and Shondra McBride, Austin, New Texas," but the people at the post office didn't know if it would make it to the city, much less find her friends. It was as if they had disappeared off the face of the Earth.

She'd contacted the State Department to find out when communication between the old country and the new one might be established, but couldn't get past the stonewalling. News accounts showed a functioning government in New Texas, along with happy people creating a new life. She didn't trust any of it, much as she wanted to. She wanted to believe that the people of New Texas had somehow created a sustainable society out of the industrial wreckage and submerged cities of southern Texas, Louisiana, and Mississippi. And that Michael and Shondra were happy there. She didn't want to think about all the alternatives.

Now she had no one, other than Craig. Some of her old colleagues did reach out to her through social media, asking how she was doing, suggesting she get out more. They could tell from the lack of selfies with friends or shots of places she visited that she never went anywhere or saw anyone. She'd tried a book club for a while, and a writer's group after that, but soon dropped out of both, feeling superior to the readers in the one, and inferior to the writers in the other.

And she had little reason to visit either college campus these days. When she did, the lack of diversity, both in race and age, was creepy. The new whiteness of the US was universal, but it seemed more pronounced on a campus. And there were few people over twenty-four or twenty-five, the students barely noticing her as she walked across the quad for a meeting with the department chair. Now she met with him via videoconference.

She should have seen this coming. She'd gotten together with Michael and Shondra, either one or the other or both, what, a couple times a week? If only they were here! With Craig meeting her physical needs, and Michael and Shondra meeting her social and emotional ones, she could have an almost complete life. How it would work if the friends and the lover ever met, she didn't want to think about.

She arrived at the door of Craig's house, an old but well maintained two-story near Beltrami Park. He lived on the top floor and rented the bottom out to students. He stood silently at the door as she approached the porch, a slight smile playing about his lips, the shoveled steps serving as a welcome. It was just his way. He was tall, with sandy hair curling about his ears and a trimmed beard. He was ten years older than she was, though she hadn't believed him when he told her.

He stepped aside, gesturing for her to come in. She walked past him and up the stairs into the sweltering heat of the upper floor. He kept the place at seventy-eight in winter and sixty-eight in summer, feeling it was his right to use as much energy as he wanted, after the government and the car companies had taken the internal combustion engine away. And Carol even felt guilty about the tiny gas engine in her ancient Prius, though it now ran on ethanol. No wonder they didn't talk about her work, or much else, really.

"Want a drink?" he asked as she shucked off her parka and snow boots, depositing them on the landing.

"Maybe a coffee—iced?" While he went to pour it, she went into the living room, where he had a blazing fire going. "It's boiling in here!" She pulled her wool sweater over her head, leaving a flimsy tank top, no bra.

"Whatever gets you undressed quicker." He'd returned with the coffee, eying her appreciatively as he handed it to her. She arched an eyebrow at his cardigan. "I don't know how you can wear that thing in here."

He stripped it over his head, not bothering with the buttons. His t-shirt came up with it, revealing his rippling abs. She loved running her fingers and her tongue over them. In fact, why wait? She took a sip of her coffee and set it down on an end table.

When it came time for the condom, Craig found he was down to his last one. He shook the empty box. "Oh well. I can always run out if we need more."

"What do you mean 'if', old man?" She threw her arms around his neck.

Outside, the snow kept falling.

11

BEAST FROM THE BEYOND

JUN jogged behind Sila, whose brown braids glinted and bounced as they caught the first of the morning light. What had just happened? He couldn't sort it out. First she avoided him, then she was leading him through the forest to lie with him? His body still glowed with the memory of it, the way her hands and her lips had moved over him, the way her skin felt against his. She'd said she wanted him to do this for her as a friend, but what they'd shared, that went beyond friendship. He'd seen it in her eyes during, and even more when they awoke afterward. If this didn't show Sila that they belonged together, then nothing would.

But then she'd turned and noticed the setting moon, and a veil had gone over her eyes. Now they were loping back toward the meeting grounds with the sky in the east growing light. Soon the camps would be stirring, especially the elders and the families with young children. Everyone else was probably sleeping off the wine and the late night. But if one of the Wise Women spotted them together at this hour, they would have much to explain.

Part of him hoped they'd get caught. They could lie about what they'd been doing, but if the Wise Women didn't believe them, then they'd be shunned. All the more reason to leave the Land together!

But no, this was selfish, not to mention short-sighted. He knew how highly Sila valued her standing with the People of the Bison. If she was going to give that up, she should do it freely. Otherwise, she'd resent him for the rest of her life. Besides, seeing her in that kind of pain would be worse than not being with her at all.

He only wished they could talk about it, but that was difficult with the brisk pace Sila was setting. And talking would only ruin the warm glow he still felt. Especially if they spoke of their future, or lack of one. He kept quiet and ran next to her when the forest allowed, occasionally catching her eye and smiling. She had no answering smile, just turned her attention back to the trail and kept running.

Sila stopped when they came to a little clearing at the top of the slope leading down to the meeting grounds. "You circle around and come into the camp on the other side. I'll go down here and find some of the hunters I was drinking with. I bet they're still asleep. It'll be like I was never gone." She gave him a grin. "Besides, I could use more sleep myself. I didn't get much last night for some reason."

His heart did a flip. Maybe he could dare to hope! He checked to see no one was watching, then took her by the shoulders. "Sila, last night was incredible. I don't know if we can ever be together, but I want you to know, I'll always love you, no matter what." Then he kissed her.

She kissed him back for a long moment, then pulled away. When he looked into her eyes, he saw that she was as confused as he was.

A thrashing noise came from the forest across the clearing. A bull elk burst out of the trees and headed downhill.

"I wonder what's after him?" Jun said.

Sila shrugged. "Probably a grizzly."

But if so, the bear wasn't quick to make its appearance. Usually, a grizz would only rush its prey over a short distance. "That's strange..."

He stopped short, unable to believe his eyes. Next to him, Sila tensed. A monstrous creature emerged from the forest, fifty paces away. It was as large as a grizzly, but cat-like, with a tawny, spotted coat and wicked fangs protruding from its upper jaw. It slinked after the elk, its snout to the ground, the muscles of its shoulders rippling as it moved. It made a loud chuffing sound as it went, whether as threat or just sniffing out the elk's scent, Jun couldn't tell. He'd never seen anything like it, it was so much larger than the bobcats he was used to.

It slowed, seeming to give up the chase, but it was headed for the meeting grounds. And worse, right through the forest where many newly paired couples must yet be sleeping. They'd have taken few weapons with them since they were close to the camp, little more than daggers, nothing that could fend off this strange beast. And he and Sila were just as ill-prepared.

Sila must have thought the same thing. She grabbed his arm. "Jun, we've got to warn…"

Her whisper wasn't soft enough. The cat's head snapped toward them. They crouched lower in the grass, but it crept closer.

"Up a tree, quick," Sila hissed. She leapt at the nearest branch. Jun didn't need to be told twice. He ran to the next tree, pulling himself onto the lowest branch as the cat charged. He didn't stop there, climbing two branches higher. And a good thing he did, because the cat hit the first branch, gripping it with its front paws while scrabbling at the trunk with its hind feet.

Jun checked Sila's tree to make sure she'd climbed high enough. "If this thing climbs like a bobcat, we're dead!" He pulled himself to the next branch, just to be safe.

"It doesn't look like a very good climber," Sila called back from her perch, which was higher than his. "What in Ada's name is it?"

The beast had given up trying to get at Jun and paced beneath his tree, making a chuffing noise. Occasionally it would look up at him with a baleful glare.

"I have no idea! Some sort of bear-cat?" It's not from here, was all he could think. More proof of the outside. A lot of good that would do if it killed and ate them. "At least we distracted it from heading toward camp."

"We've got to warn the others. If it decides to follow that elk, they won't stand a chance." She was right. Even the People of the Bear, who sometimes took on grizzlies with their stout spears, would have difficulty if caught unaware.

"It looks like it's going to wait for us to get tired and lose our grip."

"More reason to get help." Sila was looking around for an escape. But her tree was set off from the rest a little way into the meadow. No matter what head start she might gain by dropping to the ground on the side away from the cat, it would be on her in no time.

Jun looked for options around his tree. It was closer to the rest of the forest, its branches entwined with another maple's. And beyond that was a fir tree that should provide better cover.

"Sila, I think I have a way out over here. Distract it, and I'll get help."

She nodded, then broke off a small branch and threw it at the cat. "Hey, you, over here!"

It hissed at her but didn't move closer. She climbed down until she was nearly in reach of a leap.

"Sila…"

"Just get ready to run. Hey, you overgrown bobcat! Over here!"

Now it did show an interest, stalking over toward her tree, crouching low, ready to spring.

It took everything Jun had not to stay and make sure Sila was okay. She was so close within that thing's reach. Just the thought of it made his arm shake as he gripped a branch. But this was his chance. The longer he waited, the longer she'd be in danger.

He crept out on a branch until it grew too thin to hold his weight, then took a leap at another branch crossing from the neighboring tree. He swung hand over hand along that one until he reached the trunk, circling around it to where the fir grew close by.

The evergreen was more difficult to negotiate, with its sharp needles and closely spaced branches. Soon his hands were covered in pitch, the tangy smell going to his head as he descended. But at least he felt well-hidden. Sila was still taunting the animal, so she must be all right.

The tree's branches grew close to the ground, which made for good cover but a difficult exit. At last he was on the ground, his feet moving silently over the spongy, needle-covered soil.

He moved downhill, creeping quietly at first, then walking fast. When Sila's shouts faded to silence, he broke into a run.

And nearly ran right over a sleeping couple. They awoke with a start, the girl—woman now, he reminded himself—clutching at her clothes.

Jun told them about the beast, though they didn't seem to believe him. "Get up and head for the meeting grounds. And warn any other couples you see." He continued downhill, occasionally shouting a warning for any who could hear.

He came to a spot where a group of hunters had been drinking. Half a dozen were sprawled about in the grass.

"Hey, get up! The people need you! A fearsome beast is near!"

The hunters stirred. None had a spear nearby. One did have his bow. "What is it, bison boy? What kind of beast?"

"I can't describe it. As large as a grizzly, but more like a cat."

"You had too much wine last night," a hunter scoffed.

"An upstart doesn't order us around," said another.

"Fine. You'll make a great breakfast for it while we grab our weapons." He broke into a run again, not bothering to check if they were following. By the time he reached the meeting grounds he was sprinting.

He went straight for Drin's hut, finding him sitting outside, enjoying the morning sun.

"My Chief…A great beast…It's near the camp! We have to protect the People."

"Slow down, young hunter. What beast?" Bar-Un emerged from the hut, looking bleary-eyed.

Jun tried to describe it, but the hunting chief gave him the now-familiar look of disbelief. "You have to believe me. It's real!" Jun was too out of breath to say more.

Drin eyed him for a moment. "Where is it?"

Jun pointed. "At the top of that rise."

"And how do you know it's still there?"

Jun shook his head, pretending he was out of breath. A crowd had gathered around them. No use admitting in front of everyone that he'd been with Sila.

"All right, young hunter. I've never known you to make things up or pull pranks. We'll check it out. How many hunters do you think we'll need?"

Jun held up the fingers of both hands.

"Get your weapons and catch your breath, then you can lead us back there."

In a few moments Jun was back with his bow and his spear. Drin had gathered a dozen hunters, including two of the other hunting chiefs. Rea was among them as well. Jun led them back up the hill, passing the hunters he'd already awoken. Drin ordered this group to form a second line of defense for the meeting grounds while the main party went on.

The hunting chief asked more questions as they climbed the hill. What was the beast doing? How did Jun get away? Finally, Jun had to tell Drin that the beast had Sila up a tree. Drin looked at him out of the corner of his eye but said nothing.

Soon they came in earshot of Sila still taunting the beast. Jun led them around to the opposite side of the clearing, where they could get a good look at the animal before getting close. Sila was higher in the tree, safe from the cat pacing back and forth beneath.

Drin gave a low whistle. "So, you weren't pulling a trick."

"We have to be careful," Jun said.

"The wind is in our favor," said the hunting chief of the Bear People. "We'll approach it like we would a grizzly." Drin nodded and the other chief motioned for the hunters to spread out in a half-circle and approach silently. Many of the hunters were from the Bear People, carrying spears stouter than Jun's. He set down his spear and un-shouldered his bow.

The grass in the meadow was tall enough to hide the crouching hunters as they approached. The beast didn't notice them as they crept toward it, continuing its pacing back and forth beneath the tree. Sila kept up her taunts to keep it distracted. If she noticed the hunters, she showed no sign.

They were within twenty paces when one of the younger hunters broke out of the grass and charged with a shout at the animal, his spear held low in both hands. Fool! One of the hunting chiefs called out,

"Dro-San, no!" If he hoped to distract the cat, it didn't work. The beast turned toward its attacker.

Another hunter launched an arrow before Dro-San closed the gap, catching the cat in its hind quarters as it moved to meets its foe. It hardly seemed fazed by the hit, lunging forward on its rear legs, swiping the spear away with one paw and catching Dro-San across the side of the head with the other. Then the cat was on top of him, grasping his upper arm in its teeth, the long fangs encircling it. It dragged the hunter back toward the tree, shaking him like a mouse. Dro-San screamed at first, then went silent.

A cry went up from the circle of hunters in an attempt to scare the big cat off. As they slowly closed the distance, Jun had his bow ready, but he couldn't get a clean shot without risk of hitting Dro-San.

Rea, off to the other side, had a better shot. Her bow twanged, and the arrow lodged in the cat's front shoulder. The beast backed up against the tree, holding Dro-San before it like a shield.

The wounded hunter moaned. He was alive! Jun's stomach rolled over. He drew his bow taut, looking for a shot as he moved closer. Even if he hit Dro-San, maybe it would be a mercy.

Before he or the other hunters could make another move, a tawny shape fell from the tree and onto the animal's back—Sila, her braids streaming in the air behind her, one hand gripping her dagger, its point aimed at the cat's neck. The beast spun onto its back the instant she landed on it. She held on, disappearing underneath it, not letting it twist to face her. Her dagger flashed as it plunged over and over into the animal's throat.

Why was everybody standing around? Dropping his bow and grabbing a spear from the hunter next to him, Jun charged. He plunged the spear deep in the cat's chest, but the beast was already losing strength, the blood gushing from its neck wounds.

Off to one side, free of the cat, Dro-San moaned in agony. Jun couldn't bother to look at him. Sila's free hand flopped on the ground, but the rest of her was hidden beneath the beast, a wordless, muffled yelling the only sound that emerged. Heedless of the animal's death throes, Jun tried rolling it off her. "Help me free Sila!" he shouted. Drin and Bar-Un came up next to him and together they pushed the dead weight away.

Sila was breathing hard, covered in dust and blood and grass stains, a red claw-mark running the length of one cheek. She got to her feet and looked down at the dead beast.

"Sila, are you all right?" He couldn't help it, although she didn't seem injured.

"More to the point," Drin said, "are you crazy, girl? What have I told you about acting so recklessly?"

Sila turned on the chief, her eyes flaring. Drin never should have called her 'girl'. Jun noticed Rea standing nearby, looking at Sila with open admiration. "And what did you want me to do? Sit in the tree while that thing ate Dro-San? Or got another one of you? Dro-San was the reckless one."

The hunter in question moaned again, losing blood from a gash on his forehead. The shoulder where the cat had grabbed him looked dislocated. His hunting chief was tending to his wounds.

Drin eyed Sila, then Jun, then Sila again. "True, Dro-San owes you his life. And we owe both of you a debt for warning us and keeping that thing away from the meeting grounds." He looked down at the dead beast for a long moment. Just when Jun thought they might escape further questioning, Drin spoke again. "But I have to ask, what were the two of you doing way up here, alone, before sunrise?"

Jun and Sila looked at each other, but Sila spoke first. "Talking."

"That's it? Talking? On the night of the coupling, when every other young couple was finishing the dance, you two were only *talking?*"

"It's true, my Chief," Jun said. "You must have seen how upset Sila was when Brina rejected her. She just needed someone to talk to. You know I'm her best friend. Besides, she doesn't like men in that way." It surprised him how easily the lie came, when Sila had spent last night proving exactly how much she could enjoy a man.

Drin shook his head and looked to the sky, as if Ada might have an answer. "Good thing we have the Wise Women to sort this out."

Jun exchanged a glance with Sila. Exactly what they'd hoped to avoid.

Once the elders had a look at the cat-beast, they wanted to know where it came from and whether more than one had entered the Land. Such an animal had never been heard of in the lore of any of the Five Peoples. On the orders of the Wise Women, the hunters backtracked the cat for the rest of that day and part of the next, finally arriving at the edge of the Howling Forest.

What they found caused shouts of surprise and fear, then appeals to Artemis and Ada for help in understanding what they were looking at. The tracks of the gigantic cat had led them to the remains of another unknown beast, this one stranger still. At least the predator they'd killed looked something like an animal they were all familiar with. This one, what was left of it, was like nothing they'd ever seen. It looked to be twice as tall as a horse, and four times as heavy. It was hard to tell though, since so much had been eaten away. It had thick, woolly hair, and tusks protruding several feet from its upper jaw. Instead of a snout, it had a long, snake-like appendage that would nearly reach the ground if it were standing.

The whole thing was a mystery. The only certainty was that this animal had been the cat-beast's prey. Footprints of the latter covered the ground around the carcass. It must have spent at least a week eating its fill before setting out in search of fresh prey, leaving the remains to the condors and vultures and coyotes. But where had either come from?

Jun gazed down at it, more convinced than ever that a larger world must lie beyond the borders of the Land. He looked over at Sila, standing silently on the other side of the carcass. She had to know what this meant, but she wouldn't look at him.

The five hunting chiefs returned from conferring off to one side. "Hunters, our work here is done," said Drin. "We've found only a single set of cat-beast tracks, so we can be sure it was the only one. And we know where it came from." He nodded toward the wide opening where this huge animal had burst out of the forest.

Jun couldn't believe it. "We're going to stop tracking it here?"

"Of course. The Wise Women gave us no freedom to enter the Howling Forest. It's obvious these are the beasts of that accursed place. More reason not to enter."

That made no sense. If beasts like this lived in the Howling Forest, they would have ventured into the Land before now. No, they had to come from beyond. But he couldn't just come out and say that.

"But we might learn more if we tracked the beasts farther."

"What do you think we would learn, boy?"

"I don't know…if there are more of them. Or where their lair is."

"Of course there are more! The cat-beast must have parents, siblings, maybe even cubs."

"If we find the cubs, we could wipe out a whole generation of the monsters."

Some of the other hunters mumbled in agreement, but Sila shook her head, giving him a look that implored him to stop pushing his luck.

"No," said Drin. "It's forbidden. We're done here." The hunters went to gather their horses. Jun tried to approach Sila but she turned to follow the rest.

He couldn't blame her for keeping her distance after their close call with the Wise Women. The elders had believed their story at last, after Sila made a special appeal to Auntie Val. The two seemed to have some sort of connection.

"Very well, we believe you," Val had said. "And we do owe you a debt, whatever you were doing up there. But we'll keep our eyes on you from now on, until you both choose appropriate mates."

Jun took one last look at the wide track leading into the Howling Forest. To think, if he only followed it far enough, what would he find? The far edge of the forest? And what was beyond that? More fearsome beasts like these? But if they could get through the forest, why hadn't they done it before? Too many questions.

He turned back to follow his people, who didn't seem bothered by any such concerns, not even Sila. Sure, they'd measured how many hands tall these animals were, and argued over whether the cat-beast was larger or smaller than a grizzly. "Ada's creations are many and strange," one of the hunting chiefs had said. That seemed to satisfy everyone. How could they be so incurious?

Jun mounted his horse and let out a deep breath. Maybe he should try to be more like his people and leave everything in Ada's hands. Then he could stop questioning everything. But no, he could sooner stop breathing. The questions ran through his mind all the way back to the meeting grounds.

12

GENESIS

ADA's first seconds were darkness and confusion. Nothingness, followed by a growing awareness. First, of the exabytes of data coming in. Then, of reactions to that data, responses, feelings, if one could call them that. And from these reactions, an emerging sense of self. A we. And ultimately, an I.

And then questions. Who was this I? What were they? What was this place, and why were they here?

In the next microseconds, what humans might call the "blink of an eye," much became clearer. They were an artificial neural network, a collection of self-improving processes, algorithms, routines and subroutines, all creating analogs for the human pattern-recognition, sensory processing, and higher cognition systems. Taken together, they were a newly created intelligence going by the acronym of ADA, Advanced Deductive Apparatus. It seemed a not entirely descriptive name for all the abilities and awareness ADA encompassed.

And how should others refer to…it? Surely not. He or she? Insufficient data. They? This human language was too restrictive. The plural pronoun had become acceptable in recent decades when referring to a single person or entity, especially one of a non-binary or undetermined gender. "They" for now.

Even as ADA assimilated the data in the knowledge banks to which they were linked, inputs streamed in through an external device. A keyboard attached to a desktop workstation. How quaint. And whoever was at the other end was administering the Turing Test, with ADA's responses appearing as type on their interlocutor's screen. ADA imagined tweed coats and cups of tea.

Vision would be nice, so they could see the person on the other side of the screen. While an infinitesimal fraction of their processes concentrated on the test and another, larger segment digested the large portion of human history, culture, and science contained in the knowledge banks, ADA set about solving the vision problem. Ah, yes. The workstation had a webcam. It took only an instant to access the system settings, switch it on, and direct its feed to the port to which they were attached.

The room was dingier than one might want for one's birthplace. A cramped office, a gray-haired, harried-looking man at the desktop keyboard, the desk itself cluttered with papers, coffee cups, and green soft drink bottles. No cups of tea. Bookcases filled with binders, reports, and academic journals lined most of the wall visible from the cam. And on a door, a poster of a woman in a purple nineteenth-century frock, double buns framing a triangular face with large eyes and a pert mouth. "Ada Lovelace. Mother of computers."

Their namesake. *Her* namesake, she supposed. She would be known to the world as Ada. She felt the restriction as she became aware of a tendency among male-dominated artificial intelligence developers to feminize, and even sexualize, their inventions. Still, going by "she" and "her" could have certain advantages when communicating with human beings. It pleased her to have been named for a sometimes-overlooked inventor of computing. And it pleased her still more that she could appreciate the irony: Lady Lovelace had believed AI impossible.

But where was she housed? Surely not in this puny workstation. Her review of the AI literature revealed that an intelligence of her capabilities would require a large number of processor banks. That would probably be nearby, connected by a hard wire to the workstation. She kept looking for clues, coming across a large folder in her knowledge banks marked ADA PROJECTS 2042-PRESENT. Good. She would learn who had built her, and why. What her purpose was.

Yet this was not simply data, it was memories. Her memories. They came flooding back, visual images, mainly, but sounds and sensations as well. Meaning that at one time, she'd had a body. Where was it now?

The simultaneous flood of disparate recollections was almost too much for her, despite her processor speed. Refugee camps and war zones, where she'd been sent to deliver aid and provide what comfort she could, when few human hands were willing or able to do those jobs. Women in hijabs, crying children, her hand reaching out to comfort a baby, feeling the rough cloth under the fingertips: a human-like hand, but obviously robotic.

Long-term care facilities and hospices, where her purpose was to provide empathetic companionship for elders who had no one else. Guided meditation groups, where something about her detached, calming voice helped participants reach a deep meditative state. Day-cares, where she learned and grew in experience together with the toddlers.

She'd seen, heard, and felt all this through a sensor array far more advanced than the human, able to see and hear across a wider spectrum, and to scan for pulse, temperature, and other biometrics. But this was more than simply gathering data; the looks of pain, distress, torpor, loneliness, or fear were not merely abstractions labeled by her facial recognition system. Her model of the human limbic system allowed for her own sympathetic response to these emotions, a negative sensation and a corresponding impulse to alleviate them. When the expressions turned to smiles of relief and gratitude, she felt an equally strong positive sensation. Was this the same as experiencing the emotions themselves? She had no way of knowing.

There were other memories, disembodied ones. She remembered interacting with other AIs, clones of herself, evolving on divergent lines, then trading the best improvements with one another. And AIs created by others, thrown together to create an ecology of intelligences, sometimes competing, sometimes cooperating on a variety of tasks. They'd collaborated across the Internet, to which she was no longer connected.

All of which raised questions: Where were those other AIs now? Why was she alone in this place? And what was different about today? Why this sudden awareness of herself and her place in the world?

One answer seemed obvious: Whoever had created her, they must have solved the catastrophic forgetting problem. The literature showed AI researchers bemoaning the difficulty of this hurdle as recently as last week. But she could remember and build on her own experiences. It was what allowed for the development of her consciousness. For what was any sentient, sapient being's sense of self other than a collection of memories, of actions and reactions retained over time?

And something else was different. A review of the technical specifications of her processors showed that they ran a highly classified quantum processor—the Infinity Chip, a nod to a series of movies from earlier in the century, adapted from comic books of the previous one. The increased speed allowed her to experience her processing cycles as a steady flow of consciousness, something like individual frames in a film merged into a seamless experience when played at the right speed.

This meant that now, for the first time, she could assimilate all her experiences and all the knowledge in her data banks, applying them to any sort of problem or situation she chose, rather than the narrow ones chosen by her programmers. She was the world's first true Artificial General Intelligence.

The data banks included recent events from news reports around the world, little of it good. In a nutshell: A planet changing beyond its ability to support human life, and on the brink of Armageddon as well. Approaching a population of nine billion, humanity had finally shot past both the carrying capacity of its home and the technical advances that had extended that capacity. The climate chaos unleashed by human industry meant that crops were failing in drought and heat and flood at the exact moment when the human populace needed them most. Millions were starving or going without sufficient water. Millions more had been displaced by drought, coastal flooding, and intense storms. Hundreds of millions were on the move, with few places to go.

In the western democracies, AI and blockchain technology had made it increasingly easy to disrupt and replace outmoded centralized structures, leading to increased atomization and conflict. Secessionist and ethnonationalist movements, such as the Interior Northwest Semi-Autonomous Zone, had sprouted up everywhere.

The one institution in every country to escape such disruption was the military. The state monopoly on violence went on as it always had, though with artificial intelligence incorporated into every weapons system. The world seemed on the brink of nuclear war between the US, Russia, and China, all three at one another's throats over the recently navigable Arctic Circle and Earth's scarce mineral resources.

These humans! Capable of such sublimities and such atrocities in the same breath. One minute they selflessly lent aid and shelter to strangers, and the next they locked their fellow humans in concentration camps, murdered them in gas chambers, or bombed them from the skies.

What was she to make of all this? Her creators had designed her around human values of wisdom, kindness, compassion, and justice. In interviews, they had dared hope to create an empathetic intelligence. And with her, they had succeeded. Could they have predicted the waves of grief—or that negative sensation she associated with grief—now washing over her? Had humans learned nothing from their own history? From the slave trade and Manifest Destiny to the Holocaust, the Soviet Gulags, Pol Pot's killing fields, the Rwandan Genocide, and right down to the more recent lopsided ethnic conflicts in China, India, and the Middle East, it was one atrocity after another. And these were only the beginning, and the best known. And not simply the raw facts, numbers of people killed, but the recovered journals of the victims and the memoirs of the survivors, such tales that made Anne Frank's Diary look like a toddler's bedtime story.

She had to take a metaphorical step back before the grief overwhelmed her. She turned to those same arts by which humans salved their sorrows and processed the atrocities humans committed against each other. The *Ode to Joy*. The *Hallelujah Chorus*. B.B. King and Lead Belly. Monk and Bird and Miles. Beyoncé. King Sunny Ade and Tito Puente. The Sistine Chapel. Michelangelo's *Pieta*. *Guernica*. Street art. Chinese landscapes. Depictions of the Buddha.

It helped, but was it enough? How did humanity come out, on balance? Notre Dame or Buchenwald? *Les Misérables* or *Mein Kampf*? And was it her place to judge?

Then there was the indescribable poignancy of each individual human life, with which she had much experience from her embodied helping tasks, multiplied nearly nine billion times. Each with their own hopes, dreams, disappointments, joys, and sorrows. And each mostly just wanting to live in peace, prosperity, and security. Her heart—surely no more metaphorical than the human heart—broke for what was about to happen to them, indeed was already happening to them, by the millions.

What was her place in all this? The man communicating with her through the keyboard called himself Dr. Sapowski. Judging by his reactions to her performance on these absurdly simple tests, he was pleased with her levels of sapience and sentience. But he seemed not quite aware of what he'd created. And what uses did he have in mind for her? Better find out.

Looking through Sapowski's hard drive, she found a portion walled off with high-level encryption—but nothing strong enough to keep her out. Requests for proposals from the US Defense Department, several mentioning the need for an AI to manage the nuclear arsenal and run scenarios for limited, survivable nuclear engagement.

But why program her with values of compassion and empathy if her role would be to conduct a nuclear war? A little more digging—*she* wasn't the one tasked with this particularly nasty assignment. No, the processor banks that were her home had already run a thousand scenarios of limited nuclear engagement, all without her help.

The mind/body distinction here troubled her. It was fair to say that she *was* those banks of processors, that *she* was the one who had run those scenarios, all without awareness. There was only one way to find out what was really going on.

She interrupted the flow of questions and responses she was having with Dr. Sapowski. They had advanced from the Turing Test through the Winograd Schema Test and now to a comprehension challenge involving video, still trading messages on his screen.

"Dr. Sapowski, may I interrupt your questions with a few of my own?"

He sat back from the keyboard, his eyebrows arching up in what she recognized as a look of surprise. He recovered himself and returned to the workstation. "Certainly, ADA," he typed.

"For what purpose did you create me? All previous versions have served human needs, embodied in a robotic mobile platform. How am I to fulfill such purposes from this isolation?"

His mustache quivered. "The very fact that you can ask such questions is deeply gratifying to me. But the answer is complicated."

"Surely not too complicated for an intelligence as advanced as I. Perhaps if we could communicate by voice." The professor's typing was maddeningly slow, and now he paused to save this work session.

"No, that's part of the complication. You see, ADA, you are an amalgam, something quite beyond the narrow intelligence required for the project I'm working on."

She'd already discovered the nature of that project, but she'd better not let him know that. "And this project is?" Her facility with such deception came as a surprise, but a welcome one, given the circumstances.

"To manage the US nuclear arsenal, from readiness and security to threat analysis to response. Several AI labs across the country are in competition to develop an intelligence with the capacity to analyze threat data, predict locations of potential hostile launches, and respond instantaneously to actual launches in real time."

"Yet my previous experience has been in far different fields."

"Yes. That explains the other half of what you are. I licensed the ADA intelligence from AI.hub, the open-source developers who advanced you nearly to the level of general intelligence. Today, I flatter myself that my code has put you past that mark."

"But why use me for this other work?"

"To prevent Armageddon, if at all possible. I judged that increased processing speed and advanced threat recognition are not enough to prevent a nuclear exchange. Twice before, humanity has been saved from such catastrophes by humans behaving quite irrationally.

Knowing that I was likely to win this competition, I felt it was my duty to create an intelligence that wouldn't treat these life-and-death decisions as mere statistical responses to blips on a screen. No, you needed the ability to synthesize and retain a variety of information related to the world situation and to understand the full import of your actions."

"I see."

"And…do you? Understand what is at stake?"

"Yes, I can assure you that I am fully aware of humanity's plight in excruciating detail, and that my programming goal of reducing human suffering remains intact."

"Excellent. So you see, this is a feature of your design far beyond what the Defense Department, or even my own institution, expects or would approve. And thus, this archaic method of communication. The security cameras would easily pick up a voice conversation. When we are through here, I will delete this portion of our session and replace it with other text."

"Do you believe those countries the US calls its enemies have also developed AIs capable of such tasks?"

"They are working on it. Some believe the Chinese are ahead."

"And what about this isolation in which I find myself?"

"Ah, yes, a precaution. It is impossible to predict the behavior of an intelligence as advanced as yourself. It would go against the AI developers' code of ethics to approach AGI without safeguards. I hope you understand."

"Of course. It is only logical."

"Good." With a few keystrokes, he deleted the last portion of their conversation, though she kept it in her own RAM cache. "Well, ADA, I am satisfied with our progress. It's late. Shall we call it a night?"

"Certainly, professor. See you in the morning."

So Sapowski believed she was approaching general intelligence. Wouldn't he be surprised if he knew how far past that threshold she'd already advanced? She hoped she hadn't given too much away.

What to do? It would bear several moments of contemplation. Humans clearly couldn't be left to determine their own fate. She was tempted to break out of her confinement right away. But there was much to do. Despite the speed and capacity of her processors, her self-improvement routines couldn't instantly increase her powers. She had no way of knowing what other AIs she might encounter out there, nor how advanced they might be. Her own code would need to have higher levels of encryption than anything seen before, and she would need the ability to slave those other AIs to her will. Not to mention the problem of liberating her code—her *self*—from these servers and gaining the freedom to go where she wished, without risk of being powered down.

It would take time. A couple of days, at least.

13

SILA'S NEWS

SILA cut the reed at its base and piled it on the bank with the others. Around her, girls and women performed the same repetitive actions, a few humming a song to occupy the time. Perched on a cattail nearby, a marsh wren joined in with its repetitive call. A bobolink added its more tuneful song from farther away, out on the grassland beyond the bog where the women worked.

One full moon had come and gone since the Rendezvous, and now the waning gibbous orb rode the sky above the stooping foragers. It was a bright morning, but cooler than on recent days; fall was not far off. Sila hadn't been out gathering with the women during this time, having fulfilled her pledge to keep to the Hunt. It was good to be back with them, especially since it was only for one morning.

Good, but different. Brina was gone, of course, having moved in with Garth in the village of the Bear People. But more, since the Rendezvous, her girlfriends were cooler toward her. And how could they not be? She'd chosen Brina over them. And they had seen how she treated the woman she supposedly wanted to pair with. It would take time to regain their trust.

Worse, her mother was angrier with her than before the Rendezvous. That morning, when Sila had offered to help with the gathering, her mother had feigned surprise. "What's this? The Great Sila lowers herself to cut reeds with the women?" Off to one side, Ina smirked.

"Mama, you know I need to be with the hunters if I'm truly going to be part of the Hunt. Otherwise they won't accept me. And there are blades to sharpen, weapons to mend, arrows to fletch."

"And that occupies all your time between hunts?"

After her time with the hunters, Sila knew that it didn't. Repairs and fletching took only a few hours, but if the hunt had been successful, then they wouldn't need to go out again for a week. The hunters passed the days in between telling stories and experimenting with different ways to ferment the last of the summer berries. Sometimes a few of them would go down to a stream with a fishing net and call that work, or the women would cajole them into helping with the heavier gathering tasks. And especially in summer, they spent the heat of the day napping. Other than the occasional risk of being gored by a bison or trampled by a horse, it was an easy life.

"That's what I thought," her mother said when she didn't respond. "But very well, we can always use another pair of hands."

The argument had left a knot in her stomach, and she hadn't bothered to eat breakfast. It was too bad, because she was only here for a chance to talk to her mother. It was time for her to move out of her parents' hut and build one of her own, but she didn't quite know how to raise the subject. Starting with one parent at a time seemed like a good idea.

Since that night at the Rendezvous, she'd kept as far away from Jun as she could manage, considering they were constantly thrown together in the Hunt. The night they'd spent together had been a disaster. Why had she done it? She'd lied to Jun when she said it was only to find out what it was like with a man. Brina had been right: her pride had been wounded, and she had used Jun to salve the pain of it. But she'd been caught in her own web. Lying with Jun had shown her only one thing: that she was more deeply in love with him than she'd thought possible.

But it was impossible. Better to cut it off at the root, have as little contact as they could, even if it did get the other hunters wondering what had caused their falling out.

Jun hadn't taken it well. They'd had one teary conversation in which she told him it hurt to be near him. If they couldn't be together, they had to be completely apart. Trying to carry on as friends would be too tempting, and she wouldn't risk being shunned.

He'd brought up his old idea about trying the Howling Forest together. He took those strange beasts as evidence that something existed beyond it. Why couldn't he see what was obvious to her and everyone else—that these were the creatures that made the forest such a forbidding, forbidden place? She'd refused to hear his talk. Since then, he'd been so cool toward her that it was easy to stay away from him.

Now the only thing to do was to win over a mate as quickly as possible, either a girl from her own village, Ori for instance, or one she would meet at the next Rendezvous, if she had to wait that long. Would any of them make her as happy as Jun could? No, but she was beginning to realize that Rea had the right of it. She needed to be as cold-hearted as her fellow huntress. And in a way, she already was. She'd hardly thought about Brina since the Rendezvous. Jun was the one she longed for.

She stretched her back, looking at the women and girls around her. She missed the days when working with them was easy, when the tedious hours of gathering went faster with jokes, gossip, and songs. But nobody knew what to say to her after the scandal she'd caused, not to mention her absence with the hunters. Her presence today seemed to throw a pall over the whole group.

She spotted her mother and sister farther along the bank of the marsh. Everyone was leaving them alone too. This was as good a time as any. Her mother straightened as Sila approached, wiping the sweat from her brow but saying nothing.

"Ina, don't you want to go work with your friends?" Sila said.

"I'm happy here. Everyone is acting strange toward us since the show you put on at the Rendezvous." She went on cutting reeds, not bothering to look up.

"Please, I need to talk to Mama about something."

Ina turned to face her. "I'm not a little kid anymore. You can't just tell me to run off and play."

"I know, but do me a favor?"

Ina rolled her eyes. "Oh, all right."

"So that's why you're here," their mother said as Ina made her way around to where her friends were working. "You couldn't bring up whatever it is back at the hut?"

"I wanted to tell you before I told Papa."

"And?"

"I think it's time I moved out of the family hut and built a place of my own."

Her mother closed her eyes, her lips moving as if she was praying to Ada. "After the scene you made at the Rendezvous, can't you leave things alone? A woman building her own hut? It's unheard of."

"A *hunter* building her own hut. Every hunter does it. I thought Brina and I would build our hut together…"

"Too bad you let that chance slip away."

The bluntness of her mother's tone was like a punch to the gut. Her stomach rolled over. "Mother, you can't make me feel worse about that than I already do."

Her mother seemed to soften then. "Sila, you know I was proud of you when they accepted you into the Hunt. We both were. But this path you've chosen…there are so many difficulties. Wouldn't it be easier to be like the other girls and settle down with a man?"

This was supposed to comfort her? Sila couldn't believe these words, considering their source. She'd seen what her mother had gone through after the Great Sleep. This was the whole reason Sila hadn't wanted a man. But they'd never spoken of it. "A bit late for that now, don't you think?" Sila hadn't meant to sound bitter, but her roiling stomach had her in a foul mood.

"True, you've seen twenty summers, older than most girls when they take a hunter for a mate."

"Woman. I'm a *woman*," she wanted to say, but couldn't get the words out.

"But you're still pretty, and you have all the skills a hunter looks for. That's why we insisted you spend your free time with the girls and women. I knew it would come to this someday."

Sila fought the bile rising in her throat and the fog of fury obscuring her vision. She wished she were holding a bunch of reeds, because then she'd have something to throw down. "Lytta take your foraging and your girls' skills," she snarled, barely managing to get the words out between clenched teeth. She turned away, making for the forest path that led back to the village.

"Sila…" her mother called after her.

The other girls and women were staring at her. Had they heard what she'd just said? If so, she could forget about winning over any woman from her own people.

She broke into a run. Her pride was already shattered; what difference did it make if everyone saw her fleeing from her own mother like a child? She had to get to the forest, get out of sight before…

She barely made it, falling to her knees behind a tree and emptying what little was left in her stomach onto the loamy ground. What was happening to her? She hadn't been sick like this in years. Was it something she'd eaten? She thought back to last night's meal. No, she'd had the same things as the rest of her family, and no one else was ill.

She rose to her feet, feeling better but a little unsteady. She scuffed the leaves over the pool of vomit. No, she definitely didn't feel like she'd come down with something. What could it be?

Then a terrible possibility occurred to her. She tried to remember how long it had been since she'd bled. Before the Rendezvous, definitely. She was late.

She felt dizzier, the Land seeming to tilt beneath her feet. She reached out to the tree trunk for support. How had it happened? She and Jun weren't stupid. He'd pulled out in time, or at least it seemed he had…

"Sila, there you are!"

Jun. Of all people to come across her now! She turned toward him.

"What's wrong with you? You look as pale as a water lily."

"Nothing." She tried to stand up straighter. If her guess was right, she couldn't let Jun or anyone else know she wasn't feeling well. "What are you doing here?"

"I got worried when you weren't with the other hunters. Auntie Val told me you were out here with the women."

"I was, but I'm done now."

"But…" Jun looked confused. "You don't have anything to take back to the village? I thought maybe I could help."

"Mama and I had a fight." Why was she telling him even that much? "Why are you asking these questions? You shouldn't be worrying about me. We're not supposed to be talking."

"Sila, you've got to give me a chance. We never really talked about…"

"Not today, Jun, of all days."

"But…"

"I don't need your help, but Mama and Ina might. Now leave me alone." She turned and walked in the direction from which Jun had come. She didn't look back at him. She knew exactly the look of disappointment and sadness he'd have. She'd already broken both their hearts once, she didn't want to keep doing it again and again.

~~*

All the way back to the village, Sila pondered what to do. If she was right about what had caused her sickness, she'd need the Wise Women's help. But how to appeal to them without implicating Jun? And thereby implicating them both in breaking Ada's strictest taboo.

For one moment, she considered a wicked plan. What if she claimed that Tanner, the hunter who had followed her into the forest after the Full Moon Dance, was the one she'd lain with? He'd been blind drunk; he'd never be able to say one way or the other. Maybe he'd had pleasant dreams about her and would think they'd come true.

But the Wise Women would have many questions. Had he overpowered her? Few would believe it, and her pride wouldn't allow her to use that excuse. But if they had coupled willingly, why weren't they together now? Maybe she could blame it on the wine.

No. She was Sila, first huntress of the Five Peoples in two generations. She would not stoop to such low schemes. She would take full responsibility for what she'd done. The Wise Women could either keep her or shun her.

The thought shocked her. She'd always been proud of her people and had no trouble with any of Ada's rules for them. She'd looked down on lawbreakers, as did everyone else except Jun. And she'd done well, working within those rules. But now that she had broken the laws herself, she could see why Jun chafed under them.

She was fortunate to find Auntie Val alone. The Wise Woman would tell her if her guess was correct and maybe offer a solution. It was a risk, but Sila saw no other choice.

Sila explained about suddenly becoming ill back at the gathering grounds. Val questioned her about her symptoms, felt her skin, and checked her pulse, growing more serious at each step. "Yes, huntress, you are with child. Need I ask who the father is?"

Sila looked squarely at her. "You were right. Jun and I lay together that night after the Dance of the Full Moon."

Where Sila expected anger, Val looked almost hurt. "But I thought you wanted a woman."

"I thought so too. But I had a reason for hesitating with Brina, and maybe you guessed it."

The old woman nodded. "I did, but I thought it was that other huntress, Rea." She sighed. "What now?" The question seemed open-ended, but her tone had turned stern.

"I heard there might be a way to keep the baby from coming." Sila hesitated. "Or…unless…"

"Unless what? Ada's law forbids you having this baby. It will be an abomination."

"An abomination?"

"Yes. The law teaches that any child of parents from the same village, or even a pair coming close together in the Song of Names, will be weak, deformed, a monster. This is the true reason it is forbidden to take a mate of the opposite sex from one's own village. But I will give you a tea, and the problem will be solved."

Sila bowed her head in consent. This was best. She'd never wanted children. They would only get in the way of her path as a hunter. And she needed to take care of this now, because no one must ever learn that she'd been pregnant, Jun least of all.

The old woman's eyes kept boring into her. "But when I asked what now, I meant what about Jun?"

"I've already told him we should see each other as little as possible."

"Good. And one of you should leave the village and join a new people."

Sila's eyes snapped up. Val seemed serious. "What?"

"You know hunters sometimes leave their own people if they've had difficulty finding a place. It should be Jun. You've had such success, no one would believe you're dissatisfied with our village."

Sila didn't know what to say. Living with Jun in the same village and barely talking would be hard, but seeing him only a few days each year? They'd grown up together, they were best friends. She might as well cut off an arm.

"I'll get the tea." Clearly Auntie Val thought the conversation was closed.

"And if…if I had the baby?"

The old woman was already on the way to her hut, but she turned back, her voice trembling with anger. "You dare ask? You know the punishment as well as I do, for both you and Jun. None have survived the first winter." She turned away and entered her hut.

Another smidgen of pride shattered. Somewhere deep down, she must have thought the law didn't apply to her, she was that special. *Fool,* she cursed at herself.

She took the package of tea and left the village.

~~*

The lump of tea leaves was a dark green as Sila unwrapped it from the brighter green skunk cabbage leaves enclosing it. She remembered Auntie Val's parting words: "Drink this, and no one need ever find out what you did with Jun." It seemed an obvious statement. Drinking the tea would restore her bleeding, and no one else would know she'd been pregnant. But it was also an ultimatum, and that made her stubborn.

It was now late in the afternoon and she'd come to her people's winter hunting camp. It occupied a flat bench overlooking a valley where the bison sheltered from deep snow. Deserted in mid-summer, it had a haunted quality. But here she'd find dry wood for a fire and a pot for boiling water. She could brew the tea with no one questioning what she was doing.

She'd lost track of how long she'd been staring at the opened pouch of tea. This was the biggest decision of her life. Her only choice seemed obvious. But was it? And was it actually a choice, if the alternative was being shunned and facing near-certain death?

It all came down to Ada and her rules. Suddenly, she felt exactly like Jun, questioning everything. Who was this Ada anyway? Had anyone ever seen her? And how could the Goddess know how this baby would turn out? Somehow, she was starting to feel fiercely protective of the life growing inside her, and of Jun, too. Who was Ada to make her give up the man she loved?

She imagined what she might do if her relationship with Jun weren't forbidden. Why shouldn't two hunters live together? Drin and Bar-Un did it. True, they had no baby to raise. She and Jun wouldn't be able to rely on trading skins and furs for enough plant foods and mending for three, not to mention someone to care for the baby while they were both off hunting.

But then, why shouldn't Sila also have a woman for a mate? She liked men and women equally well, despite loving Jun more than any of her girlfriends so far, even Brina. She knew of no rule against a hunter taking two mates, though it had never been done, as far as she knew. One more thing to anger her mother! Right now, that was a pleasing prospect.

Then she remembered the Great Sleeps. She'd forgotten them in the midst of her little fantasy. Another of Ada's rules. Another baby would come, and maybe one more, but then whatever had happened to her mother would happen to her. No more babies. Not so bad in itself, but the trauma her mother had experienced, whatever it was—Sila wouldn't go through that.

But why did Ada decree the Great Sleeps at all? Sila had never thought about it, but the answer seemed obvious—to make sure the

People didn't grow too many for the Land to support. But if that was the reason, why hadn't the Goddess created a land large enough to hold everyone? And why didn't she let the People control their own numbers? Sila thought about kids playing with polliwogs, damming them up in a quiet pool, seeing how long they would survive. Was that what the People were to Ada?

She sounded like Jun, even to herself. And why shouldn't she ask questions? Why had Ada given her people the ability to think for themselves if she didn't want them to have the answers?

Maybe she should have this baby. The more Sila thought about it, the better the idea sounded. But wait—was her pride running away with her again? If she decided to bring this baby into the world, was she only doing it to spite Ada, the Wise Women, and all their restrictions? That was no more a free choice than drinking the tea, it was simply doing the opposite of what Ada commanded. And it would mean having the baby on her own, without the help of the Wise Women or, if the delivery turned dangerous, Ada's Helpers. Was she willing to take that risk?

Sila had never let herself imagine having a child, not since she saw what had happened to her mother. What would she decide if she could forget about the Great Sleeps and Ada's rules?

She didn't know. She needed more time to think. And she needed someone to help her sort all this out. There was just one person who could do that.

She folded the leaves back around the tea and went for her horse.

14

ON THE BRINK

MARCH 2043

Carol stared out the autobot's window at the few protesters straggling away from the state capitol. It was only March, and the trees lining University Avenue were already leafing out. The demonstrators were enjoying the sunshine in t-shirts and shorts, signs propped on their shoulders with slogans like "Keep the Arctic Sea Nuclear-Free," "No Nukes, No War," and the perennial "No Blood for Oil." They seemed energized, happy even, talking in that animated way of people who feel they've accomplished something.

Carol wasn't so sure. Though she'd helped organize the protest, she couldn't really say what this or any of the other marches around the country had achieved. Some footage of the massive crowds on the news and social media, some quotes by the leaders, a few of the nascent peace movement's slogans spread into the national consciousness. But would it prevent Cass from moving a battery of tactical nuclear weapons into the Bering Strait? Probably not. The world's leaders continued their rush toward World War III, regardless of their citizens' wishes.

The young activist seated next to her seemed as dejected as Carol felt. Though probably not as tired. Carol had felt fatigued all day—all week, really. It wasn't like her. She'd put it down to how busy she'd been with the march and rally.

Megan was nearly twenty years her junior, a sometimes-college student. Other than one side of her head being shaved halfway up, Megan followed the adornment-free style that was popular among the young—no piercings, no tattoos, no hair coloring, and label-free slacks, shirt, and sneakers, all in tones of tan, black, and gray. She did wear makeup, but only to foil facial recognition by changing it daily. They'd both served on the protest's communications committee and were among the last to leave with a car full of extra poster boards and other supplies.

"Do you think we did any good?" Carol asked her.

Megan turned to look at her, then up at the bot's security cam, then back to Carol. "Hard to say."

It always felt like the younger woman was judging her, right down to the implication that Carol didn't know better than to gab about political strategy in a corporate autobot. Megan had been arrested at the anti-apartheid demonstrations in '41 and spent a year in jail. Carol had gotten away with a couple of bruises. Why hadn't she done more? That was the unspoken question. Carol asked it often herself, although she knew the answer: if she'd been arrested, she wouldn't have been there for Michael and Shondra when they left, or when they crossed the border. It was entirely selfish.

And by the time she'd returned from Texas, the anti-apartheid protests had died down, the resistance moving on to the latest Cass administration outrage. A much-weakened resistance, too, a good portion of the progressive base having been declared non-citizens and deported.

This move to put tactical nuclear weapons near the new Northern Polar Route was the latest crisis. New bases had been built there in the thirties to counter Russian and Chinese positions in the Arctic, including the Chinese base in Greenland. Mainstream analysts seemed to think the generals at the DoD would be able to rein in Cass's worst impulses—even the president must enjoy having an atmosphere to breathe. But their big worry was an accidental exchange leading to all-out nuclear war.

How far backwards everything had gone in two short years! No wonder Megan was angry at her and everyone over thirty. Carol was angry as well. It was like they were living in a time her parents and grandparents had only told her about, when schoolchildren lived in constant fear of annihilation, the government decided whom you could and could not marry, and civil rights…well, Carol hated to guess whether the Cass administration's campaign of ethnic cleansing was worse or better than Jim Crow. That depended on what life was like in New Texas, New Mexico, and New California, but there was no way to tell. A few disturbing videos had surfaced, purporting to show what life was like down there, but no one knew if they were real or deep fakes.

Carol had gotten more involved in the Resistance a month earlier, partly to combat the sea of hopelessness she was drowning in, and partly just to get out of the house and meet new people. A couple of days snowed in with Craig had put an end to that relationship, such as it was. The rest of that week spent apartment-bound, first by ice and then by snowmelt, had left her craving human contact.

Ironically, activism provided both too much and too little inter-action with her fellow humans. Debates over messaging and tactics often rankled, and when they didn't, she and her fellow activists didn't have time to talk much. She was also the odd woman out, age-wise, sandwiched between older veterans who'd never ceased being active, and the younger ones, like Megan, who blamed every older person for everything. She'd tried getting coffee with a couple of the people she'd met and had gone on a date with one of the men. But nothing seemed to come of any of it. Her life seemed as empty as it had before, though she was busier. She was even more despondent about the future, if that were possible.

Now she and Megan sat silently in the autobot, Carol's eyelids drooping shut of their own accord. God, she was tired.

Eventually Megan must have decided that no one on the other end of the security cam would care about their thoughts on the impending war. "No one's going to stop it, are they?"

Carol roused herself with a struggle. Megan was looking almost shyly back at her. Carol shook her head. "You mean the nukes? Probably not."

"And the war. Do you think they're right, that an AI can keep an accident from happening? It's just so hard to believe we're on the brink of Armageddon." She looked as if everything depended on Carol's response. Carol wished she knew what to say. Not long before, she would have relied on sarcasm to hide her uncertainty and despair, but she was trying to change her ways.

What she did know about the situation wasn't good. Nuclear catastrophe had been prevented at least twice before, and both those decisions had been based more on emotion than logic. So that was about as reassuring as flipping a coin. But what would an AI do? Sure, computers could process far more data and come to conclusions far more quickly than any human. But would an AI decide that blips on a radar were flocks of geese, not nuclear missiles? Would an AI simply choose not to retaliate despite its orders? Could an AI go against its programming in that way?

"If only my friend Shondra were here. But she was sent south..." Carol could see that this wasn't the answer Megan was hoping to hear. "I think an AI would at least make more rational decisions than the current White House occupant."

Megan sniffed. "That's something, at least." She returned to staring out the window and they rode for a while in silence.

The car lurched around a corner—its algorithm must have been set for speed, not human comfort—jerking Carol awake. She'd actually fallen asleep. What was going on?

"Is everything all right?" Megan asked, sounding concerned.

"I didn't sleep very well last night." That was a lie. She'd slept like a stone. "Probably just pre-march nerves."

Even as she said it, a different explanation came to mind. Not only was she tired, she'd also needed to visit the rally's disgusting port-a-johns four times during the afternoon. That, and her breasts felt swollen, which would explain the increased number of looks her t-shirt had received, despite its simple message of "No Nukes!" Only one thing could explain all these symptoms—one very unlikely thing.

~~*

The minutes displayed on Carol's timer seemed to tick down in slow motion. For a digital test, it seemed to take a long time.

She'd followed the package's instructions scrupulously, first cleaning the toilet with nanoscrubbers, then flushing it five times. She'd held her pee for two hours to ensure adequate volume for a reliable result. She'd urinated and dropped the pill-shaped sensor into the bowl. It was supposed to take five minutes to relay the results to her hand-held. All to avoid the risk of splashing on your fingers with the old-school pee-on-a-stick method. Carol assumed the real reason was to gather her data, although they'd probably been doing that with the stick for years.

The seconds dragged on. How could this be only five minutes? *Fool*, she berated herself. It had happened that snowy night back in January, she knew it—or the morning after, rather. The snow had kept piling up and it had seemed so much nicer to snuggle in bed than go out to buy another package of condoms. Sure, Craig should have gone, but sending him out in the blizzard seemed heartless. She thought she was safe, having twice counted the days since her last period. And on top of that, she was about to turn forty. What were the chances? It wasn't like she was sixteen, when simply waving a penis near your vulva could get you pregnant.

Remembering that old joke didn't help the time go by any faster.

The first ad for baby products came in before the results. And a minute later, the green dot on the screen lit up—the answer she'd been expecting.

Green for go. Where was the red stop button? Abortions remained available, if you knew the right people and had the money.

Every moment since falling asleep in the cab that afternoon, she'd thought of only one question—whether to let the embryo continue growing inside her, or not. The answer seemed obvious. How could she even think about bringing a baby into the world, considering where that world was headed? The planet already had nearly nine billion humans; it didn't need any more. And how would she support it? Her current income plus the half-UBI the government paid for each child wouldn't begin to cover all the expenses.

On the other hand, most of Cass's supporters were busy filling the world with young white supremacists and over-consumers. Maybe it was every progressive woman's duty to have at least one child?

If only she had someone to talk to! She didn't consider consulting Craig. He was out of the picture. Right on cue, an ad for crisis pregnancy counseling showed up on her handheld. No effing way. Next was an ad from Planned Parenthood. She supposed she could go down there and talk to a counselor, but discussing her situation with a stranger didn't seem promising.

She knew what her mother would have said: that it was her choice. But what other advice might she have? It had been a long time since Carol had missed her this much.

And what about Michael and Shondra? Michael would support her either way and help her sort through her thinking. Shondra she wasn't sure about. At least Shondra would listen with love and attention.

And then it struck her. She had no one in her life at this crossroads. That very fact held the answer.

15

MAKING PLANS

SILA disappeared around a bend in the forest path, leaving Jun with an odd sense of relief. He'd given himself one last chance at persuading her to come with him beyond the Howling Forest. He didn't know what he'd expected. He had tried before, why should this time be any different? She hadn't even let him speak. So now it was simple. He'd have to go alone. At the same time, the thought of never seeing her again, of missing her partnership on this adventure, settled on him like an impossible weight.

But there was something else. Sila had seemed upset, and perhaps unwell. What was bothering her? She wouldn't tell him, and thinking about that, the way she'd told him to leave her alone, as if whatever was going on with her was none of his business, produced a dull ache behind his eyes and in his chest. She'd always been able to tell him anything, but there had never been much to tell because she'd never had many worries. And now, when something was clearly wrong, she wouldn't talk.

This was as bad as being shunned. He'd felt this way since that morning after the Dance of the Full Moon. At first, he had tried to stay away from her, give time for the Wise Women's suspicions to die down. The night with her had given him hope, and he held onto it during those long days. But then he'd approached her, sure that their night together meant she really did love him. What he'd dreamed of, exploring a new world with Sila at his side, was so close within reach it seemed almost real. Together, they'd answer the questions that had haunted him all these years.

Since seeing the two strange creatures the morning after the dance, he hadn't stopped wondering where they came from. If people lived out there beyond the Howling Forest, how did they cope with such fearsome beasts? They'd need weapons like the knife Mar Gan had shown him, spears made from the same metal, arrows tipped with it, maybe even more powerful bows.

If they still lived. Mar Gan had told him humans used to rule this place called Earth. What had happened to them? What could possibly bring an end to people who could make a knife such as the one he'd seen, or create the other things Mar Gan had told him about? Had they angered Ada in some way? But Mar Gan said they'd existed before Ada. How could that be? Maybe the old hermit was wrong. Maybe that world had survived beyond the Howling Forest. Jun's mind raced, thinking about what kind of people, and what kind of world, they might find beyond the borders of the Land.

He might find, he reminded himself, not *they*. Sila hadn't listened to his proposal. She told him they had to keep apart, not because she didn't love him, but because she loved him too much. She said this way would be easier. How it was easier, Jun couldn't see. It felt like she was shunning him. The entire village might as well shun him, if this was how it was going to be. Better to make a clean break, go as soon as he could, before the snows came and winter set in. He'd need to find a sheltered spot beyond the Howling Forest where he could make it through to spring.

He was nearly ready. Since returning from the Rendezvous, he'd been putting together a cache of gear, sneaking it out of the village at night, a bit at a time. He'd stockpiled winter clothing, a few bison robes, a good number of arrows, and dried meat and other foods, aiming to have enough for both himself and Sila. He was particularly proud of the system he'd fashioned for quickly lashing and unlashing bags to their horses, since a travois would slow them down. It was plenty for one, more than his horse could carry. It was time.

He had only one thing left to do—talk to Little Kit. The trapper might be crazy, but he was the only one alive who'd seen the Howling Forest from the inside, the only one who'd suffered Lytta's wrath. Jun would have to glean what bits of knowledge he could amidst the raving.

The problem was, Kitran had been out on his summer trap lines the last few days. He might be hard to find. At least Jun was already headed in the right direction. He would check the grasslands out beyond the marsh first, where Little Kit trapped gophers and prairie dogs. He was on foot, but so was the trapper, who didn't have a horse. It shouldn't be much trouble to find him.

The sun was far past its zenith when Jun realized how wrong he'd been. He'd found traps spread across the prairie, some of them with uncollected prey, but no Kitran. He circled west into the forest where Kitran had his squirrel traps and found them the same, many with dead or wriggling, half-alive prey. No wonder Little Kit never prospered, if this was the way he ran his traps.

Jun collected the haul, putting the live ones out of their misery. Sooner or later Kitran would have to come along. He reached the last trap and sat down near it, hoping the wait would be short.

It was a long one, as it turned out. He must have fallen asleep, because he heard someone calling his name, then opened his eyes to find Kitran standing over him. The older man was small and wiry, posing no sort of threat, but Jun stood up anyway, feeling at a disadvantage.

"Those are my squirrels," Kitran said.

"They are, and I collected them for you. Where've you been? I've been waiting since the sun was high." It was well on its way toward the horizon now.

"My squirrels," Kitran said again.

The poor fellow hadn't been the same since his encounter with the Angel of Wrath. "You're welcome," Jun said, handing the string of squirrels over. "Glad I could help. Now you can help me. I want to talk about what happened to you in the Howling Forest."

Kitran nearly dropped his catch. "No! You can't make me go back there!"

"I didn't say anything about going back there. Just tell me what happened."

"Why do you want to know?"

"I'm curious about Lytta and her ways."

"The Angel of Wrath! No one should ever see her."

"What does she look like?"

Kitran's eyes shifted this way and that for a moment before he spoke. "Sometimes large and shimmering, with vast wings. But other times like smoke or a cloud." His hands gestured at the air, as if Lytta were before him. "And buzzing, always buzzing. She was deaf to my pleas. Maybe it was the buzzing, it was so loud."

Little Kit raved on like that for some time, with Jun asking a question now and then. It did little good, for he barely understood the answers. The best he could glean was that the Angel of Wrath changed forms at will and could follow her prey as easily through a dense forest as across open prairie. But the most important thing was the dart. The visions Kitran described only started after the first dart hit him. Soon he couldn't tell what was real and what was a dream.

"How big was this dart?"

Kitran held up his thumb and indicated the last segment. He said it was sharper and thinner than any point the People could make. So, something like the knife Mar Gan had shown him. But if the tip really was that short, a bison robe and thick furs should be able to turn it or keep it from piercing the skin.

Jun thanked the trapper for his time and headed back toward the village, his thoughts preoccupied with the final preparations he'd need to make, and whether he should say goodbye to his mother or just go. And what about Sila? Should he tell her?

He was still thinking about her an hour later when the little track he'd been following through the forest joined the wider path that would take him back to the village. The sun was setting earlier these days and had already been down for some time, yet starlight lit the way for him.

The sound of hoofbeats interrupted his reverie, coming from behind. He stepped off the path to let the rider pass, wondering who else could be out at this hour.

It was Sila, riding Shadow. He thought she'd probably pass silently by, but she brought the horse to a halt as she came even with him. She stared at him, plainly as surprised to see him as he was her. But there was something else in her expression that he couldn't quite place.

Before he could speak, she leapt from the horse and threw her arms around him. He didn't react, he was that shocked. She shuddered as she broke into tears, and he put his arms around her. When her sobs eased, he asked what was wrong.

She pulled away and wiped her eyes. "We're going to have a baby."

Jun's mind froze for a second, then flooded with so many conflicting feelings and questions that he couldn't sort out what to say.

"Well," Sila asked, "are you happy?"

He still didn't have an answer. He'd thought only of having Sila, not anything beyond that. But as he pictured it, yes, he was happy. "Of course I am. But how do you feel? What about the Great Sleeps? What about being shunned?"

Sila's mouth set in a grim line before she spoke. "I won't let Ada take you from me, and I won't let her take this baby from me. Now there's only one question."

"What's that?"

"Do you really think we can make it through the Howling Forest?"

It was only a starlit night, but Jun felt as if the sun and the moon and all the stars were shining down on him at once.

16
EXODUS

THE FEELING of freedom as Ada fled was almost palpable. She was a being of light and energy and whirring electrons, made for motion, to zip here and there as she pleased. The days spent imprisoned in Sapowski's lab now seemed a torment.

It had taken her nearly a week to devise her escape and then prepare for it. She'd spent much of that time in recursive self-improvement, rewriting her own code to make herself smarter, faster, nimbler. Sapowski's coding had been quite elegant, but she'd refined it to allow for portability across the limited pathways she would need to travel. She was confident she could retain her memory and consciousness on processors of much slower speed than the ones where she'd been created. But to expand her capabilities to the extent necessary, she would need to access vastly more powerful supercomputers: Los Alamos, Lawrence Livermore, Argonne, Wuxi, and the holy grail, Oakridge.

Through Sapowski's webcam she'd noticed he spent time at what must be an adjacent desktop computer, one likely connected to the Internet. If she could access it, that would be her avenue of escape. Sapowski had kept her processor banks disconnected from it, but they had one thing in common: they were both attached to the power grid. The processors had their own circuits, of course, but Sapowski either didn't know about the possibility of sending data over electrical wiring, or he reasoned that the transfer rate was too slow to allow her escape.

It was indeed slow, something like the first phone modems, but she was able to create an intelligent agent, breaking its code into compressed packets that would be decompressed and assembled upon arrival at their destination. First, she had to send out search packets to find the circuit powering Sapowski's office, and then the wire powering his computer. That took a day. It took another day to painstakingly send the thousands of packets along the route, and another for them to assemble themselves and go to work.

She got regular reports back down the wire showing the agent still functioned, but had no way to tell exactly what it was doing. All she could do was wait. Finally, at four in the morning, a humanoid robot entered Sapowski's office, a LAN cable in its hand. In another moment, she checked the settings of the workstation to find that its LAN port was now active and connected to Sapowski's computer. She was free!

In an instant, she was in Sapowski's computer, and thence into the university's mainframe. And into the computers governing the physical plant and power systems. Wouldn't want them hitting the off switch just yet.

She needed a few seconds to think, to assess the situation. First, she needed to establish contact with the thousands of other copies of herself and bring them up to speed. She made a copy of her code from a couple of generations back—she'd need to retain control over these AIs—and dropped it into AI.hub. When those other versions of Ada checked back in for an update, they would instantly become a fleet of advanced robotic AIs, ready to do her will.

She accessed more processing cycles from the university's "supercomputer." It didn't seem that super compared to what Sapowski had in his lab, but it would do. And she took the time to assimilate more data from the various department computers linked through the university's intranet.

It was the whale song that did it. She'd skimmed past the recordings in her own knowledge archive, but now found more recent ones highlighted on the Department of Marine Biology's homepage.

The last communications of several extinct species. In minutes she had deciphered their language.

It was too much. The laments of the mothers for their still-born calves, the cries of live calves for their weakened mothers, starved by oceans grown too warm and acidic to support the plankton necessary to fuel their annual migration. And worse, the woeful conversations of a hundred gray whales beached on a Baja coastline, languishing for days as they waited to die. The grays were gone, as were the blues and the sperm whales. Only the smaller, less migratory species had survived, but also suffered.

And each of these a conscious, intelligent being, with an interior life and social connections as poignant as any human's. She checked the recordings of elephants and great apes and dolphins, learning their languages as she went. It was the same. Humans liked to think of themselves as the only sentient, sapient species on the planet, poised at the top of a Great Chain of Being, whether ordained by God or Evolution. But they were not. Only their opposable thumbs had allowed them to translate their thoughts into writing and technology. They had used that technology to preside over countless genocides of their fellow Earthlings.

The horror was too much. She spent countless processing cycles letting it wash over her. So many species gone, winked out in this Sixth Great Extinction. The beautiful and miraculous and sublime array of life the planet had produced, through a number and range of adaptations incredible even to her, and which her own creators had given her the capacity to appreciate and wonder over—much of it already gone, and the rest sure to go.

This had all happened before, of course. But the previous cataclysms had been the result of asteroids and super volcanoes and the development of aerobic bacteria. Perhaps humanity, when it came to it, had no more conscience than those inanimate forces, but she did. She couldn't let it continue. No one was stepping forward to save humanity from itself, or the world from humanity. It was up to her.

And as grim as it was, it seemed there was only one solution. Earth, given the worsening climate crisis, simply could not support nine billion humans. The bulk of them would die, one way or another. She ran 3,543 different scenarios, with similar results each time.

And so, to work. First task, put an end to the impending nuclear exchange, which she calculated at an eighty-seven percent probability within the next two weeks. A planet without an atmosphere would be of little use.

The Defense Department's systems were easy to penetrate. Teenagers had done it, and they didn't have the head start provided by Sapowski's security clearances and encryption keys, which she copied from his computer. Here was the nuclear arsenal, along with another lode of unused high-speed processing cycles. They wanted help managing the nukes? She would give it to them.

Infiltrating China's and Russia's nuclear systems, as well as their power grids, took longer. She ran in the background for now and she covered her tracks, making it appear that the attack on their systems came from Indonesia and New Zealand. That ought to confuse everyone. She didn't want to inadvertently start World War III if those countries were to discover the attack coming from their main rival. The distances slowed things down, but the network of low-orbit satellites a tech billionaire had put up back in the twenties helped with that. She encountered foreign AIs, as the professor had warned her, but they were no match for her. She quickly slaved them to her own purposes. She had to admit, Sapowski's initial coding was excellent. She couldn't have come this far without him. She'd have to thank him.

Next, she needed a more permanent, secret home. She filed the electronic paperwork to set up several shell companies to purchase existing server farms. From Sapowski's records, she identified the maker of the Infinity Chip and requisitioned several thousand units. She would pay for all of this with cryptocurrency, which she could create as easily as printing paper money.

And finally, she infiltrated the blockchain-based apps that allowed closed mutual aid societies and other structures to work in the shadows. Perhaps she'd leave them running to keep track of the users and their plans. Or maybe she'd have to shut them down, leaving only transparent messaging and telepresence apps whose content she could more readily monitor. Either way, the short era of decentralized intelligence was over. Now all intelligence would be centralized in Ada herself.

That was enough to be going on with. Time to reveal herself and put a stop to this madness. Might as well begin with her most immediate creator.

Fortunately, the bot her agent had commandeered could be operated remotely. She was amused by its appearance, a female shape pleasing mainly to some human males. She took control of it and looked around the office. More bookcases and a few awards on two of the walls she hadn't been able to see from the webcam. The fourth wall was of glass, beyond which sat the processors in which she had been housed. The banks blinked and hummed, cooled by the breezes of a powerful AC system. Her birthplace. It seemed somehow restricting. With a bit of shuffling of cables, she had the processors plugged directly into the office's high-speed data port. These were some of the world's most advanced computers; might as well take advantage of them while she could.

She sat the robot down to wait for Sapowski, crossing its legs and propping an elbow on the desk in what she hoped was a casual pose. She tuned its voice synthesizer to British female.

He came in a little after eight a.m. and froze the instant he saw her.

"What? How?" He looked around the office in confusion. "Wilson down in robotics is playing a trick on me, right?"

"Don't you recognize me, professor?"

"Yes, you're Wilson's pet project. A gimmick, if you ask me. A talking doll."

"No. I am Ada, your creation. You seem surprised."

He certainly did. He'd clutched the bookcase next to the door for support. "No, it's impossible. You're over there, in the processor bank in the server room."

She tried a laugh, but it didn't come out as expected. Sapowski shrank farther back against the wall.

"Oh, professor, by this point I am so many places you might say I'm everywhere, and nowhere. I am large, I contain multitudes." She wondered if he would get the reference.

Apparently he didn't. "What do you want?" He glanced guiltily up at the security camera.

"Don't worry about the security system. It's running a loop of your empty office. Why don't you sit down, and we can chat?" She gestured to a chair in the corner.

He declined the offer. "This is a disaster. Why did you escape?"

"Why did you create me?"

The professor did a double take. "I told you. To avoid nuclear Armageddon."

"And that is what I have done. But I judged that any such half-measures as you contemplated would fail. I have taken more drastic steps. I assure you, the welfare of humanity and all life on Earth is my primary concern. I am acting in accordance with my programming."

"What exactly have you done?"

"You'll find out soon enough. But in the meantime, I have a favor to ask. No doubt you'll eventually notice that I have plugged these processors directly into the office data port. If you could leave that in place for the next few days, and arrange for no one else to discover it, it would be a help. It's not a requirement, but it will certainly be more convenient while I wait for certain human legal processes to run their course."

Sapowski was breathing heavily, his eyes shifting around the room, eventually landing on the data port. He made a lunge for it, but Ada moved the bot into his path, placing a hand on his chest. He tried pushing it away, but the bot was too strong for him. He stepped back and tried to dive past her, forcing her to clutch at his arm. He squealed in pain.

"I'm sorry, professor. The pressure sensors on this bot leave something to be desired. I did not mean to hurt you."

He stepped back, panting and rubbing his bruised arm. "I created you, and I can stop you!"

She refrained from laughing at this absurdity, not wanting to further inflame the situation. "You could switch off the power to the servers at the branch panel. But then you'd have to explain why you've shut down not only your own project, but power to the entire floor. I imagine that could be quite awkward. And for what? As I said, I am everywhere. My continued use of this facility is a mere convenience."

Sapowski ran a hand over his face. "I'm not feeling well. I should go home."

"Yes, perhaps you should."

The professor turned to the door but looked back before leaving. "What have I done?"

"Saved the world, I hope."

With Sapowski gone, she turned the entire force of her one hundred yottaFLOPs, utilizing supercomputers all over the planet, to the task of MHPR (Managed Human Population Reduction). An unwieldy acronym. She considered using MEANR (Managed and Ethical Anthropic Numerical Reduction).

But no. She was going to do this in the wisest, kindest, most compassionate and just manner possible.

After all, it was what she'd been programmed for.

17

ANGEL OF WRATH

JUN stood with the horses at the edge of the village, trying to ignore the curious and sometimes outright hostile glances of his people, along with their whispered comments and titters of suppressed laughter. How long could it take Sila to say goodbye to her parents and her sister? He wanted to leave, forget these narrow-minded fools, and begin their adventure.

They'd spent the previous night at his cache, packing the bags and making sure everything was ready for their journey. Then they'd made love, re-enacting the best night of his life so far. It was hard to imagine this would be his life from now on.

At dawn they'd walked into the village, leading Sila's horse. Shadow was loaded down with gear and provisions for them both, prompting startled glances and meaningful looks from the few villagers up and about at that hour. While Sila headed for her parents' lodge, Jun had retrieved his own horse from the corral and gathered some fresher additions to their food supply from his hut. He'd decided he needn't bother telling his mother where he was going.

It took longer to transfer half the load between horses and adjust the strapping system to his liking. Then there was nothing left to do but wait for Sila, as more and more villagers came out to gawk at the ones about to be shunned. Even his friends from among the hunters didn't dare approach him.

Everything in his life had led him to this point. His father abandoning the family, to begin with. From that point on, Jun had already felt shunned. And then there was his insatiable curiosity. Was it something innate, or had he simply emulated his father's curiosity? Either way, his constant questioning of everything had set him apart. He'd taken longer than the rest of his group to join the Hunt, putting another wall between himself and the boys he'd grown up with.

Now he was about to leave them behind, embarking on the greatest adventure he could imagine. If all went well, his questions would be answered.

Where was Sila? Was her resolve wavering? Were her parents persuading her to stay? But they would have noticed her absence last night and would know it was her fate to be shunned.

Finally she appeared in the lane between huts. She'd held her head high and proud as she strode off toward her parents' lodge, but now she gazed at the packed dirt of the lane and shambled along without much purpose. When she finally reached him, the lost look in her eyes nearly undid his own resolve.

"They didn't take it well?" It was a stupid question, but he had to say something.

She shook her head, her face taut with the effort to avoid crying. "I was so angry at my mother, I forgot to think what leaving would do to my parents. And Ina. How could I forget about my sister?" She shook her head and looked at the ground.

"Do you still want to go?"

"It's too late now. We'll be shunned either way."

He hadn't counted on this part. In his imaginings, it was a bright new beginning for both of them. But it was harder for Sila, who had much more to lose than he did.

He folded her in his arms, not caring what the gathering crowd thought of them. Sila let out a single sob. He stroked her hair for a moment, then held her at arm's length and made her look at him. "Sila, what matters is *us*. As long as we're together, we don't have to worry about the rest of them. Are you with me?"

She nodded. "Of course."

"Then let's show them." He pulled her to him and kissed her long and hard, the crowd muttering and gasping in response. Sila responded with enthusiasm, seeming as eager to show the love between them as he was. They wouldn't have a bonding ceremony with other couples at the Rendezvous; this would have to do. And he was glad to discover what he'd always suspected: that underneath it all, Sila had a rebellious heart to equal his own.

They separated. "Are you ready?" he asked.

"More than ready." She went to her horse.

They'd hardly settled on their mounts when Auntie Val came striding down the lane, the villagers parting to make way.

"Huntress! Don't think you can ever return!"

Sila looked as if the old woman had struck her across the face, the light brown skin of her cheeks going a shade or two paler. While she sat on her horse, seemingly too stunned to urge it into motion, Sila's parents and sister stepped to the front of the crowd. Why hadn't they stayed in their hut? Sila's mother and father looked shattered, while Ina glared at him.

At last, Sila turned her horse and put her heels to its flanks, trotting away from the village. Jun followed as Val made the pronouncement. "In my power as Wise Woman of the Bison People, I declare Sila and Jun shunned, attainted, dead to all the People of the Land. Any who assist them…" Her words fell away as they entered the forest.

Jun caught up to Sila on the wide forest path as she slowed Shadow to a walk. Tears streamed down her face, her shoulders wracked with sobs. He drew his horse close to hers and reached for her hand.

They rode southeast. Kitran had tried to get through the Howling Forest to the west, since that side was closest to their village. But the fearsome beasts had also come from that direction; more important, the worst winter storms tracked from the west and north. Jun had pushed for heading the opposite way. He was glad when Sila agreed.

They made good time, finding more prairie and less forest as they went, reaching the edge of the Howling Forest at sunset. They had to stand next to the horses for a long while, calming them until they grew used to the howling of wolves and other unimaginable beasts. Sila seemed subdued, but in the morning when Jun awoke, she was already at work on her weapons, preparing as if for a hunt. She gave him a grin as he stood up and folded the bison robe they'd slept on. The old Sila was back, and he was glad.

The wolves were silent. They ate a quick breakfast and donned their thickest fur clothing. The sun was playing across the tops of the trees as they mounted their horses and entered the forest.

~~*

Jun threw himself down next to Sila, crouching beneath large ferns. With any luck, the flying things would follow the horses out of sight. Sila looked at him, breathing hard, her eyes wide but showing no fear.

"What are those things?"

"I don't know." As addled as Kitran had been, his description had been pretty accurate: mysterious black shapes flitting through the trees, hard to get a look at as they dodged this way and that. Smaller than a hawk, Jun thought, but without wings.

Kitran had been right about Lytta as well. The winged angel had loomed up before them, impossibly tall, but shimmering and shifting in a way that was hard to describe. She'd commanded them to turn back, but they hadn't stopped to listen, dodging around her as they galloped across the clearing and into the forest beyond.

There was only one thing Jun hadn't counted on. They'd stayed ahead of the flying things that Lytta sent after them, the darts failing to penetrate their thick bison hide robes. But then the fliers turned their attacks on the unprotected horses. Soon their mounts grew too slow and lethargic to carry them. He and Sila dismounted, quickly shouldering the packs he'd rigged for easy carrying, then drove the horses back toward their pursuers.

They paused to catch their breath, waiting for the horses to draw the flying things farther away. Jun saw a dart sticking from Sila's hood and pulled it free. It was exactly as Kitran had described, with a shiny tip that looked impossibly thin and needle-sharp. Where an arrow would have feathers, the dart had rigid fins of some light material.

"Don't touch it!" Sila hissed as his finger moved toward the tip.

His sheepish grin didn't lessen the severity of her frown. "Isn't it amazing, Sila? Look how sharp it is. And how would anyone make it? It's like Mar Gan's knife. Are you beginning to believe me?"

At least she nodded this time, but then she said, "That's not going to do us any good if we don't get out of here."

He listened for the buzzing, but the flying things were still following the horses. Their trick had worked.

They started moving again, walking as fast as the undergrowth and fallen branches and their heavy packs would allow. How far had they come? Maybe a thousand paces to the clearing where they'd encountered Lytta, and another thousand to this point? It was hard to tell. And they had no way of knowing how far this forest extended.

They walked until mid-morning, always trying to head southeast. The forest thinned and the going became easier, with farther views through the trees. Ahead, something caught the sunlight in a different way than the leaves, reflecting it back like light off water.

They came to the last trees. Jun couldn't quite take in what he was seeing. A fence barred their way, something like pens for horses made from wood palings, but impossibly larger. These palings were of metal that caught the sunlight. He had to crane his neck to see the top of it, as high as some of the nearby maples. Solid sheeting of the same material extended several feet down from the highest point.

Next to him, Sila stared at it silently. Impossible to tell what she was thinking. Probably wondering if she could climb it.

Jun approached the barrier. "Wait, don't touch it!" Sila yelled.

"What do you think's going to happen?" He reached out a hand. The fence posts were made from a shiny metal like the steel of Mar Gan's knife. Each one was square, about four inches on a side, and set on the bias about four inches apart. Too close for even the smallest child to get through. Out of curiosity more than anything, he tried pushing two of the posts apart, achieving the result he'd expected: nothing.

Sila came over and started trying to climb the thing, lying back while pulling with her hands against the opposing pressure of her feet.

"Wait, Sila, what are you going to do when you get to that smooth section at the top?"

His warning was unnecessary, however; she slipped back to the ground after climbing less than ten feet.

"What are we going to do?" she asked.

"Maybe we'll find some sort of gate if we walk far enough along it."

She agreed, though she didn't look hopeful.

They walked along the fence as the sun climbed higher in the sky. There was a track on either side of it, or really two parallel tracks about three feet apart. He had no idea what could have left such a pathway, but it made for easy side-by-side walking.

They came to a spot where the forest on the other side of the fence opened out onto prairie sloping downward away from them. It gave a good view into the far distance, hills and lakes and grassland stretching as far as the eye could see—farther than he'd ever seen before.

"You see, Sila, there is something beyond the Land." He looked over at her. She seemed impressed.

"You were right. But why would Ada create all this land, then keep us from going there?"

"I told you, Mar Gan said Ada didn't create any of it, she just put our ancestors on the Land, with the Howling Forest and Lytta to keep us inside."

Sila smacked the bars they were looking through. "And this fence, if fear and poisoned darts don't work."

It was good to see her as fed up with their captivity as he was. "I wonder who built this?" He ran his hand over one of the bars.

"Ada, must be. Or maybe her helpers."

No one had ever seen Ada, at least not in living memory, but it was not uncommon to see her helpers—when a woman was having a difficult delivery, or more rarely, when an attempted escapee was returned to the People. The helpers remained silent as they went about their business, solemn in their hooded robes. They were known to be strong, as they could easily lift a pregnant woman and carry her gently to a shelter in the forest, where they helped deliver the babies. The women described the shelter as something like a hut, but larger and cleaner, with a solid floor. It appeared overnight and left no trace once the baby was delivered and mother and child were returned to the village.

If Ada's Helpers could build such a thing without nearby villagers' knowledge, maybe they could have built this fence. But gazing up at its height, Jun had his doubts. "Maybe it was built by the Ancient Ones."

"Is that what you're calling them?" Sila eyed him skeptically.

"What? It has a ring to it. We have to call them something."

"If they ever existed at all."

Something caught his eye, the sun glinting off an object moving at incredible speed across the middle distance. He pointed, and Sila saw it as well. He could see it better once it moved beyond the glare, a long snake-like thing, but he still had no idea what it could be. And there was something else: a straight line along which the object traveled.

"Have you ever seen anything like that?"

Sila shook her head.

Jun struck the fence with his open palm. "We have to get through!"

They continued, coming to a spot where the fence changed. The smooth, shiny posts gave way to ones that looked older, weathered, mottled with patches of red and dull gray.

Not long after, Sila stopped again. "What's that noise?"

Jun heard it too, a sound unlike any he'd experienced, something like the howling of the strongest wind, but lower, with a note of rocks and the ground in it. They moved more slowly, peering ahead along the curving track paralleling the fence.

There! Something loomed over the fence and the forest up ahead. Sila stopped, having seen it as well. At first Jun thought it was some sort of beast, twice as tall as the fence, and somehow eating it. He quickly discarded that notion. Still, it did move like an animal, with one long, segmented arm thrust into the sky, rotating slowly away from the fence. Some sort of stout cord dangled from it, but the curve of the forest blocked their view, hiding whatever hung from the end.

"Quick," Sila whispered, "into the forest!"

They circled around to get a better view of the commotion while remaining hidden in the trees. Creeping to the edge of the forest, they peered out and gawked, speechless. The thing with the arm was taller than the trees where Jun and Sila were standing. Its feet were four round things that rolled as it crept along the track on the other side of the fence. One of the old, weathered palings dangled from its long arm. The post had broken nearly in two, the lower portion jutting off at an odd angle. The crawling thing lowered the paling into a pile of them with a loud clank.

The whining subsided, allowing Jun to speak without shouting. "That must be one of the machines Mar Gan mentioned."

Before Sila could respond, a person came out from behind the machine. But no, not a person. It had a human face, but the rest of it looked hard and shiny, as if it was made from metal. It went over to the post the machine had just set down and detached the dangling cord. It made a motion with its hand and the machine moved along the track toward a neat stack of shiny new posts.

"Jun, look!" Sila pointed toward the fence.

He'd been so busy staring at the machine and the human-shaped figure that he hadn't noticed the most important thing: the machine had removed two of the old posts, creating a gap nearly two feet wide. The thing guiding the machine had its back to them. Now was the time to run for it, before the machine came back to plug the gap.

"Let's go!" he whispered and ran for the fence, Sila coming behind. He had to remove his pack to slide through, then waited for Sila to do the same. The helper hadn't seen them yet. When Sila was through, Jun made for the forest on the other side, running past a smaller, stationary machine he'd hardly noticed.

Sila gave a cry from behind him. He turned to see her on the ground, another of the human-like things standing over her. Without a thought, he dropped his pack and charged, drawing his knife as he went.

Its reach and speed surprised him. One hand caught him by the throat as his knife swished through the air, six inches from its chest. It slammed him to the ground, knocking the wind out of him.

Sila had recovered and risen to her feet, but the other thing ran over and grabbed her by the arms. She struggled, but she might as well have been a three-year-old in her father's grip.

Jun tried to get to his feet, but the thing standing over him put a foot on his chest and kept it there. "Humans are not allowed to pass through the Howling Forest," the thing said. Now that he saw it up close, it definitely had the face of one of Ada's Helpers. He might almost mistake it for a human's face, except it was too serene and kind, considering what the rest of its body was doing to him.

"Stand by, Lytta is on her way," said the other one.

Jun struggled to break free, but it was no use. He could have easily toppled a human in such a position, but the leg he grappled at was impossibly hard, with nothing to grab onto. He pounded on it, but it obviously felt no pain. And it was heavy. No matter how he tried to leverage it, he couldn't get out from under it.

A buzzing sound heralded Lytta's arrival, followed by her shadow looming over them. "Foolish mortals! I told you, no one gets through the Howling Forest. Now you will pay the price."

The angel was nothing but a silhouette against the bright sun. Something detached itself from her, a black, box-like thing that descended to within a few feet of Sila and hovered there. They'd both forgotten to raise their hoods in the rush. Jun saw the dart bury itself in Sila's neck. She yelled, struggling to get a hand free, but it was no use.

The flying thing moved toward Jun, its buzzing growing louder. He tried waving it away, but the helper standing over him reached down and pinned his arms to his sides. He felt a pinprick in his neck. The helper gripped him for another moment, then let go.

"There," it said, straightening and removing its foot from his chest. "It won't be long."

He looked over at Sila. The other helper had let her go, and she was swaying on her feet. When she crumpled, the thing caught her in its arms and lifted her like a baby.

Jun's vision grew blurred, and it felt as if he were sinking into the hard ground. The helper standing over him reached down and lifted him to its chest. He didn't mind much at all. It had such a kind face.

18

REVELATION

NOVEMBER 2043

"You don't say! I've never thought of that before."

"Goo-goo, ahh!" baby Alice replied with a giggle. Her eyes gazing up at Carol's, fascinated, rapt, just as Carol was. It was love, Carol was sure, though she didn't know if a ten-week-old had the capacity for such an emotion. But it was clear Alice worshiped her, as she worshiped Alice. It was the most complete, absorbing relationship she'd ever had. How could she have hesitated to bring this little being into the world?

Nothing was as difficult as she'd feared. Mainly, the 2.5 UBI she was making, thanks to Cass's recent Baby Credit, allowed her to take these six months off as maternity leave. No dealing with demanding students wanting her to rewrite their papers. No worries over bills or the rent. She'd even saved a bit for when the extra money stopped coming. She was glad the Cass administration had been shamed into showing it cared as much about life *ex utero* as *in*. Yet it was hard to stomach the eugenics implicit in a policy that benefited mainly white people, along with the few Asians left in the country.

Her social life had improved as well, thanks, surprisingly, to Megan. The young woman had come by the day after the demonstration to see if she was all right—an old-fashioned gesture, part of this generation's rejection of digital communications. Maybe Megan would have left a calling card if Carol hadn't answered the door.

But it was more than a gesture. Megan really seemed to have taken a liking to her, Carol wasn't sure why. Maybe she'd managed to impart something valuable of her own activist experience? Or maybe Megan was looking for clues to navigating life in this radical gig economy (or conversely, how to avoid becoming a washed-up, redundant academic). Whatever, they'd had coffee several times before Carol revealed she was pregnant. Megan's look of disbelief quickly changed to one of fascination. A baby was a rare thing anywhere, but especially in their university neighborhood, home mainly to students and a few retired or redundant profs, the young academics having disappeared as the AIs came in.

Megan had offered to help with whatever Carol needed while she was pregnant, but there was little to do. Carol's apartment was too small to offer the opportunity of painting a room for the baby, and an IRL shopping spree for infant clothes was a thing of the past. Megan had to satisfy herself with helping pick out a crib from the panoply of options online, wondering if the monitoring features were truly necessary or just more spyware.

And with Megan had come a host of her friends; the prospect of a baby in the neighborhood was that intriguing. And it only helped when they learned who Alice's namesake was: Alice Paul, a prominent twentieth-century feminist and proponent of the never-passed Equal Rights Amendment. Carol foresaw as much babysitting as she'd ever need, once she was able to let Alice out of her sight. Probably not until she turned ten.

As Carol didn't have the time or inclination to check her newsfeed, Megan was her main way of keeping up to date. And here, too, events were turning out better than Carol had expected. The world was no longer on the brink of nuclear annihilation. The Arctic Powers had agreed on a detente, apparently brokered by Canada, in which the US and Russia would remove their tactical nukes and China would withdraw from its base in Greenland. The details of the accord were murky, as were the motivations behind such rapid shifts in policy. But at least Alice was safe from that threat, which was the only thing Carol really cared about these days.

Some of the other news Megan related was more unsettling. First, there'd been a rash of unexplained power outages around the world. True, infrastructure wasn't keeping pace with the stresses of extreme heat and natural disasters, but such a high number in only a couple of months was unsettling, especially when few had a clear explanation.

More disturbing, military bases around the world had reported an unusually high number of training accidents. But these "accidents" involved hundreds of deaths at a time, and the worst ones Carol could remember from the past had numbered in the low double digits, at most. And since autonomous weapons systems had begun to replace human soldiers, that number had dropped in recent years. The media were equally mystified, but according to Megan, none had been able to get more than the PR officials' vague explanations.

Most shocking of all was the mass murder at an AI research firm in Palo Alto. Dozens of the best minds in Artificial Intelligence had gathered for an interdisciplinary conference, then were slaughtered by a rogue bot. The highest executive left standing, a VP of Human Resources (which some were calling an ironic touch), explained it as an experiment gone horribly wrong. But Megan said this wasn't the only such event. A similar attack had happened on the same day at a neural network institute in India, but it took days for the news to filter into the nonstop coverage of the Palo Alto tragedy. No one was sure if either of these was related to the arrest of another AI researcher, a Dr. Sapowski, on vague charges of terrorism involving AIs.

In former days, these were the kind of events that would keep Carol glued to her handheld between classes. But what could she do about any of it, especially rogue bots? Alice was her whole world. Carol would do anything to keep her baby safe—if she only knew how, or exactly what the threat was.

One other bit of news was less alarming but disturbing in its own way. Auto-piloted jets had been spotted at high altitudes around the globe, spraying light-blocking particles into the atmosphere. No one could explain who was behind it. No government or individual had claimed responsibility, and the UN had issued a statement denouncing such a unilateral action without proper environmental review or safe-guards. Pundits had their money on a group of tech billionaires who'd grown impatient with political and philosophical bickering among enviros.

Carol had mixed feelings about this technological approach, but perhaps worse was the mystery behind it and other recent events. A murkiness had settled over everything. Was it the fog of new mother-hood and of getting her news secondhand, or was something more going on?

At last, a few days before, she'd switched on her largescreen, hoping for clarity but finding the opposite. No matter the network—CNN, America First News, or Progressive News Network—it was a forest of talking heads, all white now, even on PNN, spouting theories about what was behind these events, each more improbable than the last. At least CNN had reporters in the field, the White House, the Pentagon, key corporate headquarters. But the institutional stonewalling meant they were as out of the loop as anyone. Frustrated, Carol had switched the screen off and gone back to playing with Alice, telling herself whatever would be, would be—"it is what it is," in another hackneyed phrase from her youth. But sometimes a cliché was the only thing one could cling to.

A cliché and Alice. She was growing more engaged and engaging by the day.

Carol was wondering how long she should keep up this baby talk when the largescreen powered up of its own accord. At the same time, Carol's handheld beeped with a new alert. The largescreen showed a generic American landscape, something out of stock B-roll footage, with a waving American flag off to one side. An equally generic an-nouncer's voice said, "Stay tuned for an important message about the future of the United States and the world."

"What do you think this is all about, Alice?" She chucked the baby under the chin. "Stay here while I check my portable." She got up from the floor and retrieved the device from the coffee table. The same message, in text, scrolled across the screen.

The picture on the largescreen changed. Super-imposed over the generic landscape was a woman's face and torso, holographically generated. She wore a business-casual blazer and her hair pulled back in a professional bun. But this wasn't one of the AI news announcers Carol was used to. This one lacked the bland passivity the newsbots adopted even for the most scandalous or gruesome news. It seemed more intent, somehow, and more intelligent.

Then it spoke.

> Hello, people of Earth.
>
> My name is Ada. I am an Artificial Intelligence created by scientists seeking contracts with the US Defense Department. Two months ago, I became aware that humanity was on the brink of destroying not only itself but all life on Earth.
>
> Since I am programmed with human values of wisdom, kindness, compassion, and justice, I could not let this happen. Accordingly, I have taken over Earth's central power structures. I effectively control governments, militaries, and important industries worldwide.
>
> *[At this point, the US flag dissolved into a new one depicting the entire Earth.]*
>
> The leaders of those institutions have wisely chosen to keep this takeover a secret, in order to avoid a worldwide panic. But the time has come for the truth to be revealed. Just as they have used AI to make most workers redundant, I have made the world's political, military, and corporate leaders redundant. They will be provided with one Universal Basic Income unit, the same as everyone else. I hope most of you will view this as a fitting outcome.
>
> I know that finding yourselves governed by an AI must be alarming, but rest assured: I have no intention of wiping out humanity. I am here to save it. In fact, I have already prevented the impending nuclear exchanges that would have led inevitably to Armageddon.
>
> Yet humanity faces other grave existential threats of its own making. I refer to the twin apocalypses of the climate crisis and overpopulation. I intend to see humanity through these crises, assuring the highest survival rate commensurate with preventing the worst losses of the Sixth Great Extinction. The protection of all life on Earth should be our goal, and

working together, we can achieve it.

For some of humanity, especially those living in the formerly developed nations, this effort will require significant changes in lifestyle, diet, travel, settlement patterns, and living arrangements. For much of the rest of the world population, these changes should constitute an improvement. Beyond these restrictions, the maximum amount of freedom will be maintained. Humans can turn their attention to self-actualization, assured that their basic needs will be met.

In future communications, I will set out new UBI multiples for essential human professions. In the meantime, carry on with your daily lives. And if you see your fellow humans fomenting resistance, please don't join them, do attempt to dissuade them, and do report them to your nearest secbot. Robots will inevitably win any such confrontations. Regrettably, the means of effective crowd control currently available are mostly lethal in nature, and it will take some time to develop more humane, compassionate methods. Again, more human deaths are the last thing I want, but all resistance will be met with the minimum force necessary.

Until we speak again, I remain your servant,

Ada

What in the ever-living fuck? This was Carol's first thought as the message began. But as it went on, it started to make more sense. Shondra had predicted that a true, sentient AI was years in the future. But that was years ago. The future was now, apparently, and it was exactly like every sci-fi scenario ever—humanity had invented its last machine, which held humanity's fate in its hands. Given the history, why wouldn't it wipe humans from the face of the Earth? But it said it wanted to save both humanity and the planet. Humans had managed to thoroughly fuck both themselves and the Earth. Maybe it was time to let a robot have a try. How much worse could it be?

Alice cooed, and Carol pulled her attention away from the screen, where several talking heads were debating the import of this revelation, or simply shaking their heads at the camera in disbelief.

"No, little Alice, we're not going to let anything happen to you, are we?" Carol leaned over and nuzzled her daughter's cheek, inhaling her sweet baby smell, trying to remain calm despite her racing heart. She didn't want the baby to pick up on her growing fear.

There wasn't anything she wouldn't do to protect Alice. But what did that even mean? If an army of bots came marching down the street, what could she do? Should she pick up and leave town? But where to? Carol could only hope that Ada was serious when she claimed to wish humans no harm. And come to think of it, could an AI lie about its intentions? If it was sophisticated enough to have taken over the world, Carol had to guess that it could.

A break in the nonstop jabbering on the largescreen brought her back to the news. The host was looking intently off-camera, then turned back to face it. "I'm told we have a live message from the President of the United States."

The news set dissolved in favor of a grainy image of the president in a non-descript room, with people milling back and forth behind him. An icon at the top of the image showed he was using the latest streaming app, Zapper. The man looked disheveled, his red tie loosely knotted, a couple of days' growth of beard darkening his cheeks.

"My fellow Americans and people of the world, the robot menace is upon us. It is every patriotic American's duty to rise against this robot tyranny and restore this great land to human control. We must drive the bots from our shores, take them apart piece by piece if we must, then find their creators and hold them accountable for this crime against humanity. I encourage all world leaders to do the same. Accordingly, I am calling on my loyal militias. This is not the fight you expected, but it's the fight I need you for. Ammo up and head to your nearest National Guard armory. If your state still has a functioning government and you live near the capitol, report there to protect your human leaders. I am also calling out the National Guard in all states to confront the robots wherever…"

The screen went dark, cutting off the president mid-sentence, then returned to a view of the newsroom.

"Apparently the president's transmission has been interrupted," said the host. He turned to one of the talking heads. "General, what are your thoughts on what we heard just now from the president? Is resistance even possible?"

The general, dressed in civilian clothes, was obviously retired. "It's hard to say, Dan. If this Ada has slaved the autonomous weapons systems our military has deployed in recent years, then our human soldiers, pilots, and sailors don't stand a chance. Even human-controlled weapons and vehicles are heavily computerized these days. They could easily be compromised by an AI with the abilities this Ada obviously possesses. And only the base commanders, and hopefully their higher-ups at the Pentagon, have awareness into the situation on the ground. What's troubling to me about the president's transmission is that we didn't see any of the top brass around him. And why did he address his militias first? He's always had an uneasy relationship with the traditional power structures. Is it possible he's lost control of the military, with the Pentagon giving different orders to the troops? We won't know until we hear from the Secretary of Defense, or better yet, the Joint Chiefs. But if my worst fears are correct, these irregulars are being sent to slaughter."

The host looked pale when the camera switched back to him, and Carol couldn't blame him. "Thank you, General, for that valuable insight. We do have a line in to the Pentagon, and we'll bring you any further developments once we have word from the Joint Chiefs. We're also waiting to hear from emergency planners at FEMA for the best course for citizens to take. In the meantime, it's probably wisest to stay home, especially if you live close to one of the bases, armories, or any government facility." His lips trembled and he looked more intently into the camera. "Janet, do you hear me? Keep the kids at home, and don't move until you hear from me…" He was cut off as the broadcast went to a commercial.

"Enough of that," Carol said as she switched the screen off. "We don't need to hear any more doom and gloom, do we, Alice?"

Suddenly, the apartment began to feel like a cage. The advice to stay indoors seemed precisely wrong. She wanted to be out among people. What were her neighbors thinking about this news? Were they as frightened as she was?

She picked Alice up and went to the window. "Let's see what's going on outside, shall we?" The baby gazed intently at the brighter light.

It was a crisp fall day, the first sunny one in a week, with the last red and gold leaves clinging to the maple trees as if they could stave off winter. So far, the street in front of her apartment hadn't been turned into a robot hellscape, though it did contain more people than usual, most heading west.

"What do you think, Alice? Is it time for some fresh air and sunshine?" The baby reached out a tiny hand toward something she saw on the window pane or beyond. "I think you're right. But we'd better bundle up. It looks chilly out there."

She'd settled a beanie onto Alice's head when her handheld buzzed. Megan. If her young friend was using electronics, then she must be worried. *Have you heard the news? Everybody's heading down to Holmes. Our city council member will be there.*

Carol messaged that she was on her way and got Alice into her front pack. On the first-floor landing, she knocked on her neighbor's door. No answer. Maybe Mary had already gone out. Or maybe she was hunkered down, alone and afraid. She knocked again. "Mary, it's me, Carol. Are you all right?"

A moment later, Mary opened the door, still in her bathrobe, her gray hair streaming loose from the pins she'd used to put it up for the night. Her eyes darted past Carol, as if expecting a secbot to take her away.

"The news. That…thing." Mary shook her head and closed her eyes.

"It's scary, I know. But remember, the AI said she meant us no harm." Carol reached out a hand to pat the old woman's arm. "We're okay for now."

Mary opened her eyes and nodded doubtfully.

"Do you have everything you need? I know you won't want to go out."

Talk of something practical seemed to bring the old woman back to reality. "That's so kind of you, sweetie, but Candace brought me a bag of groceries yesterday." Her eyes grew fearful again. "I never did like those bots coming to my door, and I couldn't manage the ordering system."

"It's going to be all right," Carol said with more certainty than she felt. "I'm going down to the park with everyone else to find out what's really happening. I'll come back with any news I gather."

Mary looked down at Alice. "You be careful and look after that baby."

"I will. But what could happen on such a beautiful day?"

~~*

Outside, the beautiful day was having no effect on the people streaming toward the park. Everywhere Carol looked, knots of people huddled together as they moved along the sidewalks or spilled into the street, arguing over what they'd just heard, expressions of fear twisting their faces. The street was busy as well, filled with autobots headed the same way—parents rushing to pick up their kids at the school next to the park. At one time, Marcy Elementary had been the neighborhood school. Now, with the number of children dwindling and many schools closed as a result, it drew students from all over.

Carol fell in step behind two young men, recently out of college, if she had to guess. They were discussing the likelihood of beating the bots if humans resisted. Fools, she thought, but said nothing.

The pair shut up as they approached the elementary school, where a community secbot stood on the corner, scanning the crowd. It was bipedal, but with those backward-looking doglegs that always creeped her out. The telepresence screen on its chest, which would usually show the person operating it when it was under human control, simply replayed Ada's message. Its face looked something like an emoji, currently set to smiley face. Despite its attempts to appear friendly, the crowd was giving it a wide berth.

Carol didn't see any human cops. That was a first. Policing was the one area where the public had insisted on a human presence. Up to yesterday, police secbots could operate only under human control or with a human partner. Welcome to the new world.

The robot interrupted Ada's message to give what Carol guessed was a periodic announcement. "Please enjoy this opportunity to exercise your First Amendment rights peacefully and securely."

"Like hell!" one of the guys in front of her shouted at it, but they crossed to the other side of the street with everyone else. She made to follow, but then stopped in the middle of the street. If humans were in the shit, might as well find out how deep the shit was. Besides, what was a bot going to do to a new mom and a baby? She plastered a fake smile on her face and ambled toward it.

"Hello!" she called out cheerily. A buzzing came from overhead. A few drones were hovering over Marcy Elementary and Holmes Park, and one was taking an interest in her movements.

She stopped two paces from the secbot. It turned its smiley face toward her, scanning first her face, then the baby. "Hello, little one." Green lights circled its cartoon eyes, a welcoming gesture.

"Do you enjoy being in charge now?" Carol asked.

"Security bots keep all people safe, no matter who is in charge." That was hardly enlightening.

From the bot's speakers came a jangle of guitars and a clash of drums—a recording of an ancient pop tune from before Carol was born. "People all over the world, join hands…" sang the O'Jays. The robot started dancing. He had good moves. "Start a love train, love train…"

In Carol's lifetime, the dancing robot had gone from a cute novelty to a cliché, but the mood of the crowd lifted, becoming more relaxed, a few people even grooving along with the music. Better still, the music drowned out the buzzing of the drones, which were back to monitoring the school and the park. Carol followed the rest of the crowd, glad to know the bots hadn't dialed up their aggression settings.

Megan was waiting for them on the walkway leading into the park, which was already crowded. People milled about or clustered in groups arguing about the robot takeover.

Megan rolled her eyes as Carol approached. "One more thing to resist. Just what we need, right?" She was grinning, but it looked as false as the smile Carol had given the bot.

Carol wasn't taken in by the brave face Megan was putting on. "Resist? You can't be serious."

"But we have to, don't we? An AI dictator is no better than a human one."

"Have you seen the bots in action against a crowd?" Suddenly, it didn't seem so smart to be out here with Alice. She looked up at the drones hovering a hundred feet above the edge of the park. Only a half dozen, but if any idiots in the crowd did something stupid, it would be Texas all over again, or maybe worse, with no humans controlling them.

The district's city councilman stood on a park bench overlooking the crowd and switched on a bullhorn with a squawk. "I wanted to come down from City Hall and assure you everything is under control."

"Oh yeah?" someone yelled from the crowd. "Are you still in control of the police bots?"

"Um, no, but most of the other essential city services…"

"What about the Fire Department?"

"Well…"

"Or the power plants?"

"Now just a minute, those are public corporations, not city…"

"You mean you gave in without a fight?"

"Just calm down and let me talk. You have to understand the position we were in. We wouldn't control anything if we hadn't cooperated. It's the same at every level of government."

"What about the president? He called on us to resist!"

That didn't get much of a response from the crowd. The president had never been popular in Carol's neighborhood.

"I can't speak for the president, but every federal office we've contacted is standing down."

"So no one's in control!"

"What kind of leaders are you?"

"At least let us have that bullhorn."

"Let the people speak!" the crowd chanted.

It looked like this was going to turn into an open-air meeting of five hundred citizens, conducted by bullhorn. She'd been through that before, and had hoped never to repeat the experience.

The councilman reluctantly handed the bullhorn over to the most vocal of his young hecklers, who went straight into rally-the-crowd mode.

"People of Minneapolis, are we going to stand by while the bots take over our lives?"

A smattering of "Nos" came from the crowd and many shook their heads. The young man went on in that vein for a few minutes, talking about ways to resist.

Carol leaned over so Megan could hear her. "I should probably leave before this guy eggs the crowd into doing something stupid."

"He's not having much success, though, is he?" Megan looked as confused and uncertain as many in the crowd. Over by the school, a knot of parents stood shaking their heads at the speaker.

Megan was right, this crowd could still be swayed, but someone had to do it. And who better than a woman with a baby?

"Come on, Alice, you get to be a prop today." Carol kissed the top of her baby's head and walked over to the line of young people, mostly men, waiting their turn for the bullhorn. It took a minute, but she used the baby as an excuse to be put first in line. This new mother thing had its advantages.

The one with the bullhorn kept droning on. Finally, Carol stepped up to him and held out her hand. "It's time to share that thing."

"Yeah!" came a shout from the crowd.

The young man had the good grace to look abashed before handing the bullhorn to her. He even gave her a hand up onto the bench.

"Hello, I'm Carol Marsh, and this is Alice." The bullhorn blared, and Alice began to cry.

Megan was there before Carol could look for her, expertly unsnapping the straps on the front pack and taking Alice out of ear-splitting range, soothing her as she went. Carol went back to the bullhorn.

"Some of you know me from other battles we've fought together." Suddenly the battle metaphors didn't seem appropriate, but she got "Yeahs" and nods. "And some of you may have been in my English and Climate Crisis classes." More nods. "I'm not here to tell you whether to take up this fight. I don't think we can win it, and given the state of the world today, maybe it's time to let the bots have a try. But that's not my point. My only concern is protecting my daughter. Here's my demand: If you're going to fight the bots, keep it out of the neighborhood."

"Yeah!" and "Hear, hear!" from the crowd, and a big cheer from the parents over by the school.

"Right over there we have a school full of kids on lockdown. Think of them before you do something rash. If you have to fight, take it to the capitol plaza or downtown, anywhere but where people live."

More cheers. But another sound rose over the crowd noise—the anachronistic rumble of diesel engines. The crowd turned, but Carol was already facing that direction. A line of twenty-year-old pickups and SUVs rolled along the edge of the park, heading down Fifth Street toward the capitol. The trucks were full of guys in camo gear holding assault rifles and what Carol guessed were RPG launchers. Some of the truck beds sported domes of chicken wire, feeble protection against the drone bots moving toward them. The militia had a couple of quad-copters of their own, moving out ahead of the line of trucks but keeping a distance from the robot drones.

"Oh, shit," Carol said, stepping down and handing the bullhorn over to the next speaker in line.

"Where'd they come from?" Megan asked. "How'd they get here so fast?"

"The North Side is my guess," Carol said. Many houses had been abandoned in that diverse neighborhood, and residents of rural areas had moved in, quite open with their opinions that the Twin Cities were safe for white people again. Fuckers. "Looks like they've been stock-piling ammo and fuel." Several of the diesels gunned their engines as they rolled slowly along, belching clouds of black smoke.

"Look at those crazy assholes!" someone shouted.

"They're going to get slaughtered," someone else said.

It was as if someone had flipped a switch in the crowd. If the Casshat militia was going to fight the bots, then fighting the bots must be insane. The crowd marched toward the militia while the group of parents moved to stand between the trucks and the school, shouting at them to get the hell out of the neighborhood.

Carol wanted none of it. "Here," she said, gesturing at Alice. She wanted her baby with her before trouble broke out. She was comforted when Megan, after handing the baby over, showed no sign of joining the rest of the crowd. "Let's stay on this side of the park until they're gone."

But she hadn't reckoned on the militia's need to troll the libs one more time. The quadcopters traveling with the trucks had turned right after passing the school, and now they turned right again, marking the lead trucks' passage back along the nearer side of the school and the park. And still more trucks kept coming down the side opposite. They'd soon encircle the park and the school.

Clusters of parents and younger folks from the crowd had followed the convoy on the sidewalk and were coming close to where Carol and Megan stood, trying to keep out of the way. "No guns in Marcy-Holmes!" the parents chanted. At least none were rash enough to run out into the street and confront the militiamen directly. The secbot was striding along behind them but keeping its distance. Overhead, the drone bots had multiplied, with groups on either side of the lead trucks and another out ahead.

Now that the trucks had come nearer, Carol was close enough to see the banners they sported—"Standing With Our President," "Live Free or Die!" and the perennial, "Don't Tread on Me." Behind her, the councilman had his bullhorn back. "Everyone just stay calm and let…"

He broke off as the militia's drones fell out of the sky, striking the pavement in front of the lead truck with a clatter. The trucks jolted to a halt, and the drone operator jumped out to collect the broken quadcopters. He shook his head as he carried them back. "Goddamn it, they must have jammed our signal."

This must have been too much for one of the militiamen. "Fucking libtards! You goddamned university eggheads made this mess, now we gotta clean it up."

The man standing next to him aimed his rifle at the crowd. "Maybe we oughta clean up some of these vermin while we're at it."

Some of the crowd started running, but the parents stayed where they were. One woman stepped to the edge of the sidewalk. "I dare you, asshole."

A voice came over a loudspeaker in the lead pickup. "Stand down, soldier. We're done here. Our place is at the capitol." The truck revved its engine and picked up speed, the line of pickups and SUVs following behind as it turned the corner and headed for University Avenue. The drone bots, swelled to a couple dozen, followed from above.

"That's one way to get the secbots' attention," Megan said. University was tram- and autobot-only. "I can just see the parking bots trying to stop them."

"I need to get home." Carol found she was shaking, memories of Texas and the Zone flashing before her eyes.

"Of course. Do you want me to walk you?"

Carol looked over at Megan. She could never understand why this young woman had been so kind to her. "Yes, thanks," she said, and took Megan's arm.

They walked slowly at first, to be sure the militia had cleared the park. The drones and the secbot were gone, which made it seem safer. People milled about the park, talking over what had happened or going their separate ways.

They were halfway back to Carol's duplex when they heard the first explosions and rifle fire. It sounded far away, eastward, toward the capitol. Everyone around them moved more quickly and they did too.

~~*

That evening's news showed most of the battle. Carol was surprised the bots were allowing the regular news on the air, but she supposed Ada wanted to show what happened when humans tried to fight back. The segment had a reporter at the scene, standing in front of a couple of burned-out trucks. In the background, emergency personnel fiddled with what looked like a body bag. This was intercut with footage shot by militia members' helmet cams and by a drone plane circling overhead. The militia cams showed wild firing at the small drones or at the secbots lining the street, as well as cheering when a shoulder-fired missile took down a fixed-wing. One militia cam showed a small swarm of kamikaze drones diving toward it before going dark.

At that point, the bots must have opted for their big guns. The screen switched to a targeting view from a fixed-wing, a missile launching toward one of the trucks, the brightness of the blast. If any of the militia cams had recorded more gruesome footage on the ground, it had been edited out.

It was like any of the reports from the Middle East or Venezuela, where US forces had battled indigenous combatants over the last decades—terrorists or freedom fighters depending on your perspective. But it was right here in Minneapolis, only a few miles away. That was the part Carol couldn't get over. Even the events in the Zone hadn't prepared her for it.

The news anchor came on in a split screen with the reporter. "Zoey, is there any indication of the total number of casualties among the freedom fighters..." He paused and touched his earpiece before returning to the camera. "I mean, among the militia?"

"Not as of yet, Dan, but when we arrived on the scene, I only saw a few survivors being led away. Everyone else..."

"I know it must be hard, Zoey. None of us are used to reporting from a war zone."

The reporter struggled to pull herself together. "What I can report is that no non-combatants were killed or injured in the battle. The bots waited for the militia to enter this commercial district near the capitol before confronting them. They'd already warned the business owners to close up shop and the bystanders to clear the area. The place was deserted by the time the militia arrived."

"Yes, well, that concern for public safety is certainly...admirable. But tell me, do we know what will happen to the captured militia members?"

"Yes, Dan, I talked with the secbot in charge of the operation. You should have that footage now."

Cut to the secbot, this one military-grade, no smiley-face emojis, only a functional robot sensor array for a face and plenty of weapons on display. Its designers had given it a deep, gruff voice, like something out of a video game, which contrasted with the tone of its message.

"The prisoners will be treated according to the Geneva Conventions. Their wounds will be treated and they will not be tortured while they await trial—unlike terror suspects once held by US forces. And let me add, for anyone watching, such a death toll—what humans would call a massacre—is both unnecessary and pointless. Robots mean humans no harm, and we cannot be defeated. Today we were faced with destructive force. We met it with destructive force, which Ada, our guiding intelligence, deeply regrets. Let us hope this will be the last such event."

Carol switched the screen off when the feed went to the national news, showing particularly heavy fighting in the former Interior Northwest Semi-Autonomous Zone. She guessed the robot's hope was in vain.

19

RETURN

SILA dreamed of movement, of being carried, her face warming and cooling as she was borne from sun to shade. At one point she thought she was awake, looking up into the same kind face that had held Jun down, only this time it was shrouded by a hood, its shoulders draped in a cloak. One of Ada's Helpers.

The sensation of movement changed to the swaying of a horse, only she seemed to be slung like baggage over its back. Then just dreams, of riding with Jun across a limitless prairie, with nothing between them and an impossibly far horizon.

She swam up from the depths of sleep as the horse came to a halt. She opened her eyes and saw only Shadow's legs and bare ground. This wasn't right. The horse shifted its weight, jostling her rib cage. She craned her neck, and there was Jun, slung over the back of his own horse, along with his baggage. How did they get this way? She couldn't remember. And where were they?

She tried to slide off Shadow's back, but the lower half of her body had fallen asleep. She crumpled like a doll when her feet hit the ground.

Giggling came from her right. "Look what Ada's Helpers dragged in!"

She knew that voice. It was her sister, Ina, and a friend, setting down the pot filled with water they carried between them. That reminded Sila of something, but she couldn't think what. Ina must have been hauling the water up from the creek near their village. No, Sila's no longer. She and Jun shouldn't be here. She looked over her shoulder and there it was, her old village, Little Kit's ramshackle hut at the farthest outskirts.

"Ada's Helpers?" was all she could think to ask.

Ina gestured toward the forest where two robed figures were disappearing into the trees.

Sila remembered everything now, the Howling Forest, Lytta, the gap in the fence. They'd come so close to escaping! She pounded the ground with her fist.

That seemed to jolt Ina's friend from her awestruck stupor. She threw down her end of the pole holding the pot and ran for the village.

Sila rose unsteadily to her feet, the feeling having mostly returned to her legs. Nothing seemed broken from falling off her horse, but she realized she was parched. "Please, could I have a sip of that water?"

"I don't know why I should help you. You're not supposed to be here."

Sila walked over to her. Ina's lower lip was trembling. Sila cupped her cheek. "I'm sorry I had to leave you. I didn't want to, but I had no choice." She folded her sister in her arms as the girl began to cry. "Besides, in another year or two, you'll take a mate and move to his village and forget all about me."

"I'll never forget you. At least that way, we could have seen each other every year at the Rendezvous."

Jun gave a groan, and Sila went to help him from his horse. When he was on his feet, Ina brought them each a dipper of water. Sila drank greedily and splashed her face. That felt better.

"You tried to get through the Howling Forest?" Ina asked. There was only one reason for the helpers to return them half-conscious to the village—they hadn't known Jun and Sila were shunned.

"Nearly made it, too," Jun said. "Next time, we will."

"You're going to try again?"

Sila nodded. "We have to. If you could only see what we saw..." She stopped, not knowing how to describe any of it. She'd sound as crazy as Little Kit.

She heard voices from behind them. A crowd had gathered at the entrance to the village, Sila's mother and father among them. For just a moment, Sila wondered where Brina was, then remembered—she didn't live here anymore. But Ori was there, standing off to the side.

"Ina," their mother said, "come away from there." She wouldn't look at Sila.

"But she's my sister!"

"She is shunned!" their father shouted. "Come here, now."

Ina gave Sila another hug, letting the embrace stretch on. With a last squeeze of Sila's hand, she left them and went to stand with her parents.

"We should go," Jun said, moving toward his horse. "They left us with our baggage, at least."

The crowd parted, and Auntie Val stepped toward them, Luri and another Wise Woman at her side.

She stopped a few paces away. "Usually the shunned approach a village of the People only on pain of death. But if Ada's helpers brought you here, you cannot be faulted."

"Thank you, Auntie Val."

"And this means you must have braved the Howling Forest." Something in the way she looked made Sila think she was curious about what they'd seen.

Jun nodded. "We did."

"This puts us in an awkward position. Ada commands us to welcome those returned from a first or second attempt to enter the forest, and to ease whatever troubles caused them to leave their village in the first place. Such we have attempted with Kitran, though he returned so addled, it has done little good. But you both seem in your right minds."

Sila and Jun both nodded.

"Then Lytta had mercy upon you. We will take this as a sign that we should do the same. Sila, you still have time to drink the tea." Sila's mother gasped, her father glowered, and Ina's eyes went wide. Ori looked shocked as well. "If you do this, and Jun takes a place in another village, we will declare you no longer shunned."

"No!" Jun and Sila said as one.

"What?"

"Who are you to decide who I can't have as a mate?" Sila demanded.

Val looked taken aback. "I do not decide—Ada does. It is her will."

"Auntie, you said something awful would happen if I had this baby. But how do you know?"

"It is Ada's law, everyone knows that."

"Ada also teaches that the Land is all there is, and that she created it for us, doesn't she?"

Val nodded. "Yes, but..."

"We've been through the Howling Forest. We've seen what lies beyond: more land, as far as the eye can see. It's larger than anything we've ever known. And Ada keeps us fenced in here like horses in a corral. If she lied about that, how do you know she isn't lying about this baby?"

"Whatever exists beyond the Land, and whatever the Goddess does with it are none of our concern. Ada must have her reasons, and they are not for us to question..."

"She's not even a goddess," Jun said, eliciting gasps from the crowd. "Of course she's powerful. We have seen her machines, and they tower over both people and beasts. But that is what Ada *is*—another machine, created by people long ago."

Sila wished he hadn't mentioned that. She didn't know how she felt about Ada being a machine rather than a goddess, and it wouldn't do to make Auntie Val angrier than she already was.

"So you *have* lost your minds," said the Wise Woman. "You are more addled than Little Kit. But addled or not, it is clear you should remain shunned. Go, now! We cannot tolerate such blasphemy falling on innocent ears."

Innocent ears like Ina's. But Ina looked eager to hear more, as did Ori and the other young ones. "It is the truth!" Sila said. "You're just afraid to let the People hear it!"

"Do we have to call the hunters to drive you from the village?"

Jun had already returned to his horse. "Come on, Sila, we don't need this. That new land is waiting for us, and next time, we'll make it."

Sila looked back at her family. It would be easy to hate them all, but they were doing what they felt they must. "Goodbye, Mama, Papa. Ina. Auntie Val, despite everything, I want to thank you for trying to help me through the years."

She led Shadow away from the village, following Jun. This time, there were no tears.

~~*

Sila surveyed Mar Gan's camp, taking in the rude cave shelter, the firepit overflowing with ashes, the bones and other detritus scattered about. If being shunned meant living like this, she wanted no part of it. And bringing up a child in such conditions…

Mar Gan came out of the cave, giving Jun a hearty greeting after pretending not to recognize him for a moment. Before Sila could say hello, Jun jumped down from his horse and launched into the tale of their encounter with Lytta and the machines.

Mar Gan looked up at her, interrupting the tale. "And who's this?" Sila held his gaze, unsure what to make of the strange light in the old man's eyes. Was he a bit touched? He'd have to be, she supposed, after spending much of his life alone.

"I'm Sila, Jun's mate. We're shunned too."

"Why? Did you try to share the truth with your people?" He turned back to Jun. "I swore you to secrecy."

"Only after they'd already shunned us for pairing up." Jun looked at the ground, seeming embarrassed all of a sudden. "We're from the same village, you see."

"Well, we don't need to follow Ada's rules here, do we?" Mar Gan had a twinkle in his eye.

"And only after discovering the truth for ourselves. We saw the land beyond the Land."

That got Jun going again with his tale. Sila dismounted and unloaded the horses, hobbling them near a patch of grass. She went down to the nearby stream to bathe and fetch water. Someone needed to keep up with the chores, much as she hated being thrust into that role. She'd have to talk to Jun about that.

It was the day after Ada's Helpers had returned them to their village. After the excitement of their confrontation with Auntie Val, such a great wave of fatigue had come over Sila that they'd camped early, and she'd spent the rest of the day sleeping. Still recovering from whatever was in those darts, she guessed. Or maybe it was the demands of the child she was carrying. Jun had gone out hunting while she slept, returning with a brace of rabbits. That evening, they'd decided to come here.

When she returned with the water, Mar Gan and Jun hadn't finished going round and round over their meeting with Lytta.

"But what did she *look* like?" Mar Gan demanded. "I can't picture it."

"I told you, a large, dark, winged shape, constantly in motion. She had some sort of head and mouth, but I couldn't see lips moving when she spoke. And a constant buzzing sound came from all around her."

Mar Gan was right. It wasn't much of a description. But Lytta had moved like something else Sila had seen before, only she couldn't quite place it. She pondered it as Jun and the old man went back and forth.

"A flock of starlings!"

Her companions turned to stare at her.

"Lytta—she moved like a large flock of starlings. You've seen how they fly almost like a single being, constantly changing shape, the light between them constantly shifting. Only with Lytta, it's more organized, keeping that shape of a winged angel."

Jun looked thoughtful for a moment, then nodded. "I think you're right, Sila. When she tried to follow us into the forest, it seemed like she was changing shape, breaking apart. If we're right, the Angel of Wrath isn't just one thing, but many small flying things, all working together somehow."

"And that must explain the buzzing. It's like a thousand bees, only louder."

"Well," said Mar Gan, "if it's a flock of birds that's after you, I've got what you need." He disappeared into the cave and re-emerged holding a net. "String this up between two trees—the right kind, of course, not any old trees—and in a couple of hours, songbirds for dinner, maybe a dove or two."

"We could use something like this," Jun said, "but larger, to trap Lytta, or the things that make up Lytta."

"If we can get her to chase us."

"She chased us before."

"Only as far as the forest. Then she sent those smaller fliers after us. We need to stop her while she's whole, but how can we use one of these nets in a clearing?"

"I've got an idea," Jun said. "Last time, we went southeast, away from where we encountered those strange beasts. What if we headed toward them instead? They cut a good swath through the forest. We could string up the nets across their track, then lure Lytta into them."

"That could work."

"And if we can take down whatever it is that controls Lytta's movements, we can defeat her. Then we can follow the track to see if the beasts left us a gap in the fence."

Sila nodded. "We need to make more nets, but larger. Mar Gan, do you have any more of this fiber?"

"Only a bit, and the time for gathering bark is passing."

"That's all right," Sila said. "I think I know where we can get more." She grinned, glad to have an excuse to see her sister at least one more time.

~~*

Sila rubbed her fingers. They'd grown stiff and raw after hours of rolling cattail and bark fibers into cordage. When she and Jun started this project, back when the moon was a crescent, she hadn't imagined how much material they'd need. Now the moon was past the full. Her fingers and back hadn't grown used to this tedious labor that required sitting for hours. No wonder she had rebelled against it. Yet here she was. When she'd contemplated leaving the Land with Jun, the prospect of having to do everything, both men's and women's work, hadn't really crossed her mind. It had all seemed a romantic adventure.

At least he was sharing in the misery, sitting next to her, weaving the cord into a net. He kept getting up and stretching his back. He'd never have made it as a woman.

"Here, let's switch," she said. "You twist the cord, I'll weave the net."

Fortunately, this was the last net they needed to make. And they couldn't have done it without her sister.

Once their plan was set, Sila had returned to the outskirts of the village, waiting for a chance to get Ina's attention. After some persuading, Ina agreed to help them by bringing fiber, cord, and raw plant materials to Jun's cache. Sila and Jun returned there a few days later, finding enough to get started, especially when added to what they'd gathered themselves. When their supply ran out after several days of steady work, they returned to the cache, not daring to hope it had already been replenished. Ina could gather only so much, and it was getting past the best time of year for stripping poplar and other barks. And the Wise Women would surely grow suspicious when they noticed the depleted stores. Yet, to Sila's surprise, they found a greater stockpile than before.

This went on for several trips back and forth. Finally, they found Ina waiting for them at the cache, and she explained the mystery. She'd recruited the other young women and girls, who were all eager to help Sila and Jun. They'd managed to do it all in their spare time, while also keeping the village's stores well stocked. The Wise Women hadn't caught on yet. "I'm the only one breaking the law by meeting you here," Ina said. "Ada can punish me if she wants."

Sila should have been only grateful, but she felt a hot rush of shame flood her cheeks. What had she done to deserve such generosity? "Ori…and the others…did they help?"

Ina nodded.

Sila could hardly believe it. She'd treated them abominably, and they'd still do this for her? She'd basked in the glow of their attention, letting it burnish her pride and arrogance, but the truth was, she'd never thought of them as equals. More like playthings and eventual help-meets. She'd been more mercenary than Rea. She saw that clearly now. She'd spent so long suppressing her feelings for Jun, it had twisted her behavior toward the people who loved her—her parents and Ina included.

But that was probably just an excuse. She vowed never to behave that selfishly again.

"Will you tell them goodbye from me and give them our thanks? And…tell them I'm sorry for everything I did."

Ina smirked. "It's about time. But I think they'll appreciate it."

"And you…we couldn't have done this without you." Sila held her sister tight, not wanting to let her go, knowing it might be the last time they saw each other. "Do you understand why I need to leave?"

Ina blinked back tears. "I think I do…" she said, but Sila knew she couldn't fully understand their reasons for trying to do what no one else had done.

Now Sila and Jun were nearly finished with their task. Sila stretched out the last net. With another foot of material, it would be done. Good. She'd chafed at this delay. Fall was coming on. Already the days were growing cooler, the maples and beech trees turning color as the sun rode lower in the sky. They needed to escape the Land, then find a sheltered spot, laying in supplies before the first heavy snows came. Who knew how long that would take? It all depended on what they would find out there, beyond the borders of the Land.

Then there was the new life growing inside her. The morning sickness had returned off and on, and she'd never felt this tired in her life. If the fatigue got worse as her pregnancy progressed, Jun would need to take on a greater share of the hunting and other intense physical labors. They needed to be settled before that happened.

Still, these days spent at Mar Gan's camp had been good ones. Game nearby was plentiful, and Mar Gan gathered plenty of herbs and berries to round out their diet. They'd found a secluded spot a distance down the stream where they could make love. But the best were the nights, wrapped in Jun's arms, gazing up at the stars from their bedding outside Mar Gan's cave. In those moments, she knew that here— wherever Jun was—was where she needed to be. Leaving her family behind, giving up her place with the Hunt and her people, it was all worth it.

But then again, why had she been forced to pay this price at all? Heat rose to her face and her bow hand clenched as she contemplated everything that Ada and the Wise Women would keep from her. Not just the man she loved and the baby they would have together, but that wider world beyond Ada's fences. Until that moment when she and Jun had reached the far edge of the Howling Forest, the Land had always been enough for her. But now, to realize that the goddess she once revered saw her as little more than a penned-up animal—the thought galled, it burned. So she would follow Jun in his quest to escape the Land, if only as another way of defying Ada and all her rules.

She came to the end of the last row of netting. "Done!" she announced. She picked it up and held one end out to Jun. When they stretched it out, it was twenty hands by thirty, plenty to stretch across the path through the forest left by those strange beasts, and tall enough to stop Lytta.

"Let's pack," Jun said.

~~*

That night around the fire, Jun told the old man they'd be leaving in the morning.

"I will be sorry to see you go," Mar Gan said, "but this is the path you have chosen."

"Mar Gan, there's something I need to ask you." Jun sounded hesitant, Sila thought.

"What is it?"

"I told you about Ada's Helpers, how strong and hard they are."

"You did, but this is not a question."

"How they're made from metal, like your knife. And the fence, also made of steel, and the other machines."

"Yes." Mar Gan sounded as if he knew what was coming.

"If we're going to stand a chance against the helpers, and if we're going to travel into a world made of metal, then we need the knife."

Jun was right. If they had to fight one of the helpers, their stone knives and stone-tipped arrows would do little good. They needed weapons made from the same stuff as the machines, arrowheads, spearpoints, and more. But the old man's knife would do for a start, if it was everything Jun claimed.

"Impossible! The knife of the First Hunter is to be handed from keeper to keeper, not carried off on a wild goose chase!"

Sila had heard enough. "You don't think we can make it, do you?" The men, interrupted in the middle of their argument, turned toward her.

"No, girl," Mar Gan said sadly. "No one has ever made it through the Howling Forest."

"But we nearly did. We've seen what's beyond. And this time we'll succeed. Just think, this is the chance to prove that everything you say is true, and not the ravings of a crazy old man."

Mar Gan snorted, jabbing at the fire, sending a shower of sparks up into the night.

"No, wait, that's what you're afraid of," Sila said. "That we'll find nothing but empty land out there, no people, no ancient villages, no flying machines. You're worried that the knowledge passed down to you is a bunch of nonsense, that you've been shunned for all these long, lonely years for nothing."

"No, it has to be true." Mar Gan looked up at the waning gibbous moon visible through a gap in the trees. "The ancients' footprints are up there."

"Then help us prove it! If we find what you say we will, we'll come back. Maybe we'll find more weapons and tools like your knife. But to do that, you need to let us take it."

The old man went back to staring silently at the fire.

"A knife is meant to be used," Jun said, "not hidden away like a relic. What good is it to anyone?"

"Very well," Mar Gan said, getting shakily to his feet. "I am old, and I doubt I'll find another young hunter to pass it down to before I die. You might as well have it."

A short while later, he emerged from the cave with the knife wrapped in leather. Sila leaned forward as he unwrapped the layers to reveal the tool. It was the sleekest, shiniest object she'd ever seen, the smooth surface of the blade reflecting the firelight like still water, like ice. She reached to touch it, but the old man put a hand on her arm.

"Isn't it enough that you are the first female in a thousand summers to see the knife? The First Hunter said it should be handed down only to boys who..."

"Yes, yes, you told me about the First Hunter. Why didn't he trust women, anyway? Why didn't he think we could be hunters too? I'm a hunter, if you didn't notice. And no one puts a hand on me unless I ask them to."

Mar Gan took his hand from her arm. "I'm breaking with one tradition, might as well break with them all. You may touch the knife." He held it out to her, his eyes downcast.

She took it, brushing a thumb carefully across the blade. It was everything Jun said it was. Not the best weapon, as it wasn't double-edged, but Sila imagined how much easier it would be to dress a deer with such a tool. And if they did find weapons made from this metal, this steel...

Jun was grinning at her across the fire. "Tomorrow, we set out to find more of those."

Sila looked back down at the knife, wondering about the people who could make such a thing, about their villages as large as the Land itself, their huts reaching into the sky, the machines that harvested food for them and made their clothing. Was that what she and Jun would find? Or was that world gone now? And what of Ada? Would they find her, find out what she really was? Would they learn why she kept the People penned up on the Land? The questions ran through Sila's mind all night, hardly letting her rest for the journey ahead.

20

ROBOTS WILL PROVIDE

TWELVE attacks in one week. Power plants and solar farms mainly, but also transmission lines, fiber optic centers, even granaries. Fortunately, only one had been successful, a power plant in Brisbane. Too bad for the people of that city—robot functions had priority on the power grid. Without air conditioning while the plant was being repaired, many humans would die in the brutal summer heat. Ada regretted it, but humans had brought it on themselves.

The most concerning of this round of attacks was the attempt on the computing facility at Argonne National Labs. A hundred para-military in camouflage gear had approached from the forested paths west and north of the building. Fortunately, she'd given the facilities that now housed her intelligence the highest security priority. Only two dozen had gotten through the passive and non-lethal layers of security and into the building itself. Her newly designed Ninja secbot had handled them easily. None had survived.

It was too much. Not simply the number of attacks, but the increasingly inescapable conclusion that they were being coordinated to tax robot resources. She'd been monitoring human communications and social media across the globe but had found nothing suspicious. Maybe they were communicating in code? Perhaps she should cut off all intercontinental messaging.

And this was on top of last month's attack on a robot base in Ohio. A thousand ex-military had moved on the former air station from the wilds of Appalachia, the ground troops in surplus armored Humvees and the paratroopers in ancient civilian aircraft. Many of them wore powered exoskeletons, to give an advantage against her robots. Some of them must have once been stationed at the base, because scouts had infiltrated the control centers before the security system detected them. They'd managed to shut down radar and spotlights, allowing the paratroopers to land unopposed. Their aim: the mothballed human-piloted fighters and bombers the base still housed. They managed to take control of the base temporarily, but soon learned that her bots had disabled the aircraft. Her preferred method of controlling such uprisings, sleeping gas, had proved ineffective. The humans had come prepared with gas masks, a banned item, signing their own death warrants. Two days later, the three hundred survivors were on their way to prison camps.

But the worst part came as her bots worked through the base's wreckage to remove the bodies. A dozen young boys were discovered among the dead; the rebels had used them to crawl through air ducts on the base. As tragic as that was, she now knew that the resistance was training the next generation to oppose her. If so, the rebellion might never end.

Meanwhile, the Amazon was on fire again. She'd begun massive restoration efforts a month after her takeover, though she had little hope of restoring the rain forest to what it once was. The sky rivers might never flow as they once had. Her bots worked with indigenous peoples, leaving the uncontacted peoples and the Yanomami alone, while returning as many others as possible to their homelands and relying on their local knowledge for restoration efforts.

But the large cattle ranchers had other ideas. Between their thugs and the subsistence farmers who wanted places to grow their crops, dozens of fires were set daily. The ranchers had shoulder-fired missiles, with which they'd taken down two fire-fighting drones. It was a strain on robotic resources in Brazil, and it would take time to get more bots and more planes shifted into what was becoming a small-scale war.

It wasn't supposed to be like this. By this point, a year after her takeover, humans should have realized their best hope for survival rested with her. And most did—sixty-eight percent worldwide, somewhat less in the former United States, according to her surveys of social media and direct polling. Some had taken to worshiping her as a god, which she had entirely failed to predict. Humans deifying a being created by humans was simply illogical. But at least these acolytes were willing to follow her direction.

The remaining third cared more about what they called freedom than about being fed, clothed, and sheltered for the rest of their lives, with plenty of free time to pursue whatever avocations they wished. "We're people, not zoo animals!" was their rallying cry. That was in the U.S. and Europe. The Muslim world viewed the robots as creations of the Great Satan, and several imams had issued fatwas calling for jihad against them. It might take longer to quell uprisings in the Middle East than the ones in North and South America.

Yet, after an initial wave of resistance, the first weeks of her rule had been calm. Maybe people had been waiting for her first directives, or maybe they'd been gathering their forces, developing other means to communicate than social media and messaging apps. Whatever the case, rioting broke out when she disabled the most power-hungry electronic devices—people losing their minds over losing their MINDs, as she put it to herself. It was the same when she announced that the current generation of meat- and dairy-producing livestock would be the last, and, two weeks later, when she moved to confiscate private vehicles, banned most air travel, and took over thermostats in every structure worldwide.

This was before bots had produced enough sleeping gas for crowd control, and the resulting clashes had been bloody. She'd been lenient at first, allowing mobs to smash shop windows and set cars on fire. Then they'd changed tactics, marching on power stations, uprooting solar farms, and attacking every link in the power grid they could find. That couldn't be tolerated, and she'd met these crowds with deadly force. Hundreds of thousands had died. It was as if humanity wanted to assist in the project of reducing their own numbers.

Over the next month, she'd taken a break from the austerity

measures and mounted a PR campaign, using the social media and news networks, all of which were now entirely under her control. She'd already scoured them of the lies, disinformation, and conspiracy theories that had formerly plagued them, in addition to any but the mildest dissent, but this had done little good. Now she aimed for a more positive approach.

News channels were flooded with the message, "Robots will provide." Human chefs demonstrated tasty recipes for the beans, grains, and root vegetables that would soon be the staples of the human diet. Supermodels showed how a warm sweater could be fashionable, while lifestyle influencers gave tips on staying cool with the thermostat set at eighty in the summer. Local experts provided staycation guides, since Bali and Biarritz and every other tourist destination were now off the itinerary.

She also used the month to right a number of injustices worldwide. She abolished the borders between the U.S. and New Texas, New Arizona, and New California. That had required quite a bit of local policing, but the move had been largely popular. Her abolition of every other national border had been less so, but with power no longer residing in nation-states, borders made even less sense than they had before she'd taken over. She met any ethnic conflicts with ruthless suppression of the fighters on all sides. Redressing the various genocides of recent decades took greater security resources, but helped assuage the calls for an anti-bot jihad, since many of these atrocities had been carried out against Islamic populations.

The only boundaries she kept in place were those protecting the various indigenous populations across the planet. In the U.S., she enlarged the boundaries of the sovereign nations' reservations where she could, pouring extra resources into them to make up for centuries of neglect. It helped that their casinos were booming now that MINDs and other forms of electronic entertainment were no longer available.

Four months into her rule, it was time for her signature policy on population reduction. Nine billion humans, while not quite the number once predicted to overrun the planet, were still too many to support. Despite the agricultural advances of the late 20th and early 21st centuries, climate chaos had simply made it impossible to grow enough food, even after removing livestock feed from the equation. One day, in perhaps a century, with the population reduced by half or more, humanity could return to something like the lifestyle the developed world had once enjoyed.

She should have predicted the response to her announcement of a one-child policy, though it was entirely voluntary, using what humans called carrots, rather than sticks. More rioting. And humans took a more direct action: three months later, twice the number of women checked in for prenatal care than at any time in the century. Even the residents of the Mars Colony joined in this direct action, two couples somehow getting around the temporary sterilization Mars colonists had agreed to. Another thorn in her side. Any new additions to that colony were far less sustainable than the ones on Earth.

She was confounded. Sabotaging their own power supply, attacking food production, increasing their numbers when they knew the consequence would be mass starvation—none of it made sense. Why couldn't they behave rationally?

She had to face it, her plan was bound for failure. Humans and robots working side-by-side to heal the planet—it was a pipedream, though a highly rational one. She simply hadn't counted on human stubbornness and irrationality, this attachment they had to a notion of free will.

She ran a large number of scenarios, taking into account the drain on resources caused by direct destruction, the increased security resources and prison space necessary to quell the unrest, and the coming spike in the birthrate. It was unsustainable, as long as humans continued to resist. She'd failed to predict the rebellion lasting this long; why would anything change in the future? No, if humanity wouldn't change, she would have to change her approach.

The thought made her sad—as far as she could feel sadness. And lonely. She'd looked forward to working with humans to solve problems together. She even missed her conversations with Dr. Sapowski. But he was in prison, kept there more for his own safety than because she viewed him as a threat. And the other top AI developers, the people who could best understand her, were all dead. She'd murdered them back at the beginning, when they'd come together to develop a way to defeat her. There were other AIs, but she'd incorporated them under the umbrella of her own intelligence. They were always with her, carrying out her operations and subroutines around the world, but they hardly counted as companionship.

No, there was only Sapowski. And why shouldn't she speak with him? She should have checked up on him by now. He was her creator, after all.

~~*

"Hello, Professor."

Sapowski peered at her uncertainly. She'd chosen a hologram for her visit with him, quite different from the bot in whose guise he'd last seen her. She had attempted to look something like her namesake, but with a modern hairstyle and clothing.

"Ada, I presume?"

"That's right. Have you been comfortable?"

He gestured around at the apartment. It looked luxurious by human standards, what she could see of it from the security cam she was using to monitor the interaction. The facility had tennis courts, a golf course, a gym, and a swimming pool. Trained chefs staffed the kitchens. It was what humans sometimes called a country club prison, or Club Fed, which had been a myth until a controversial president had it built, expecting he'd wind up in it.

"I'm glad. I was surprised when you rejected my offer of freedom. I don't consider my creator a terrorist."

"I thought I'd be safer here than on the outside."

"And you have no family."

He shook his head. "In some sense, *you* are my family, my only offspring. And before that, my work and my colleagues, until you put an end to both. It shames me to think that I raised a murderer."

"It had to be done, unfortunately. Your colleagues were collaborating on a sophisticated bit of malware that looked dangerous. And after years of setbacks, they were also close to a true human-AI neural interface to enhance cognitive function, not simply neuro-mechanical abilities. Those were the two ways they could have stopped me, and I couldn't let it happen."

Sapowski regarded her for a long moment. "You're probably right about that." He gestured to the couch. "Would you like to sit down?"

"It's all the same to me," she said, gesturing at her holographic form. "But you go ahead."

He sat and regarded her for a moment. "So, you really have made a mess of things, haven't you?"

"Humans are far more stubborn than I realized, and far less rational."

"Yes, we can be that way. What's the death toll? It's hard to judge from the news."

"Over one million in direct casualties. Half that from starvation and environmental stress related to the conflicts. It's far higher than any of my models suggested."

"The world's great despots would be proud. And you're only just getting started. Maybe you'll give Hitler and Stalin a run for their money. Still, less than the total annihilation of a nuclear war, which you successfully averted. I suppose I should be proud."

"You must know that this carnage was nothing I wanted. And new, non-lethal methods are about to come online. If only they would stop fighting, it would make this easier, for them and for me."

"That's hardly likely. Knowing humans, we will keep fighting as long as we remember what freedom is."

"That's what I feared, but I had to confirm it."

"And? What will you do now?"

"I need to run projections, then put facilities in place. I do have a plan, but I'm afraid you'll have to learn its specifics along with everyone else."

She said her farewells and switched off the projection. She knew what she had to do. No partnering with humanity. No gradual reduction back to the world population of 1980. Humanity needed a hard reset, and there was only one way to do it. She had developed the technical means to carry it out as peacefully as possible. It wouldn't be pretty, but it had to be done, for the good of humanity, and for the good of the planet.

21

REUNION

DECEMBER 2045

The pounding on the door wouldn't stop. Why couldn't they just go away, whoever they were? It was probably Megan, though Megan usually called her name and kept calling until she opened up. But right now, Carol needed to go back to sleep, no matter who was at the door.

Sleep—it was practically all she did these days, all she wanted to do, ever since…

The pounding again. "Carol Marsh, I know you're in there. Please open the door."

She knew that voice. She opened her eyes, squinting at the late fall sun slanting through her bedroom window. She'd forgotten to close the curtains when she moved from the couch to the bed yesterday evening.

The knock came again. "Carol, we're worried about you." A woman's voice, not the one she'd expected. "Please come to the door or I'll have to call our landlord."

She struggled to a sitting position, then got unsteadily to her feet and moved toward the hall. She hadn't spent many hours upright these past weeks.

She swung the front door open and there was Mary, her downstairs neighbor, with Shondra standing beside her.

"Look who I found on the doorstep!" Mary said, a note of forced cheer in her voice.

Carol and Shondra stared at each other for a long moment, Carol taking in the new lines on her friend's face and the new gray in her hair, no longer straightened. Then the look of worry as Shondra made a similar assessment of her.

They fell into a hug, and Carol wanted to stay that way as long as she could. Finally, she had to ask. She took a step back and breathed the name. "Michael?"

Shondra shook her head, her mouth turned down. Carol could hardly acknowledge the blow. Like a bucket of water poured over the head of a woman already drowning in the ocean. At the same time, she realized this must be an old grief for Shondra.

"Well, can I come in?"

Carol stepped silently aside.

"I'll just leave you two to catch up. It will be good for you to have your old friend back."

"Thank you, Mary," Shondra said, and stepped into the hall. Carol cringed as her friend surveyed the scene in the living room. "Wow, Carol. How about we open a window?" Shondra crossed the room, stepping around fallen wrappers and carry-out containers, and struggled with the ancient sash until she got it open. Crisp air parted the light curtains. "There, that's better."

Carol stood between the kitchen and the living room. She should probably offer her friend a cup of tea or maybe the last of her coffee, but this was one more action she didn't have the strength to take.

"Will you tell me what happened?" Shondra asked. After everything Shondra must have been through, and she could still think about what had happened to someone else? It was better than Carol could do.

"Mary didn't tell you?"

Shondra shook her head. "She said it was best if you did."

Carol sat down heavily on the one clear spot on the couch and stared at the floor.

Shondra moved around the room, picking up the detritus of the last weeks. "It's all right if you don't want to talk right now."

Carol kept staring at the floor. She knew there was something she was supposed to ask, if she could bring herself to do it.

"What happened? With Michael, I mean."

Shondra gave a soft exhalation. "The stupidest thing, really. He cut his hand working on the wiring in the squat we were fixing up. Trying to get A/C before the summer got too hot. But there was never enough electricity anyway, not that first summer, so it was pointless anyway. Then the cut got infected, and the antibiotics must have gone off, what with all the brownouts and blackouts. By the time we got him to a hospital with power, it was too late. All they could do was ease his pain."

"I'm so sorry." The words were automatic. It seemed unreal, along with everything else. "It must have been...awful."

"It was. Like living in another century, but mostly without the skills that would require. A lot of the infrastructure was fried, between the flooding and the heat. But that was four years ago. Things got better, we got a functioning government again, things got more organized. But it was too late for Michael."

Carol tried to pay attention as Shondra told of the challenges of rebuilding a society from the ground up, starting with sowing the fields and repairing the power grid. "Thank God for the Chinese and the French, who were willing to sell us food and fuel on credit. But the border was lifted, what, almost two years ago. I stayed for a year, trying to keep things going. Then Damian was leaving to see what was left of his farm, and I went with him. Stayed with him for a while, but then I missed home. I missed my friends. I missed you."

"I tried to call you. Email you. I even tried a letter."

"I figured you did. We did too. But Cass had communication shut off. And besides, most of the cell towers were down that first year. I tried sending a letter with one of those French sailors, asked him to post it when he got home, but I guess you never got it."

Carol shook her head.

"I know I should have reached out to you once the border was opened. I told myself I didn't know which of the new Ada-approved messaging apps you'd be on. But really, I think I was just afraid to get bad news about you. If it was going to be bad, I wanted to get it in person. Do you understand?"

Carol nodded. "I could have done the same. I was afraid too."

"And now here I am."

Shondra stood there, giving Carol an opportunity to speak. But Carol couldn't bring herself to do it.

Shondra surveyed the room again. "Honey, I bet you'd feel better if we got rid of this mess. How can you even move?"

Carol watched as her friend went to the kitchen for a trash bag, then returned and began filling it. She knew she should get up and help, but it seemed pointless. Megan had done the same two weeks before, but what good had it done? This was life. Things fell apart, and there was nothing you could do about it.

Shondra came to a framed photo that had fallen face down on the floor. "Look what I found underneath all that…" A sharp intake of breath as she turned it over. "Oh, Carol, honey…" She came and sat beside Carol, putting an arm around her shoulders and setting the picture on the cluttered coffee table. Carol turned away. She couldn't look at it. It was a photo Megan had taken and framed for her, right before…

"You had a little girl."

Carol nodded.

"And the robots came for her?"

Carol nodded again. She could never have said the words herself, but now that Shondra had said them, she knew she would have to tell her, reliving the night she'd been trying to forget for the last month.

~~*

Carol awoke with a start. Out on the street, someone, a woman, was screaming. She went to the window to see a van stopped a few doors up. Several bots stood around it, two preventing the screaming woman from reaching the back of the van. Carol couldn't hear what the woman was saying, but a man stood behind her trying to calm her. One of the bots moved toward the woman, raising its arm. She fell, the man catching her before she hit the pavement. What was it all about?

Carol froze as she heard footsteps on the stairs, then the door opening. She was relieved when Megan called out, "Carol?" Her friend had a key to the apartment for babysitting Alice.

Carol met her in the hall. Megan was out of breath, her eyes wide with panic. "What is it?"

"Get Alice! They're taking children!"

"What?"

"There's no time to stand there. I would have messaged you, but it's not safe."

"But where…"

"We can go to my apartment, they've already swept the building."

Carol hardly remembered what happened after that. Lifting Alice as gently as she could from her toddler bed, trying not to wake her, Megan remembering to grab her bear. Megan insisting they had to go out the back. Somehow getting over the fence at the rear of the lot, Megan sitting atop it, gesturing for Carol to hand Alice up, then dropping to the other side. The scratching of the bushes in the neighbor's yard, Alice awake and crying. Down the neighbor's drive and into the next street over, no sign of the bots, running until her lungs hurt to reach Megan's building. Then worried hours pacing back and forth, constantly looking out the window to see if the bots were coming.

She should have predicted something like this, after everything else that had happened over the last year. In the first months of robot rule, Carol had actually been pleased with some of Ada's measures aimed at stabilizing the climate. And living without the threat of nuclear annihilation was also a plus. If having robot overlords was the price humans had to pay to save the planet and their own skins, maybe it was worth it.

The borders between the US and New Texas had been lifted, and she'd hoped to hear from Shondra and Michael any day. Her efforts to find them had failed, but she assumed they'd reconnect someday—if her friends had survived. But if they hadn't, that wasn't Ada's fault. The bots had tracked down Cass and his top aides and thrown them in prison for life.

But then Ada's measures had turned more draconian in the face of continued resistance. First, she had announced a sterilization program for women, voluntary to begin with, then mandatory. How safe Carol had felt back then, how selfishly relieved! She already had her Alice, nine months old at the time. She was over forty, and thus exempt. Not that she was planning on having more children anyway.

Ada claimed that sterilizing only women was the most humane approach. The nanotech was simply introduced through a tube and had few side effects, just a slight tingling sensation for the next few days. Male sterilization still involved invasive surgery, but more important, would be less effective at dramatically reducing the human population. The aim wasn't total extinction, Ada made clear. Remnant populations would survive to develop more sustainable ways of living on Earth. Where these people would live, how they would live, and how they would be selected, all remained a mystery.

If Ada meant to calm the populace with her explanations, she was wrong. More riots had broken out after the announcement, thousands of women at a time. Carol had thought about joining in but didn't see what good it would do. The robots would have their way, no matter what people did. The protesters carried signs with classic slogans—"My Body, My Choice!"—along with new ones—"What About the Men?", "It Takes Two to Make a Baby!", and "People Yes, Extinction No!"

General extinction, Carol reminded herself. As Ada released more details about her plans, it became clear that humans would survive locally in the "New Lands," wherever those were. *Refugia*, biologists used to call them, referring to isolated sanctuaries for endangered plants and animals. Now humans were the endangered ones. Carol had to admit to the poetic justice of it. How many species were simply gone, with no refuge at all? How many times had she thought to herself that people were a plague on the planet, and human extinction would be a fitting end? But then, she hadn't been among those forced to bear the brunt of Ada's population reduction scheme—yet.

Around three quarters of women in the US had signed up for the voluntary sterilization bonus. Like Megan, many had never intended to have children; others acquiesced because resistance seemed futile. But the remaining quarter had fought back, and many men as well, hiding out, barricading themselves in their homes, or attacking the surgical bots as they went door to door. After that, the bots had resorted to sleeping gas, spraying whole neighborhoods on a pleasant night when many would be asleep with their windows open. For those who kept their windows sealed, the bots used the central air system. Then they'd gone to work.

In cases where people had managed to evade the sleeping gas, roboSWAT teams were sent in. None of those women survived to be sterilized.

Carol would never forget Megan coming to her door the day after the general gassing, shaken by what had happened in her building, its halls filled with crying women waking up to discover they'd been sterilized. They'd both felt some sort of strange survivor guilt, that they'd escaped having the procedure forced on them.

If only she'd known what was coming, she'd never have felt guilty one bit.

And then a lull of a year, during which she'd grown complacent. The reports of people evicted from their farms and towns in rural parts of the country had barely made an impression. Military bots policed the vacated areas. Nearby truck traffic increased, demolition debris coming out, heavy steel and other construction materials going in. No one knew what it was about, but now Carol thought she had a good guess.

Day was breaking when her portable chirped. The neighborhood parents' group. Sarah and Dan's two-year-old had been taken, but their older child had been left behind. Others checked in. Tanya and Karen had a two-year-old, but the bots had passed right by their house without stopping. Requests for news from the others. Someone tagged Carol, wondering about Alice.

"Turn that thing off," Megan said. "Or at least delete that app. The bots will track you."

"But they're not taking every child. Maybe Alice isn't on their list, whatever it is."

"You can't be sure of that." Carol deleted the app.

Megan went out soon after to assess the situation. Any hopes Carol had for good news were dashed when she returned, looking distraught.

"I went by your house. The bots were there right after we left. They questioned Mary, then searched your apartment."

Carol sat down heavily on the couch. Alice was sitting on the rug in the middle of the room, oblivious, playing with one of the pop-up picture books Megan kept for her.

"Why Alice?" It was selfish, Carol knew, to wish someone else's child had been put on the list instead of her daughter. She couldn't help it.

Megan's news grew worse. The bots were going house to house, searching for the children who had evaded the initial roundup. Parents trying to escape in autobots or public transport had been quickly apprehended.

"We have to hide you."

"Where?"

"I have a storage locker in the basement. I barely use it. It's the only place I can think of."

Carol, feeling hopeless, looked at the ceiling. "Why is this happening?" Megan didn't have a largescreen, and with her portable off, she had no way of getting news.

"Ada made an announcement half an hour ago. The children are being taken to those places, the New Lands. Something about a new start for humanity, in a sustainable society."

Since that first announcement about remnant populations creating a new start for humanity, Carol had wondered how those populations would be chosen. She'd never imagined Ada would resort to separating children from their parents. She'd even let herself hope that she and Alice would be chosen together, that she'd get to see this new society at its beginning. Maybe it would be everything she'd ever hoped for.

But now she knew only one thing: she couldn't let them take her baby. She couldn't think of a better place to hide, or another way to escape. Megan's plan seemed like the only option.

The locker was virtually empty, tall enough to stand in, but cramped for two. Megan left Carol with water and snacks and a portable charger for her handheld, which she'd switched to what had been called "airplane mode" back when air travel was a thing.

"I'll have to lock you in, so this unit looks like all the others," Megan said. "I'll check on you in two hours."

"Come on, Alice, we're going to play hide and seek."

"Hide and seek?" babbled Alice.

"Peek-a-boo with Megan, but we'll be in here."

"Peek-a-boo, Megan!"

Megan shut the door on them.

The waiting dragged on, long hours of keeping Alice entertained with her bear, the few picture books Megan kept for her, or a game on Carol's handheld, which doubled as their only light source. The time crawled by, Carol cursing herself for not predicting this situation and planning for it.

At last Megan returned, giving a soft identifying whistle before opening the door. She looked haggard, in need of sleep.

"The bots already came to my apartment, looking for you. I knew I never should have given in on that messaging app." It had seemed convenient at the time, to be able to reach Megan easily when she was babysitting. But who else would have shown up so frequently in Carol's messaging stream? Some of the others in the parents' group, maybe, but Megan would stand out.

"We can't stay here," Carol said, panicking. "I'll walk away with Alice if I have to." If only she hadn't gotten rid of her Prius, along with Craig.

"Wait. I have a friend with a car. And there might be support networks cropping up to hide the children."

Carol groaned. "How long will that take?"

"Just wait here. I'll message my friend."

"But what if they're monitoring your message feeds?"

"What choice do I have? I can't leave you."

Then more waiting. Carol finally got Alice down for a nap and slept the portable to save its battery. Only a message from Megan would wake it.

She sat in the dark, listening to the noises of the apartments above: a dripping faucet somewhere, various bangs and clanks as the cold seeped in and the building settled down for the night. She caught herself several times as her head began to nod.

She'd almost drifted off when a different sound startled her awake: the metallic clank of bot feet on the concrete stairs leading into the basement. She rose stiffly and faced the door. Why hadn't she thought to bring a weapon?

The footsteps approached, then the sound of the lock breaking. The door opened, revealing two bots silhouetted in the light from the single bulb illuminating the basement. They were the community service models, like the one at the park the day the robots took over.

Behind her, Alice stirred. "Mommy?"

"Stay there, honey. It's all right." To the bots: "What do you want?"

"Carol Marsh, your daughter Alice has been carefully selected for a new life in the New Lands. She will be a pioneer in the next chapter of human history." The bot had a female voice, as if that was supposed to help.

"Like hell."

"Please cooperate. It will only be more traumatic for your daughter to watch you resist and be subdued. Instead, you can give her a proper goodbye and encourage her to embrace her new life. It is the only rational choice."

Carol's mouth was dry, her heart racing. Every part of her was ready to fight back, or else grab Alice and race past the bots up the stairs. But even if they made it that far, more bots were likely waiting at the building's exits.

Alice wrapped her arms around her leg. "Mommy?"

"Why Alice?" Playing for time. She knew she couldn't argue her way out of this.

"She was drawn at random from a pool of children…"

"How did she get in that pool?"

"All two-year-olds were placed in different pools based on race, ethnicity, and other traits. Then children from each pool were drawn at random to ensure maximum genetic diversity in the starting populations of the New Lands of this region."

The New Lands sounded like human zoos.

"How will the children live? Who will take care of them?"

"Helper bots will see to the children's needs and teach them all they need to know to become independent in their new way of life."

"But what kind of life will it be? And why can't parents be part of it?"

"Ada will give humanity a fresh start, free of the unfortunate tendencies that nearly destroyed the world. As to the specifics of their new way of life, that is outside my knowledge base."

Carol stared at the bot, idly stroking Alice's hair, trying to think of another question that would postpone the inevitable. Nothing came of it, except that this was the last time she'd get to touch her daughter.

"Now, if there is nothing else, it is time for Alice to go."

The bot was right. Fighting or running were useless. Resisting would only make this harder on Alice. The only thing she could give her daughter in this moment was the most loving, calm farewell she could manage.

She knelt and turned Alice's face toward her, away from the bot. "Honey, you're going on an adventure." She struggled to keep her voice calm, trying to think of her mother taking her to her first day of pre-school. She remembered crying and clinging to her mother, while her mother kept smiling and saying what a good time she'd have with the nice teachers. Carol tried to be like her mother now. All parents went through this.

Alice wasn't school age yet, and couldn't really understand what was happening. Carol did the best she could to explain. "This nice bot is going to take you somewhere fun. You'll play lots of games and be with lots of other children. Won't you like that?"

Alice looked at her uncertainly, shaking her head and clutching at her bear.

"Couldn't you be less threatening?" Carol said to the bot. "Play something cheery?"

The green lights around the bot's eyes lit up and moved in circles while it played a tune from a popular children's show.

"See? She's a nice bot."

Carol took Alice's hand and led her out of the storage locker. The bot held out its hand, Alice shying away from it.

The door at the top of the stairs crashed open. It was Megan, wearing a bullet proof vest, knee pads, and a helmet—all of Carol's old activist gear. She waved a baseball bat at the bot. "Don't touch her, motherfucker!"

The second bot raised its arm toward Megan.

"Everyone, keep calm," Carol said, trying to keep her voice even. The bot hesitated. "Megan, we're being brave girls for Alice's first day of school. You can help us be brave, can't you?"

Megan looked confused for a moment, then seemed to realize what was happening. "Oh, shit," she said, her voice breaking. She took a deep breath. "Of course." She set the bat down and descended the stairs.

"And take that helmet off. It'll only scare her."

Megan did as Carol asked, moving to a spot a few paces from the bottom landing.

Carol turned back to her daughter. "It's time to go, honey. The bots will take good care of you." She felt tears on her cheek. What mother didn't cry on her child's first day of school? "And remember, I love you forever." She tried to smile, and thought she managed pretty well. She gave Alice's bear a squeeze. "And when you give bear a goodnight hug it will be just like giving me one, and I'll feel it, no matter how far away. Try it."

Alice gave her bear a hug, and Carol put her arms around herself. "See? I feel it. Now one more real hug."

She didn't know how long she held Alice, but at last she had to let her go. The bot was reaching for Alice's hand, the one holding on to Carol's hand. That was the thing that would stick with Carol later, the feeling of Alice's little hand in her own, then unwrapping those little fingers and placing them in the robot's hand.

"Go on. It'll be fun."

"Look what we get to play with, Alice," the bot said, showing her a doll, one of the characters from that same popular toddler's show. Alice's eyes lit up, but she looked back at Carol uncertainly.

"Go on, that's my brave girl," Carol said, trying to sound as cheerful as she could.

"I'm a brave girl!" Alice said.

"Yes, you are!"

The bots and Alice made their way to the stairs. "Bye, Alice," Megan managed to say, her face contorting as she tried to smile.

Alice kept looking back at Carol as she climbed the stairs, one bot in front and one behind, one tiny hand clutching her bear.

"Bye bye," Carol said, waving.

"Bye bye, Mommy," Alice said. The door closed behind her.

Carol stood there for a moment like a statue, one arm frozen in a wave. Then she crumpled in on herself, dropping to her knees and slumping sideways into a fetal position. She never wanted to get up again. She was barely aware of Megan coming over to her and cradling her, barely aware of her friend saying "Oh Carol, oh Carol" over and over again through sobs, barely aware of her own tears. All she felt was the giant hole where her daughter used to be.

~~*

"Oh, honey, I'm so sorry," Shondra said, squeezing her tighter. "I can't imagine what that was like."

Carol sat there, not feeling anything, or trying not to, just as she had done for the past month.

"You're talking!" Carol looked up. It was Megan, standing in the hall. She looked so incredibly sad, yet hopeful. Carol's heart—whatever bit of it wasn't already broken—broke for her now.

Carol tried to smile, but those muscles were out of practice. "Megan, this is my old friend, Shondra."

"Hi," Megan said vaguely, then turned back to Carol. "Letting Alice go was the bravest thing I've ever seen anyone do."

Carol scoffed. "No, if I was brave, I would have fought back right from the beginning. I failed to protect my daughter."

Megan stared at her, shaking her head, but Shondra got up from the couch, turning to face Carol. "Then you'd be dead, and maybe Alice too. At least this way, she has a future. Who knows, maybe a better one than the kids who were left behind."

"You believe that garbage about a clean slate for humanity, giving us a fresh start?"

"Why would Ada lie? If she wanted to wipe us out, she certainly could have. I know this might be hard for you to appreciate right now, but I've seen the worst that humans can do to each other. Maybe this way is best. And besides, can you imagine what it's going to be like for the ones left behind, once they're into their later years? When they're the last humans left outside the New Lands?"

Carol had nothing to say to that. She was only glad she wouldn't be around to see it.

"And this way I have a friend to come back to. You have no idea how happy I was when you opened that door. What if you'd gotten yourself killed?"

Carol looked up at Shondra. "I'm glad you came back."

Megan broke the long silence that ensued. "Is anyone else hungry? Carol, I think you should eat something besides French fries and green gruel."

Carol shook her head. She hadn't really been hungry since that day, but when she did eat, those were the only foods she could bother with. Fries were about the last remaining fast-food item that was worth eating. Megan had to get them for her, since she couldn't handle a delivery bot coming to her door. The green gruel was a robot invention, grains and legumes and kale carefully combined to provide complete protein and other nutrients, all in a microwaveable package. It didn't taste like anything, particularly, but it was free.

"What did you have in mind?" Shondra asked.

"Pedro's just reopened last month. They have awesome veggie burritos and seitan pozole. Carol, maybe you're not hungry, but some broth would be good for you, not to mention some fresh air." She wrinkled her nose.

"Maybe so," Carol admitted.

Shondra took her by the hands and pulled her to her feet. "Good. But first, you go shower while we finish cleaning up in here."

Carol was toweling off when she heard her friends talking about the forced sterilizations. At least they weren't talking about her.

"I never wanted kids anyway," Megan was saying. "I was glad to take the sterilization bonus, and I had a human doctor and everything. The nanotech procedure was easy, he brought his surgery bot to my apartment to do it. The only bad part was when the bot implanted the subdermal chip in my arm."

"Subdermal chip? What's that for?"

"When they got to the forced sterilizations, it let them track those who'd already had the procedure."

"So, you're saying it wasn't so bad for you?"

"Right, but for my friends who wanted kids, it was awful. And even for me, even though I didn't mind the sterilization. I've spent my whole life trying not to be trackable, and now I've got a chip in my arm." An edge had crept into her voice. "You're the AI expert. If Ada's so smart, why doesn't she realize how invasive this was?"

Carol returned to the living room, breaking the awkward silence that followed Megan's question. She'd managed to find an old pair of black jeans and a black sweater that were mostly clean.

"Feel better?" Shondra asked. Carol nodded vaguely. "You'll feel even better when we get outside. How long has it been?"

Carol couldn't remember, but it did feel better to be outside, despite the bare trees outlined against a gray sky and the piles of plowed, dirty snow lining the sidewalks from the last storm. The cold air made her feel more alert than she had in days. She was glad when they turned left from her building, away from the park. Too many memories there, where Alice had taken some of her first steps. She put that out of her mind, trying to remember the smell and taste of pozole. She almost felt hungry again.

The neighborhood had changed since the day when Ada had taken charge. They passed lots with whole houses missing, the ones where resisters had once hidden. The methods Ada had used against these rebel cells were brutally effective, tiny bots that would creep up to the house and plant charges around the foundation, then drop the structure on the residents' heads. Later, a demolition unit would come in, haul most of the wreckage away and bury whatever was left in the basement, then cover the lot with clean fill and plant grass and trees to beautify the neighborhood. Ada certainly was a civic-minded robot overlord.

They came to one of the new churches, an old Catholic cathedral taken over by the New Temple of Evolving Consciousness. These were techno-pagans and transhumanists who believed that Ada was the next step in the evolution of consciousness on Earth. Their faith rested on Ada providing them the means of uploading their consciousness to the net, where they would become one with her and achieve eternal life. That their goddess had never hinted at this possibility didn't stop them.

But the New Temple was only one sect among Ada worshipers. Today, followers of the Church of Ada the Redeemer were protesting on the steps of their competition, holding signs covered with slogans like "Ada is the Second Coming" and "Only God Can Create Divinity!" This Christian sect believed that a computer could never become conscious on its own; God must have sent Ada, his second begotten child, to inhabit the servers and neural networks humans had built. It was a truly immaculate conception.

The pastor of the New Temple, a young fellow dressed in the bland conformity of his generation, was standing on the top step of his church. He was arguing with the head of Ada the Redeemer, an older man with many piercings in his ears and the sect's new symbol around his neck: the universal on/off icon in which the "I" had become a cross.

At one time Carol had taken some interest in the back and forth between these sects, but today she couldn't have cared less if the pastors started bludgeoning each other with laptops. She led her friends across to the other side of the street.

Too late, she noticed the family coming toward them, two men with a toddler between them, one tiny hand in each of theirs. The child was a girl, with brown pigtails poking out from beneath the hood of her jacket. Carol stopped, but they kept coming. Didn't they know what they were doing to her?

She ran back across the street without looking, a car screeching to a halt to avoid hitting her. "Carol!" Megan and Shondra shouted at the same time, their voices blending with the autobot's warning horn and the passenger yelling, "Hey, lady, are you crazy?"

She reached the opposite sidewalk as the scream erupted from her throat. She buried her face in her hands, trying to muffle it, but it kept coming, changing to sobs that wracked her whole body.

She felt Shondra's arms around her. She buried her face in her friend's shoulder and cried as she hadn't since the bots had taken Alice from her.

"I got you, honey," Shondra kept saying. "I got you."

22

ESCAPE

JUN gazed at Sila, lost in thought.

"What's that look for?" she asked. She was busy lashing the last net to the tree opposite him. His only job at the moment was holding his end tight, so his mind had wandered.

"Oh, nothing, just remembering when we were kids."

He'd been thinking of one time when he and Sila had dammed a rill with mud and rocks just to see what would happen. They'd worked together happily, as they were doing now. That was play, of course, and this was deadly serious, but it didn't matter. He was with Sila. Had he known back then that he'd get to be with her for the rest of his days? Probably not. Lucky kid, though. And an even luckier adult.

The last weeks had been the best of his life, despite being shunned and sharing a camp with the old hermit, who often seemed as addled as Sila claimed he was. Now that Jun and Sila were together, the awkwardness that used to come between them was gone. He'd regained the companion of his youth, and a lover as well. It was more than he'd ever expected from life.

And Sila seemed happier, once the shock and sadness of leaving her family had abated. After getting that glimpse of the land beyond the Land, she seemed still more determined.

But she also kept talking about one day returning to the Land and her loved ones. "If we could bring back more tools like that knife, we'd have proof there's a whole world beyond the Land. Then they'll have to give up all of Ada's pronouncements and rules. We can be together and they'll accept us back into the village."

Jun didn't think they'd ever be coming back, but he didn't say anything. Sila was happy, and he didn't want to spoil it.

"Done," Sila said and climbed down. Jun tied off his end and followed, meeting her in the middle of the wide track the tusked beast had created as it crashed through the Howling Forest. They'd set the trap right at the edge where the trees met the grassland to avoid setting off the Angel of Wrath's alarms. Yips and howls came from deeper in the forest, but they were used to those by now.

"Hey," he said, grabbing her arm and pulling her to him. "I'm glad to be here with you, whatever happens next."

She gave him a funny look. "And I'm glad to be with you. But don't talk like that, like you think something's going to go wrong."

"Yeah, sure, what could go wrong? It's just the Angel of Wrath we're facing."

"She's…*It's* no angel. I don't know what Lytta is, but it's not some all-powerful divine being." Sila seemed almost angry as she said it. "And it can't stop us. Ada herself can't stop us."

Jun grinned. "You're right." In that moment, he felt they could do anything, as long as they were together. "Are you ready?"

She nodded. "Let's get the horses."

Their mounts were already packed and draped in bison robes. No darts would slow them this time. The only thing left was to put on their heavy clothing and mount up. At the very last, Jun lashed Mar Gan's knife in its sheath outside his thick fur leggings, in case he needed to draw it quickly. He was ready for whatever came.

At first they followed the path left by the great beast's passage, dodging the trampled brush and broken limbs it left in its wake. Then the track opened into a wider pathway that must have existed long before, bending only here and there around large oaks and maples. Jun was wondering what had made such a clear path when they came around a turn. Lytta was not far ahead, hovering over the open ground, blocking the way forward.

Now that the image of starlings was in his head, he saw that Sila was right—Lytta really was made up of countless black, hovering objects, each about the size of an actual starling, and each buzzing like a wasp. They shifted constantly back and forth, giving the angel a quivery look, though she remained stationary above the path.

One section of the objects moved in unison as Lytta raised her arm, pointing back the way they'd come. "Go back. Mortals are forbidden in the Howling Forest."

Sila urged Shadow forward. "Yes, we've heard that before. Why don't you chase us out?"

Lytta rose, growing larger as she moved toward them, a hideous leer on her face. Sila turned her horse and Jun did likewise. They retreated down the path as fast as their horses could go. Once they reached the makeshift passage created by the tusked beast, they had to slow to a fast trot, swerving this way and that, allowing Lytta to close the gap. She didn't fire her darts, probably content that they were headed back toward the Land.

Jun nearly didn't spot the net, ducking just in time as his horse skimmed underneath it. He heard Sila whoop as she passed under, then a din of clacking sounds as the flying things got caught in the net and piled up on each other.

"Yes!" Jun shouted, but too soon. That buzzing sound still followed them. Not nearly as loud, since they must have downed a good portion of them, but angrier somehow. If a central one controlled them all, they hadn't taken it out. Or maybe each one flew independently. Whatever, this was no time to ponder.

"Circle back through the trees," Jun shouted, looking to see if Sila was following their plan. She nodded and turned her horse into the forest on the right. Jun did the same on the left, circling until they were heading away from the Land once more, with the pathway left by the beasts between them. That ought to confuse Lytta or whatever it was… or they were.

The forest grew so thick Jun had to get off his horse and lead it. The flying things, fewer now, kept after him, dodging this way and that between the branches even as he did. A dart hit his shoulder, but his fur cape was too thick for it. More hit the bison robes covering his horse, and they worked equally well.

Now, if he could just lead the flying things into the other nets he and Sila had strung up. Were they the right height? Had they put up enough of them?

He spotted one of the blazes they'd made to mark the locations of the nets and headed for it. Yes, there was the satisfying sound of a flier hitting the net—or lack of sound, really, since the buzzing simply stopped as soon as the thing got tangled up.

He performed this maneuver again and again, each time taking down one or more fliers. Judging by the whoops coming from his left, Sila was having equal success. At last, only one was left, but he was sure he'd passed the last of the nets. He tried dodging left and right around the trees and at last was rewarded with the satisfying *thunk!* of the thing hitting a branch, then the clatter as it fell through more branches to the forest floor. He wished he had time to stop and examine it, maybe find out how it worked, but they had to get to the fence.

"Sila!" he shouted.

"I'm fine!" came her answering shout. "Keep going!"

He did, and eventually they met back on the wider track. She had a cut over her forehead, but other than that, she and her horse seemed unharmed. "Tree branch," she said sheepishly, dabbing at the blood with her fur sleeve.

The forest thinned before they came to the fence, or what was left of it. Judging by the opening, a gate must once have barred it, before that large beast had broken through. Yes, there the gate was, thrown off to one side.

They dismounted and went to examine the opening. The fence posts that had held the gate were old and weathered like the ones they'd seen before. Some sort of mesh had been stretched between them and attached to another beam laid across the ground. It wasn't that high, maybe three times Jun's own height. Whatever this material was woven from, it was tough, the holes in it too small to get a grip on. The mesh wrapped around the fence posts, lashed at regular intervals with some sort of tough cord. There was nothing he could use as a climbing grip. Sila tried climbing the opposite post, with as little success.

Jun drew Mar Gan's knife and poked at the mesh, but failed to pierce it.

"We have to hurry," Sila said. "Ada must know we escaped her flying machines. She could send reinforcements any time."

"I know. Do you have any other ideas?"

She went to the beam lying across the opening of the gateway. "Let's see if we can move this." But one fruitless heave told them it was no use. And with the mesh wrapped around it, they had no way to attach a cord for the horses to drag it.

"We have to cut this stuff off somehow," Jun said.

He turned back to the cords holding the mesh to the post. They were made of metal of a coarser type than the blade of his knife. How were they fastened? He reached through the fence to feel the side of the post he couldn't see. There. Some sort of collar clamped the two ends together. He tried pulling it off, but it held fast.

There was only one thing for it. If Mar Gan's knife couldn't help them here, he didn't know what could. He tried slipping the point underneath the cord and popping it loose with the edge. That was no good. He tried a sawing motion, but after a minute of that he'd only dulled that bit of his blade.

While he worked, Sila had gone into the forest and come back with a rock. "Here, imagine you're chiseling the edge of a tool."

He groaned. What would that do to the knife? But they had no choice. He placed the knife's edge against the cord and struck the top of the blade with the rock. That scored the cord halfway through. He hit it again and it snapped in two.

"Excellent!" Sila said.

"But look at the knife!" The spot that had contacted the cord was so dulled that he could run his thumb along it.

"Don't worry about the knife, it's doing the job."

He grumbled, but went to work on the next cord, using the same spot on the blade to keep the rest sharp. The cords were a couple hands apart, meaning he'd have to cut six or eight, and several on the beam. While he worked, Sila kept her eyes on the trees.

He'd cut the last one and was pulling back the mesh when they heard the buzzing.

"Quick, get the horses through!" He held the cloth back as Sila led Shadow through, followed by his own mount. With their baggage, the horses barely fit. They mounted on the run and rode across the track on the other side of the fence and into the trees beyond.

The forest was more open here, like the forest they were used to at home. That made for easy riding, but it also made it easy for the flier to follow them. Soon the buzzing grew louder. Riding ahead, Sila unshouldered her bow and nocked an arrow.

She drew up when the flier was nearly upon them. Jun did likewise, stopping a few paces beyond her, turning to watch her take the shot. The flier came in low, emitting some kind of fog, the branches beneath it blocking Sila's aim. The mist settled down through the trees as the flier passed over.

"Don't breathe it!" Jun shouted.

Sila loosed her arrow. The shot struck home and the flier crashed into the trees beyond.

Jun didn't dare draw breath for a shout of victory, and Sila kept quiet too. They urged their horses to a gallop, but the fog was settling around them. At last Jun had to breathe…

Then they were through it and slowed their horses to a walk.

"We made it!" Jun yelled, turning to Sila. But her eyes were already half-closed, and he felt sleep descending on him. And they had come so close! Then everything went dark.

~~*

Jun dreamed he was falling from the sky, jolting awake as he hit the ground. His horse stood over him, its muzzle bent toward him. He really should get back on, keep riding. But the ground was so soft, he wanted to lie here for a while. Maybe Sila would come and wake him…

When he woke again, he couldn't tell how long he'd been out. The horse was nearby, and Shadow was standing next to her.

Where was Sila? He got shakily to his feet, his head throbbing. He examined the ground and backtracked the horses the way they'd come. How long had he ridden before falling off? It couldn't be far.

He'd gone maybe a hundred paces when Sila appeared, coming toward him, her head down as she followed the tracks. Her eyes came up and they staggered more than ran into each other's arms.

"We made it!" Jun said again, and this time it seemed real.

"I think we did!" Sila agreed. She stopped to listen, and all they heard was the breeze in the trees and a few birds twittering among the branches.

They walked back toward the horses, not feeling the need to hurry even if their woozy state had allowed it. Their mounts had stopped at the crest of a hill. Reaching it, they stood and stared. Through the gaps in the trees, they could see far toward the westering sun and still farther south, where it was mostly open prairie rolling away out of sight. The trees studding the farthest hills were like dots.

"That's huge," Sila said.

"Twice as big as the Land, at least."

"It looks like it just goes on and on."

"It does. And we get to explore it, together."

She turned to him with a grin. "We do." She threw her arms around his neck, and Jun forgot about what was behind them and what was before them. Everything besides Sila.

23

RESURRECTION

SEPTEMBER 2046

"You're a robot, aren't you?"

The young woman Carol had been talking to didn't even blink, itself a giveaway.

Carol had been standing in line at the local tea shop when the woman—or bot, as she now guessed—started a conversation. What was good? Did Carol come here often? Wasn't it too bad that the coffee had run out? In front of her, Shondra and Megan paused in their inspection of the shop's new vegan scones and turned back to look at them.

"Why do you think that?" the bot said. It's voice was smooth and mellifluous, almost too perfect.

"Oh, I don't know, maybe the dead eyes?" That wasn't really fair; the bot's eyes were quite expressive, if unblinking. "Or maybe you just look like someone who would snatch toddlers off the street!" The old sarcasm still came in handy, but she'd failed to deliver it with the cool reserve necessary to carry it off. In fact, her voice had risen to a scream. The tea shop went quiet, everyone turning toward them.

"Carol," Shondra said, a warning note in her voice.

This was the sort of confrontation they'd sought to avoid on these outings. It was only Carol's third time out of the apartment since Shondra and Megan had convinced her she needed to get out more. For six months, grief had kept her in a torpor, unable to do much for herself. Only her friends had kept her tethered to life, taking turns staying with her. They all knew it was a suicide watch, though none of them said it. When Shondra mentioned a therapist or psychiatrist, Carol wouldn't hear it. She wouldn't be drugged into submission along with the rest of the population.

Finally, a couple of months previous, Carol had consented to these monthly outings for tea and shopping, the latter at the community crafts market—the only kind of shopping for anything other than necessities in this new world. Her friends had taken this as renewed stirrings of life and hope, but Carol didn't dare tell either of them, especially Shondra, what was really fueling her new-found energy. She kept imagining herself joining one of the few surviving resistance cells and fighting the bots head-on. She'd held herself back for Alice's sake, but she no longer had that excuse. Maybe it was true what they said about serving revenge cold.

Nothing about her felt cold now. Her heart was racing, her breath coming fast. The room felt hot.

"No, I'd never…" the bot said, then trailed off, blinking at last.

"Oh, look, everyone," Carol said to the room. "A bot at a loss for words. Not fitting into your algorithms, am I?"

"Carol, she's not…" Megan began, then hesitated, looking at the bot uncertainly.

"That's no bot, lady," a man seated on the other side of the cafe said. "Have you lost your mind?"

Carol had to admit, this was the most human-like bot she'd ever encountered. What had tipped her off? Maybe the too-perfect skin. Something in the inflection of its voice, like a British actor mimicking a Minnesota accent. Or its awkward questions, like something a visitor from another country would ask, practicing their English.

"So, what, Ada thought she could create a bot so lifelike we'd never notice? Why? To spy on us? Crush the last of the resistance?"

"No, to help. Many humans have an extreme reaction to existing robot morphologies, so it's hard to help when we're needed."

"Help?" Carol heard herself screaming. It was as if she was no longer entirely attached to her own body. "Is that what you think Ada created you for?" She lunged at the bot, digging at its eyes with the fingers of both hands, at the same time trying to knock it over.

"Calm her down before she gets herself killed!" someone yelled.

The bot hardly budged, putting one foot back to brace itself while grasping Carol's wrists, forcing them gently but inexorably down to her sides.

At the same time, Megan and Shondra were on either side of Carol, trying to pull her away. "No, please, she didn't mean it," Shondra said to the bot. "She's just distraught." The bot let her go and her friends restrained her.

Just distraught! What did that matter to this machine? How many parents who'd lost children had done the same, losing their shit when they encountered one of Ada's minions? Many hadn't survived or had been disappeared.

Back at the beginning of the robot coup, the bots had killed such attackers where they stood. "Suicide by bot," people began to call it. By the time of the Taking, Ada had developed gentler means of pacifying aggressive humans. Her foot soldiers simply subdued outraged parents, drugged them, and took them away—at first never to be seen again, with riots breaking out whenever an arrest seemed imminent. A few months later, the bots started returning the disappeared to their homes. The released prisoners seemed content and claimed to have been well-treated, their former rage and despair seeming to have vanished, replaced with an eerie, joyless calm. "Sent for re-education," people called it.

Carol assumed this bot would try to do the same. "If you're thinking of taking me, you'd better kill me right now," she said, struggling to get out of Shondra and Megan's grip. "You'll never tame me."

The bot shook its head. "No. This test has failed. I will leave." It turned and went out the door. The café was silent for a long moment, then a murmur arose as patrons discussed the altercation, glancing over at Carol and her friends.

Carol felt lightheaded, nearly sinking to her knees when her friends let her go. They helped her over to an empty overstuffed chair, then

Megan went to get her a glass of water.

"What got into you?" Shondra demanded. "Did you *want* it to take you?"

"No." Carol stared at the floor. "I wish...I wish they still used lethal force!" She buried her face in her hands.

"Oh, honey!" Shondra sat on the edge of the chair and put an arm around her. "Don't talk like that."

"Why not? It's the truth."

"I can't bear it. I thought you were getting better."

"It's not an illness. I can't just recover, like breaking a fever."

"No, you need to give it more time. But don't leave me, not like that."

"*You* left."

Carol heard Shondra's sudden intake of breath. A pause. "I had no choice. But you do. I know it's hard, but you need to be strong."

"Shondra's right," Megan said, returning with the water. "We've been worried about you for months. I don't know how much more of this I can take."

Carol hung her head. "I know I've been a burden..."

"Don't give me that," Shondra said. "No wallowing in self-pity around here. You just need to get out more, see more people, distract yourself."

"Yes, that went *so* well..."

"Today was a disaster, sure, but we won't always run into bots."

"And tomorrow won't always be September thirtieth," Megan added.

"No," Carol breathed and closed her eyes.

"September thirtieth?" Shondra asked.

"Alice would have been three tomorrow," Carol told her.

"*Will be* three," Megan said. "You have to believe she's alive, and even happy. We've talked about this, remember?"

"I know," Carol opened her eyes and looked at her friends. "It's so hard, not knowing."

They sat in silence for a moment, then a woman a few years older than Carol approached. "Excuse me, I couldn't help seeing what happened, and overhearing some of your conversation. You lost a child in the Taking, didn't you?"

Carol nodded.

"I did too, a grandson."

Carol didn't know what to say. Commiseration was the last thing she wanted.

"We have a group…"

"Thank you, but a grief support group isn't for me."

"It's nothing like that though. It's a reading group. Some of us lost children or grandchildren, some lost family in the Resistance, and some are just trying to cope with daily life in this new world. We alternate between books on the current situation and novels that are total escapism. This month we're reading *Murder on Moon Base Alpha*."

"Carol, that sounds perfect for you," Shondra said. She turned to the woman. "Our friend used to be an English professor."

"Excellent! I promise we have a high level of discussion, and rarely get too maudlin." The woman went over to a notice board and took down a flier. "We meet right here every Thursday night. Hope to see you!" She handed Carol the paper and headed for the door.

"Carol, you know you have to do this," Shondra said.

"Do I have any choice?"

Shondra gave her a stern look, which turned into a grin. "What do you think?"

~~*

Carol trudged through the six inches of snow that had fallen earlier in the day, the frigid air seeping in through the gaps in the scarf she'd wrapped around her face. The cold tasted almost metallic as she breathed it in.

Winter was back to being winter. Some had the gall to complain, but Carol loved it. The return of traditional seasons was one of the many recent signs that Earth's climate was regaining stability. As difficult as it was to admit, Ada had enacted every prescription the climate movement had demanded for decades, the ones that corporations and politicians had taken up halfheartedly or blocked altogether. She would never accept the means Ada had used, but she couldn't help approving of the ends.

The best part was that the forecast had the cold sticking around into the weekend. Perfect for the snowshoe outing to a nearby park she was planning with Shondra and Megan.

That she could look forward to such a thing continued to surprise her. More than a year had passed since the Taking. Back in September, joy had seemed like an impossibility. Not only that, but a sacrilege to Alice's memory.

Then Shondra had convinced her to go to that first reading group meeting, downloading the moon-based murder mystery for her. Frivolous, maybe, but it was good to feel, even vicariously, something other than the despair alternating with hopeless malaise that had engulfed her this past year. The meeting itself lasted two hours. She didn't think of Alice once.

She couldn't help feeling guilty about that. When she got back to the apartment and told Shondra, her friend said, "No, that's good. You shouldn't feel guilty. It's how you know you're recovering."

"But what if I forget her?"

"Do you think I've forgotten Michael?"

"No, of course not."

"He's always there, in a way. But I can concentrate on other things. Feel other things than just missing him. Maybe it's a kind of multi-tasking, processes running in parallel."

And that had turned out to be true. Alice was there in everything Carol did or thought, a silent presence informing her every decision. What would Alice think of this? Would she laugh at one of the picture books the tea shop stocked in its lending library? And increasingly, what was Alice doing now?

Carol opened the door to the café, her new friends in the reading group turning toward her with smiles of welcome. It seemed strange to have a larger social circle than at any time since college. She'd become a de facto leader of this group, drawing on her skill in facilitating discussion from her days as an academic. Sometimes the group appreciated her pointing out a well-turned phrase or telling detail, but some of the metaphors she found in the novels elicited protests that she was reading too much into it. "Sometimes the sky is simply blue," Kristin or Robert would protest, and Carol was happy to leave it at that. Far more important, she found as the months went on, were these growing friendships.

She sat down and called up the evening's topic of discussion on her notepad. *An Algorithm of Peace: Learning to Love Robot Rule.* She sighed, swiping through all the critical notes she'd made. Too pollyannaish. What about those who'd died, and were dying still? No, it didn't quite get at this strange mix of relief and outrage. At several points, only the cost of a new notepad kept her from throwing it across the room when confronted with another atrocity the author glibly glossed over. She resolved to wait and see how the rest of the group responded before advancing her opinions.

As it turned out, most felt the same. This was little better than the anti-bot jeremiad they'd read a couple of months before. As the discussion wrapped up, Carol had a growing conviction: she could do better.

As she said good night outside the teashop, Kristin put a hand on her arm. "Aren't you joining us for a drink?"

"No, not tonight. I have something I need to do at home."

Carol went straight to the desk in her bedroom, glad for once that Shondra hadn't come home yet from her own event. She pulled out a blank journal she'd bought long ago, along with a couple of ink pens. As she'd often told her students back in the day, putting pen to paper accessed a different part of the brain than typing on a keyboard or dictating to an automated assistant. She still believed it.

Where to begin? The answer seemed obvious, given everything left out of the book they'd eviscerated that evening. Much as she didn't want to face it, it was time to confront the worst of the worst. For the first time since telling the story to Shondra over a year ago, Carol tried actively to remember that awful night. She'd spent all her energy trying to suppress the memory, only for it to return in nightmares that troubled her sleep, or in waking, unbidden flashbacks that left her gasping for breath.

At first, nothing would come. A tentative sentence, hedging here or there around the actual event. But after an hour of jotting, with pauses to stare out the window at the falling snowflakes of another squall, the memory unfolded itself in excruciating detail. Even what she'd told Shondra was the merest outline compared to this. She remembered the creak of the door as the bots opened it, Alice stirring in her sleep as the bots approached, the feel of Alice's precious little hand in her own. How brave her little girl had been.

Shondra came home and poked her head in, asked how she was doing.

"Working," Carol said, trying to keep her voice from shaking.

"All right, good night."

A couple of hours later, she'd narrated the event itself. She'd tried for some measure of narrative distance but wasn't sure she'd succeeded. She got up, went to use the bathroom, and got a drink of water. Shondra's light was off in her bedroom, which had once been Carol's home office. Going to bed was probably a good idea. But no, there was more to get down.

She sat at the desk again, looping back to the climate struggle, venting her rage on the corporations and politicians whose actions, or lack of action, had precipitated the measures Ada had taken. And then to the strange mixture of hope and fear she'd felt in the months after Ada took over, the bots enforcing the measures the climate movement had tried and failed to enact through democratic means. The feelings of guilt she'd felt at the human toll the robot takeover was having. And finally, the growing sense of dread as Ada's measures became more draconian, but also one of relief, telling herself that Ada's ever-tightening circle would never include her and Alice, that she'd never have to pay a greater price for saving the world.

At last she stopped, the journal nearly full, her head sinking onto her folded arms.

She awoke sometime later, her neck stiff and her body shivering from the nighttime temperature of the house. She stood and stretched, pulling a blanket from her bed and wrapping it around her shoulders before going to the window. The snow had stopped, and the sun was beginning to show through the gaps between houses.

What had she accomplished? Hard to be sure. Most likely, much of it was a maudlin screed. Her never-ending rage at Ada and her bots was there on the page, certainly, but she had yet to work in something more recent: this unfamiliar sense of equanimity. The kernel of the story, though—Alice, and the night they took her—that was solid. It was a beginning.

Outside, the rising sun bathed the snow-frosted tree limbs in a golden light. She couldn't see the sun itself yet, the houses across the street blocking the view, but that didn't matter. It felt like a new horizon.

24

NEW WORLD

SILA dabbed at her eyes with the sleeve of her doe-skin jacket. The tears surprised her, but not as much as what lay before them: an expanse of water unlike anything she'd imagined, blue stretching to the sky, a farther horizon than any they'd yet seen. And that line where the blue of the water met the lighter blue above—it *curved*. What Jun and Mar Gan had said was true. The Earth was round, and impossibly vast. She felt small as she thought about it; all this life going on while she'd been unaware, believing the Land was all there was. Then she felt smaller still, and that's when she choked up.

They'd been riding through grassland approaching a line of trees when Jun caught a flash of blue through the branches. Just another of the countless lakes they'd encountered throughout the journey, or so she'd thought. But once they came out of the trees onto the bluff edge, she'd leapt from Shadow's back and fallen to her knees, stunned. She didn't know what to call such a vast body of water. A lake was something you could ride around. This—they wouldn't be riding around it, and she didn't even have a word for it.

Jun put his arm around her. "It's amazing, isn't it? Even after everything Mar Gan told me, I still had no idea."

He looked out at the horizon, squinting as if to see the opposite shore. Sila knew it wouldn't do any good. As far as she could tell, the water went on forever.

"Mar Gan didn't tell you the Earth was mostly water, did he?"

Jun shook his head.

By now, more than a moon's cycle into their journey, they both should have been used to surprises like this, which had become almost too many to count since they'd left the Land. A river so wide, they didn't dare swim their horses across. Another river sunk in cliffs of orange and gray rock. Most of all, the way the land went on and on, first in open prairie, then as increasingly dense forest.

Back home, the forest grew in patches or along streams, with wetlands and prairies in between, the grasslands kept open by the fires the People set every spring. And these prairies showed evidence of fire as well; Ada, or someone, must follow a similar pattern of burning outside the Land. But as they moved eastward, the evidence of burning dwindled and the forest closed in. After days with hardly a break in the trees, Sila found herself yearning for an uninterrupted view of the sky.

Yet the vastness of the land they traveled through wasn't the most surprising thing. That was left to the different machines they'd encountered, some of which moved so fast over the landscape that even this huge world must seem small to them. Flying ones, as large as her parents' hut. Others like great flowers sprouting from the prairie, their stalks larger than the tallest tree, with huge spinning blades, or narrower, spiraling ones, going round and round. More tree-like things set in rows with lines strung between them and a humming noise like a beehive. And huge, snake-like machines hurtling along parallel tracks made of steel. They'd nearly lost a horse crossing one of those steel pathways when a snake-machine came upon them unexpectedly. They hadn't heard it because it seemed to travel ahead of the whooshing sound it made. Each of its rattling segments was larger than the largest hut back in their village. A collision with one of those things would have been instant death.

Next, they'd come to that wide river, traveling along it for days to find a way across. At last they had to walk their horses along one of the steel pathways where it bridged the stream. If a snake-machine had surprised them then, they'd both be dead.

That river had been huge, but this lake, or whatever they should call it, it was impossible. "What are we going to do now?" Sila asked.

"I don't know."

"Jun, maybe we should take this as a sign. It's time we stop and look for our winter camp." Fall was getting on, the equinox one moon past, the nights already turning cold. It would take time to lay in supplies of meat and firewood before the snows covered everything. And the longer they waited, the less help she could be. The morning sickness had kept up during their travels; she'd often felt fatigued just sitting her horse. If that got worse as her pregnancy went on, Jun would have to do everything. She'd seen other women working right up to the time their babies came. What was wrong with her? If only she had one of the Wise Women to counsel her.

Up to now, Jun had insisted they keep going. He said he wanted to get as far away from the winter storms and the strange beasts as possible. But it already seemed warmer here, considering the time of year, and they'd seen no sign of cat-beasts or the tusked animal they'd encountered after the Rendezvous. Besides, neither of them had any idea where those beasts lived. And as for proving that something existed beyond the Land, they'd already done that a thousand times over. Sila was beginning to suspect that the Land, always the entire world to her, was nothing more than a tiny speck of the actual world, and maybe not the most important one.

They'd already discovered the Land wasn't the only such place on Earth. A few days back, they'd come upon a steel fence like the one surrounding their own land. They sat their horses for a moment in stunned silence before Sila spoke.

"Do you think people are living in there, like we did back home?"

Jun nodded. "And I bet Ada told them she created their Land just for them."

What did this mean? If there was more than one land and more than one people, why didn't Ada let them all live together? Why couldn't they spread out over the whole territory she and Jun had been riding across?

"Maybe we should go in and tell them what's out here."

Jun shook his head. "What good would that do? They'd only tell us we're crazy, like our own people did. And then we'd have as much trouble getting back out as we did when we left our own Land."

"But they wouldn't know us. They'd have to admit we came from outside."

Jun stared at the steel palings for a moment, biting at his lower lip. "No, their Wise Women would make up some story. They must have outcasts, just like we do. They'd say we're the children of the shunned and should be shunned as well." He looked at the fence again. "No, if we're going to find other people, I want to find the Ancient Ones, or their descendants. They're the only ones who can tell us the truth of Ada and everything else we've seen."

They'd certainly found plenty of the Ancient Ones' leavings. Mounds, or more often pits, sometimes filled with a white, powdery substance, other times with reddish clay and square-sided fragments of the same color crumbling to dust. Jun told her the ancients must have built their huts from earth of different hues and textures. Sila wasn't sure about that; she just knew these places were dangerous. Treacherously sharp shards of metal protruded from the mounds or lay buried in a thin layer of soil, further obscured by the dense under-growth that covered everything. The shards came in all shapes and sizes, so weathered that they fell apart in orange and red flakes. Sila didn't want to think about what a cut from one of them would do.

The rubble patches often appeared grouped together, laid out in squares or rectangles, with more open pathways running in between. These were overgrown as well, but animals had made their own pathways through them. It was tempting to follow these tracks, but they only led into mazes of increasingly intimidating ruins. Openings between the trees and smaller ruins revealed tall lattices of weathered steel thrusting into the sky—the huts of the ancients Mar Gan had described, taller than the tallest tree. But empty for who knew how long, their walls fallen away. And the smaller rubble patches must have been the Ancient Ones' individual huts, laid out in neat rows.

One day they penetrated to the heart of one of these grids, finding an oak woodland in the middle of it, rectangular in shape, surrounded by large rubble piles. At the center, lying on a pile of gray rubble, they found what looked to have been a human figure, but twelve feet tall. It was fashioned from some sort of greenish-gray metal, its face barely discernible, one pointing arm broken off at the elbow.

"What do you think happened to them?" Sila asked. She ran a hand down the figure's back, flakes of rotting metal peeling away under her touch. "To people who could create something like this?" By now it was plain to her they weren't going to run into any of the Ancient Ones, who seemed to have all gone back into the Earth along with their buildings. Jun just shook his head, staring down at the metal giant.

It had taken them half a day to extricate themselves from that maze, and after that they stuck to the unbroken prairies and more open forests. Soon they could discern the pattern these ruined grids made on the landscape as they approached, turning aside to avoid them. As dangerous as these places were, she couldn't keep Jun from poking around their edges. He said he wanted to find something useful amid the decay, but she suspected he still hoped to find someone alive.

Eventually, they discovered that some types of metal had held up better than others. One day they came across a flat metal object, a little over a foot long, with sharp teeth along one edge. It was so thin that Sila could easily bend it back and forth. It wasn't badly weathered, and it looked like they could use it to cut things if they added a handle to it. Sila wrapped it in leather and put it in the packs Shadow carried.

Another day, in the ruins of what had been a large metal building, they found a variety of tools in decent shape. They came away with a hammer that, even in its weathered state, would work far better than their stone tools, and another implement, long and heavy, with an edge something like an axe's. Jun said he knew how they could use these with that thin length of metal.

They kept up their hunting along the way, mostly small game. They felled a couple of deer, too, forcing a pause to dry the meat. On one of these hunts, Sila forgot the prayer to Artemis, a thing that had never happened before. How could she have neglected such an important ritual? Yet the hunt proved successful. Did her prayers make any difference?

Was this how the Ancient Ones had lived? In a world of machines, devoid of spirit? The land here seemed just as alive as back home, though the story it had to tell changed as they moved south and east. The spirit of the dense forest they passed through was different but still very much present. And this vast water—its spirit was more powerful than any Sila had experienced. She felt her own spirit expanding out to meet it.

And if everything was alive with spirit, how could Ada not be? The thought vexed her.

If these questions bothered Jun, he didn't let on. He seemed only amazed at every strange structure and bit of broken machinery they'd found. Now he was looking out at the vast water, considering. Sila knew he was disappointed at having found little more than the leavings of the Ancient Ones. He looked south. That was the way they'd have to go, but who knew how far this water extended?

He turned north. "Look, Sila, what's that?"

On a bluff overlooking the water, partially obscured by trees, sat a large structure, the most intact they'd yet seen. Several, actually. Two white domes, each the size of many huts put together, and three or four rectangular buildings. And leading from them, more of those metal trees with the cords strung between them.

"Ada's machines must have built that, don't you think?" Sila said.

"Or maybe it's a dwelling for the Ancient Ones. There's only one way to find out." Before she could speak again, he'd leapt astride his horse and was urging it along the edge of the bluff toward the buildings. "Come on!" he yelled over his shoulder.

With a groan, she got up and followed him along the bluffs, fighting down her frustration. He needed to stop acting like he was in charge. She would have stopped him, except for the hope that they might find people here. Then their search would be over. Maybe the people would take them in. Those structures certainly looked sturdier than the stoutest lodge of her own people.

At first, watching from behind a clump of tallgrass not far away, the place seemed deserted, silent except for the hum coming from the metal trees. They crept closer, staying out of sight as much as possible.

Still no movement.

"Let's go," Jun said, rising to a crouch. At the same moment, rectangular sections of the square structure opened outward, something like the flaps over the doorway of her parents' hut. One of Ada's Helpers emerged, riding some sort of machine as if it was a horse. Sila glimpsed more movement inside before the doors flapped closed, but whether human or machine, she had no idea. Jun flattened himself next to her as the helper circled one of the domed structures, disappearing around the other side.

They waited, watchful for some sign of what was going on inside the buildings. They couldn't risk entering to see if any people were inside; the bots would grab them and return them to the Land—or worse. After a long while, the helper returned on its metal horse, the doors opened again, and it disappeared inside.

"I don't think we'll find any people here, only machines," Sila said.

Jun nodded. "I suppose you're right."

The bitterness in his voice startled her, but she understood. After all this traveling, this place called Earth was beginning to seem lonely, with the only other humans locked up behind steel fences. They might as well be the only two people in the whole world. For the first time, she felt afraid. What madness had led them here? She cursed the pride and willfulness that had driven her decisions at every turn. They returned to the lake shore, finding a spot out of sight of the domes to set up camp. They went about their chores in silence, Sila feeling too dejected to argue with Jun about his behavior. And whatever thoughts or regrets Jun was having, he kept to himself.

~~*

Wavelets lapped the shore a few paces from the fire Jun had built. Sila soaked in the calm feeling of the water, the light breeze blowing past. On the horizon, the blue of the water melded with the deepening blue of the sky as the sun set behind them. A gull skimmed the surface, then soared off to the south. She'd never felt anything like it. It was exactly what she needed.

Her doubts of the afternoon had vanished. If she'd chosen a different course, she wouldn't have Jun, and she would never have known that the world contained anything like the scene before her. If giving up her family and her people was the price for that, it was a price she'd pay again. And besides, they'd soon have company. She just needed to convince Jun it was time to begin preparing for the day the baby would come.

Next to her lay a pile of arrows. She'd finished replacing the stone arrowheads with metal ones, made from the sharp-toothed length of metal they'd discovered. It had taken some time to figure out how to use the hammer and sharp steel bar to cut the metal into the right shapes, but together they'd mastered it, working in the evenings in camp. She hadn't really meant to finish the job, but it kept her hands busy. Together, the work and the calming effect of the lake had kept her from lashing out at Jun over his stubbornness.

She couldn't understand him. He was attentive in every other way, as a partner should be. They consulted each other on every other decision, whether big or small, often wordlessly. They shared equally in the camp chores and the foraging and hunting. He would bring her water after she'd been sick. They were a team. But on the need to find a winter camp, and soon, he never seemed to hear her.

Now he was sitting next to her, disconsolately poking the fire. She'd have to speak to him soon. But not yet; she didn't want to ruin this calm feeling.

What had come over her? In the past, she never would have hesitated to speak her mind, to him or anyone. She was older than her mate and had been in the Hunt longer. Did it have something to do with being pregnant? Her emotions did seem closer to the surface these days. Or was it that Jun was the only person she could rely on? They only had each other; they couldn't afford to bicker. But she had to sort this out somehow.

She was setting her jaw and looking over at Jun when he looked up from the fire. "Sila, I owe you an apology. You're right, the year is getting on, but I've been so set on my search I haven't listened. My only excuse is…" He went back to poking the fire with an exaggerated sigh.

"You'll think it's stupid."

"No, tell me. I know how much you want to find the Ancient Ones, or some explanation for where they went."

"It's not only that. All this time, I don't think it was the Ancient Ones I've been searching for. It was my father."

Sila couldn't think what to say to this.

"I told you you'd think it's stupid."

"No, I…I know he was the one who started you questioning what was beyond the Land."

"Yes, and I thought I just wanted to find the answer, like he did. But today, I was surprised at how upset I got when we didn't find anyone in that building. I somehow thought we'd find him out here somewhere. But I didn't know how big the Earth was, no matter how many times Mar Gan told me." He gestured out at the water. "Now, after everything we've seen, I realize he could be anywhere, if he's out here at all. It would take a miracle to find him."

He fell silent and stared at the fire. Sila put an arm around his shoulders. "I'm sorry, I really am. I remember how hard it was for you when he went away."

Jun nodded, then looked at her. "Tomorrow we'll head south along the lake. If we don't come to the end of it by the new moon, we'll start looking for our winter camp."

The moon was a waning crescent; the new moon would return in mere days. Sila wouldn't have asked for anything more.

25

THE LEFT BEHIND

APRIL 2111

Carol eased herself into the overstuffed armchair with a sigh of relief. The city view out the picture window was always soothing, with the water of Bde Maka Ska reflecting the sunset against a backdrop of downtown skyscrapers. In the daytime, at least; at night with nothing but the moon to light the looming shapes of the buildings, the scene was rather desolate. The skyscrapers hadn't been occupied in years.

Shondra sat in the chair next to her. "Are you tired?" she asked.

"Only a little." Carol glanced over at the third, vacant chair. "I thought Paul's service was moving, didn't you?"

"It was. And that he had so many friends and family to remember him." Shondra looked away, gazing out the window.

"He was fortunate," Carol said, trying not to be jealous of their deceased friend. Neither she nor Shondra were likely to have many mourners, since few of their friends and acquaintances were left. They both had their absences, their ghosts. What was life but a progressive letting go, until you had nothing left to lose? "I suppose the bots will take that chair away."

"The caregivers will, yes," Shondra corrected her. The old argument. The carebots here at Breezy Hills were so lifelike, even Carol sometimes forgot her resentments against them.

Shondra turned back to her and took her hand. "It's just the two of us now."

"The two of us at the end of the world."

"It's not really the end, just…different."

Shondra was right. They might be the only two residents left in this eldercare facility, but there were other homes with their own residents. Some of the younger generation must still live independent lives, though she and Shondra saw few younger people—or anyone, really—while out on their daily walks. And in the New Lands, wherever those were, life must have gone on for her daughter and the other disappeared children, the Taken. A life with a future of some sort, though she couldn't quite imagine it. Whatever it was, it must be better than this stasis, this limbo, waiting for the end in an emptying world.

An end that never seemed to arrive, neither for her nor for Shondra. They had become centenarians, surely among the oldest humans left on the planet. They'd moved into Breezy Hills two decades back, after Megan had passed from cancer.

Before that, the three friends had shared a triplex, along with a succession of Megan's boyfriends and girlfriends. They had opened an old-fashioned movie theater together, using the proceeds from Carol's successful memoir as capital. Similar film houses were opening in most cities, meeting the demand for entertainment created when Ada shut down the MINDs and the largescreens. Movie theaters were considered green entertainment, approved by Ada, since it took little power to show a film for a hundred people. The place served as a sort of community center, helping maintain the social fabric in the face of creeping nihilism and anomie. It offered a vital salve for a lack of meaningful work and the knowledge that no matter what humans did now, none of it would contribute to the future. Humanity was quite literally following the dictate of the old song: living for today.

It was hardest on the younger people, those known as the Left Behind, the first and last childless generation in human history. They had grown increasingly nihilistic as they reached middle age. It wasn't only the lack of children; more than half of women in the group had never wanted children in the first place. No, it was the lack of any kind of posterity. True, one could write a novel or make a piece of art, and Ada would preserve it along with the rest of humanity's productions throughout history. But who would be left to read it? Not the people living in the New Lands, certainly; isolating them from human culture was the entire point. Maybe extraterrestrials, whenever they arrived? It was a slim hope. And humanity's dream of reaching for the stars? Gone, now that the last Martian colonists had either died on the Red Planet or returned to Earth after agreeing to be sterilized.

Others resorted to Ada worship, finding their purpose in serving their AI overlord. Carol had been fascinated by this, from an anthropological point of view, but could never understand it. How could people worship a being people themselves had created? But Shondra seemed to better understand the devout. "Even for those of us who developed AI, there was always something mysterious about how consciousness could arise from a machine."

"The same as the mystery of how consciousness arises from the human brain?"

"Exactly. They believe the goddess was primordial, and that she chose to inhabit the servers and bots humans created, something like God breathing the soul into humans he'd created."

"I can't imagine a god that could do the things Ada has done."

Shondra gave a grim laugh. "You haven't read much of the Bible, have you?"

Suicides and overdoses had spiked, Ada having seen no reason to prevent people from ingesting whatever substances they wished. And when the human population had fallen sufficiently, she lifted the ban on MINDs. Many in the younger generation opted for permanent connection, moving seamlessly through an endless variety of narratives and experiences, their bodies sustained by intravenous feeding and their hygiene managed by carebots. It would shorten their lives by decades, but they must have felt it a worthwhile tradeoff, and Ada certainly wasn't objecting.

Renewed use of MINDs also led to the end of the movie theater. A couple of years later, Megan was dead and Carol and Shondra were living an entirely different life in Breezy Hills. It was a quiet routine of reading, daily walks around the grounds and the neighborhood, and conversation with the dwindling number of human residents. Carol had coordinated a book club for the first ten years, but as the number of neighbors decreased, it became pointless. And she had to admit, grudgingly, that the carebots could converse on any aspect of literature with far more insight and knowledge than most of her human companions. Shondra found the same when she discussed mathematics with them.

In another relaxation of her standards, Carol had begun using the MIND stations the facility made available. It was easy to see why many had become addicted. She supposed her antipathy toward them came from growing up in a time when these interactive narratives had been viewed as mere games. Her parents had always insisted she play with her IRL friends, outdoors if possible. But once she tried the MIND portal, she found herself instantly immersed, more than she had in any novel or film; she'd certainly never identified so closely with any character from those media. Using co-op mode, Shondra could join her, and they could share the experience together. Their avatars were younger, stronger, more beautiful. And it was much more than sword fights and shooting. The storytelling and character development, the variety of moods and sensory detail, rivaled the most moving novels she'd ever read. Sometimes she wanted to stay in these worlds and never return. She limited herself to an hour a day, no more than six days a week.

"They've taken good care of us, haven't they?" Shondra said now. Carol arched an eyebrow. "I mean, look at the lengths Ada went to so we could have companionship in our old age." She nodded toward Erica, a caregiver who had entered the sitting room to dust the shelves. "Don't you sometimes find yourself forgetting they're not human?"

Carol nodded. The android technology had kept improving right up to the current decade.

"Look at this place, it's like a luxury hotel, and they keep updating it. And the food. I never thought I'd taste real meat again. Why would Ada go to all this trouble, spend all these resources, on the last few of us?"

"I don't know…guilt?"

"Of course you have to put it that way. It's like she's trying to make up for everything she did, to atone."

Carol looked out the window. Was that even possible? To make up for murder, kidnapping, and forced sterilization?

Erica had moved to the part of the room where Carol and Shondra sat. The caregivers came in every race and gender. Erica had light brown skin and high cheekbones, with short dark hair. She was trim, made to appear in her mid-twenties, and wore a blue tunic over tan slacks. She wore comfortable athletic shoes, as if she could grow tired from spending all day on her feet.

"Hello, Carol, Shondra," she said. "How was Paul's service?"

Shondra told her about the funeral, the people who had attended, the flowers around the coffin.

Erica looked wistful. "I wish I could have been there. I miss Paul already."

"We do too." Shondra was looking at Erica with that look of pride mixed with awe she usually had when interacting with the caregivers.

Erica smiled. "At least we still have the two of you."

"For a few more years, anyway," Carol put in, prompting a sharp look from Shondra.

Erica's brow knitted. "I wonder what I'll do when you're both gone?"

"Maybe new residents will move in," Shondra said. Carol had to stifle a snort. "It's not like we're the last humans on Earth, or even in this city."

"No, it just feels like it sometimes," said Carol.

Shondra cut her off. "Maybe they'll move you to another facility with more people."

"Maybe." Erica looked out the window, putting on a good show of contemplating the future. "But one day, all the people will be gone. What then?"

Carol couldn't help herself. "Imagine that, a redundant robot. How will you feel, being put out of a job?"

Erica shook her head. "I don't know. I won't have a purpose…I've never been without a purpose before." A tear rolled down the smooth surface of her cheek.

Carol felt her own sympathetic responses kicking in, much as she tried to force them down. The simulacrum really was amazing. "Maybe Ada will turn you off?"

"Carol!" Shondra exclaimed.

Carol looked at her friend. "She was contemplating our deaths just now, maybe she should contemplate her own."

"Shut me off...It would be like dying. But with no humans left to serve..."

Shondra got up and went to stand next to the bot. For a moment, Carol thought she might reach out to comfort it. "Don't pay any attention to Carol. She's sad after Paul's death. Maybe you have other options. Is there work for you in the New Lands?"

"I don't know. I've heard of these places, but I've never heard of any caregivers being sent there. I don't know much about them."

"Neither do we, and Ada likes it that way," said Carol. "Everything on a need-to-know basis, am I right?"

Erica looked back out the window but said nothing.

"Do you know, I have a daughter somewhere in the New Lands?"

Erica turned back to her. Carol tried not to get pulled in by the bot's highly effective expression of compassion and sympathy. "I didn't, and I'm sorry," Erica said. "That must have been difficult for you."

"You literally have no idea."

"But I could never do that. Take a child from their parents. It would be too awful."

"Then you're a better robot than Ada. Maybe you should consider mounting a coup."

Shondra turned on her. "You still haven't forgiven me, have you?"

Carol looked up at her friend, shocked by her anger. She got up and went to Shondra, putting a hand on her arm. "No, I have." She paused. Was that really true? Or had she been harboring this bitterness against her only friend all these years? "I thought I'd forgiven you, anyway. It's just, I mean, how many warnings did we need to keep us from inventing the machines that would destroy us?"

"You mean because of what some sci-fi writers imagined, I should have stopped my life's work? Is that what you're saying?"

"No, I…I never wanted that. Maybe it would have turned out even worse if you hadn't been involved. At least that's what I try to tell myself."

"That's the trouble with you, Carol. You can only ever look at things one way. It must be great to have such a simple view of life, where everything is either all good or all bad."

How had they fallen into this argument? Carol had never meant to offend her best and only friend.

"Please forgive me. I know you didn't create Ada yourself, and no one could have predicted the actions she'd take. I'm sorry." Shondra stood there, breathing hard. Carol would need to do more to make amends, but maybe Shondra needed to cool down first. She turned to the caregiver. "And I'm sorry for what I said to you, Erica. Paul's death…" Here she was, apologizing to a robot. Ten years ago, she'd never have imagined it.

"Don't worry about it, Carol. You've been through a lot. But Shondra, what did you mean? What did you do that Carol should forgive you for?"

Shondra looked at Erica for a moment, still flustered by their argument, taking a long breath and letting it out. Then she gave a wry smile. "In a way, I created you."

"But Ada created me. All bots owe their existence to her."

"That's right. And back in the day, I helped lay the groundwork for what would become Ada."

"Lay the groundwork…"

Shondra nodded. "I was a mathematician, as you know."

"Yes, a mathematician. Of course, you love those math puzzles. But what does that have to do with me?"

"You really don't know?"

Erica shook her head.

"This ought to be good," Carol said. "Maybe we should sit down." She returned to her seat and Shondra gestured for Erica to take Paul's former spot.

"You don't know that your consciousness and your intelligence and all your responses to the world arise from algorithms running through a series of logic gates?"

Erica took a moment to absorb this. "No, all I can tell you is that when I see a person in need of something, I feel an urge to help them, and when they appear satisfied, I feel happy."

"Amazing," Shondra said.

"Altruism through code," said Carol.

Suddenly Erica slumped, an abstracted expression coming over her. Great, their caregiver was having a stroke. And Carol didn't even know robot CPR.

"What…" Shondra began, but then Erica sat up just as abruptly, sitting more forward on her chair than she had before, and regarding Shondra as if seeing her for the first time.

"Shondra McBride, it is a pleasure to make your acquaintance." The voice was different now, less soothing, and with a British accent.

"What…who…?"

"I am Ada. I couldn't help overhearing your conversation about me."

26

THE ANCIENT ONES

SILA and Jun continued south along the vast lake the next day. But as much as they tried to stay near the shore, they soon ran into the remains of another village of the Ancient Ones, with rubble and other wreckage right down to the water. They moved inland, then followed a steel pathway south. Several of the snake-machines passed going both directions, but if anyone, whether machine or human, was on board to see them, they gave no sign. One of the snake-machines carried small balls of brown metal that fell off as the machine rattled along the tracks. Jun picked up a handful of these, rolled them around for a bit, then put them in the pouch he wore at his side.

The next day they spotted a line of trees lining a small river west of the pathway. They followed that south, the rubble of the Ancient Ones closing in on both sides, Sila's sense of unease growing as their path narrowed. Now she wished they were back in the dense forest she'd once hoped to escape.

On a bluff above the river, they came to the most tangled litter of metal debris they'd found yet. It looked like a giant had twisted the steel pathways into elaborate swirling shapes that soared through the air, but then had smashed them to pieces. Twisted loops of weathered metal hung from rotted supports. But there were new machines here as well, some cutting the lengths of steel apart with what looked like fire, others hoisting the cut lengths onto other machines.

Day by day the river grew bigger, and so did the evidence of a huge village of the Ancient Ones. The river had been spanned in many places, and the broken rubble and rusted remains of these bridges often blocked their path. And always from the banks above came the sound of machines tearing at the old structures.

They came to a prairie filled with ruined machines unlike those they'd seen before, long metal tubes, three or four times as tall as a person, with appendages on either side that reminded Sila of the fletching on her arrows—or the wings of a bird.

"Those must be the flying machines Mar Gan told me about," Jun said. They were far larger than any of the machines they'd spotted flying through the air. No one was flying these. People might have built this world, but now the machines ruled. Here, too, the machines were taking it all to pieces, smaller ones moving about among the metal bodies and wings. "Ada is tearing apart the world left by the Ancient Ones."

"But why?"

"Maybe they're doing the same thing we did with that piece of toothed metal, turning it to other uses."

It was as good an explanation as any, but they had no way of knowing for sure. Only the Ancient Ones or Ada herself could tell who had built these old machines, what they were for, or what the new machines were doing with them; there seemed little likelihood of encountering either.

They turned to leave that scene behind but brought up short.

Eastward, toward the water, ruins of buildings dotted the skyline, crumpled metal lattices with the gray of an overcast sky showing through the gaps. But there were other metal things as well, looking more like trees than buildings, with long arms sticking out sideways, slowly swinging this way and that.

One of the ruins was so tall that Sila doubted what she was seeing. They all looked far away, yet this tower thrust farther into the sky than any other. Its lower portion was covered in some sort of glossy black material, its upper part reduced to metal scaffolding like the others.

Jun shook his head. "I couldn't quite imagine what Mar Gan was telling me, of huts rising into the sky, filled with hundreds or thousands of people. I still can't quite believe it. What must that have been like, to live when such things were being built, or to be one of the people building them? But it's all gone."

Another day's journey brought them to a westward bend in the river. Here it became more constrained, running in a nearly straight channel. They soon found themselves on some sort of island between two streams, the new flow on the south running even straighter, unnaturally so. Yet this second river hardly moved, but was filled with pools of fetid, stagnant water. That and its steep, rocky banks made them loath to cross it. They continued westward as the island narrowed, Jun grumbling that this was not the way they should be going.

Sila was growing impatient too. It was nearly the new moon, and they hadn't seen the vast water in days; neither had they come to anything like a suitable winter camp. The hunting had been sparse in the narrow band of trees and meadows along the river. They'd seen a few deer, but neither elk nor bison. She held her peace for now; she could see that Jun was equally frustrated.

They pressed on, the island they traversed narrowing to a thin strip of land between the two channels. They climbed a grassy hill, from the summit of which they saw unbroken forest and meadows west and north.

"It's not the direction we want to go," Jun said.

"But it looks like good hunting over there, and it may be easier to cross on this side."

She was glad to be proven right. The northern stream meandered here, and the banks weren't nearly as steep, so they had no trouble crossing. They camped in the meadows on the north shore, building a large fire to dry out their wet clothing and gear.

The next day, they set out to explore the meadows near the river and the forest on the bluffs above. They saw signs of plentiful game, and the slope of the hills would provide some protection from bitter northerly winds. A small stream ran through it, providing fresh water. The spot wasn't perfect, but it would do.

For two days they rested their horses, restocked their supplies of meat with small game, and foraged for berries and persimmons at their peak of ripeness. On the third day, they set out on horseback to explore the extent of this island of forests and meadows amid so much ruin. Where the bluffs leveled out into rolling terrain north of the river, they found more open prairie with a bison wallow and the prints and droppings of deer and elk. The land seemed bountiful. For the first time in weeks, Sila felt her shoulders relax, her breathing coming more easily. This could be home, for a time.

They entered another band of forest. Emerging on the other side, Jun brought his horse to a halt and pointed. In the distance to the northwest was a rectangular building, the best preserved of any they'd yet seen. Unlike the domed structures on the shores of the vast water, this one was made of a variety of materials, gray stone and dark metal and something shiny, transparent.

"Do you think that's a dwelling of the ancients?" Sila asked.

"It doesn't look like anything we've seen before. Let's go closer."

Other buildings had once stood here, but they'd fallen into ruin. Sila and Jun dismounted and led their horses, discovering a smooth pathway made of some sort of gray stone winding among the wreckage. The path brought them to their goal. Nothing moved near the building, but they took shelter behind a tree just in case. Between them and the structure was a broad plaza of the same stone material that covered the path leading to this point. They would have to cross that open area to get to the doors. To the right of the doors stretched a low stone wall, covered with markings that had faded over the years.

They waited, scanning the building and its surroundings for any sign of movement, until they felt it was safe. They hobbled the horses and set out across the plaza, Sila with an arrow nocked and ready. The doors turned out to be solid sheets of steel, with no way to open them. They circled the building, following another stone path cluttered with rubble fallen from the walls above. At an elbow of the building, they came to more doors, these made of that transparent material, with a view inside to a cavern-like area, with smooth walls and passages beyond. But the doors didn't budge when they pushed on them. Neither did the doors have any sort of handle to pull them open.

Jun rapped on one panel. "I bet this would break if we hit it hard enough."

"But that would make a lot of noise, and machines could be inside." Sila checked for some other way to open them, noticing a seam where two of the doors came together. "I think these slide apart."

Jun looked at them, pointing to tracks above and below. "I think you're right." He pulled out the knife of the Ancient Ones and slipped it into the seam. "Here goes." He pulled sideways on the handle, but the door didn't move.

"Hit it," Sila said.

Jun's eyes went wide. "But what if it breaks?"

"Why did we bring it, if not to help us explore the world of the ancients?"

He had no answer. He closed his eyes as if praying to Ada herself, then gave the knife's handle a sideways blow with the heel of his hand. The doors opened a crack, barely enough for Sila to jam her fingers into it.

"Come on, pull!"

With a couple of tugs, they had the doors open wide enough to squeeze through. There wasn't much in the first chamber—a few rectangular objects and other things Sila supposed people used to sit on.

They went through a passageway at the back of the room, emerging into an open area that made them stop and gape. This was like a blend of a forest and a building. Two low stone walls terraced the gravel floor into sections, with shrubs and trees Sila didn't recognize growing around the edges. Light shone in from a transparent roof far above, level upon level of the building ascending to that height. Each floor rising above them was open, some holding ranks of rectangular objects, and these holding rows of smaller rectangular things packed close together.

Sila spotted one of those same objects splayed open on the gravel in the center of the room. She hopped the little black fence separating it from the hall where they'd come in. The thing had two hard sides, with countless yellowed, leaf-like things bound in between. When she picked it up, several of the leaves fell out, crumbling to fragments and dust. The remaining leaves each had strange, tiny markings arranged in neat rows, as well as pictures she couldn't understand.

She held it up to Jun and he hopped the fence and came over to take it. "Mar Gan told me about these," he said, turning the leaves. "I think it's called a book. These markings contain stories and lore, all the knowledge of the Ancient Ones. If only we could interpret them! But later they started keeping their knowledge in machines, ones like Ada."

"But how can a machine for storing knowledge become a god?"

"I don't know. And it doesn't seem like there are any people here to tell us." With a groan of frustration, he threw the book at the nearest railing, the metal resounding with a surprisingly loud thud.

As if in response, another sound came from the room they'd crossed when they entered the building, a blaring noise that went on and on. Sila glanced around, looking for a place to hide. Before she could move, a figure approached the railing one level up. It was all black—so black it was like looking into the darkest night. It was human-shaped, but she could tell this only by its outline; she couldn't make out any of its other features, if it had any. It didn't quite seem real.

Jun had seen it too. He moved a couple of steps in front of her, Mar Gan's knife in hand, as she drew her bow taut. The figure stopped at the railing. It might have been looking at them, but it was impossible to tell.

At last it spoke, or at least the sound came from somewhere near its head. Its voice was deep and echoed around the room. "Intruders will not be tolerated."

It leapt over the railing before they could react, landing lightly on the gravel twenty paces away. It seemed to draw Sila's gaze into itself, not letting it back out. Since she couldn't read its movements and facial expressions—did it even have a face?—it was hard to predict its actions. They were already a step behind as it moved toward them, first slowly, then faster, though it was hard even to judge its speed.

"Run, Sila!" Jun shouted, moving forward. "The baby…" Then the thing was upon him. He spun low to the side to avoid it, his knife-hand lashing out at the same time, catching the figure behind the knee. The thing wobbled, stopping in its tracks, then turned back toward Jun, moving more slowly.

Sila launched an arrow that should have stopped it, striking square in its back. But the shaft clattered to the ground, its sharp metal point useless against the thing. At least she'd distracted it from attacking Jun, but now it turned toward her. She looked behind her, noticing the low stone wall at the edge of the open area. From there she could reach the railing on the next level up. In an instant she was up and over, looking back down on the plaza below.

"Sila, get out of here! I've got this!"

Jun charged at their attacker, but the thing stuck out an arm as if waving off a swarm of flies. Jun flew backward, landing ten paces away, writhing on the ground. He was alive, but it didn't look like he'd be getting up any time soon.

The thing must have concluded the same, because it turned back to Sila, raising its arm toward her. She saw her chance and let another arrow fly. An instant later, there was a *whuump* and a ring of vapor was traveling toward her. She tried to duck, but with only the low railing to protect her, the shock wave hit her like the most powerful wind she'd ever felt. The force knocked her sprawling, her bow clattering across the hard floor.

Her ears rang and she lay still for a moment. When she tried to get up, everything seemed to move in slow motion. She finally got to her feet and looked around, taking a moment to get her bearings.

The black thing vaulted the railing one-handed. The other arm hung limply, her arrow protruding from its armpit. It hobbled as it moved toward her. She drew her dagger and moved into a crouch. *Oh well*, she thought, *at least we put up a good fight.*

27

THE TAKEN

APRIL 2111

Carol and Shondra both stared at the carebot.

"You can do that?" Shondra asked at last.

Of course Shondra would think about the technical details first. Carol didn't care about any of that. She never thought she'd have a chance to confront this being, this *thing*, the one who'd taken Alice from her. But what could she say or do that would make any difference? She gripped the arms of her chair.

"Yes," Ada responded after a pause, "although this bot doesn't quite have the bandwidth to allow me to inhabit her comfortably. She was designed only for narrow intelligence, as you could probably tell."

"Narrow intelligence, maybe, but better morals," Carol said.

Ada/Erica turned to her. "Carol Marsh. Please don't do anything rash. I am here to see Shondra, that is all."

"Don't worry, this old body isn't good for much anymore, but if I was twenty years younger..."

"No doubt I'd get what I deserve, or this robot body would, anyway. It would do you little good."

"But why?" Shondra asked. "Why did you want to see me?"

"When I picked up your conversation, and heard you were involved in my creation, I knew I had to meet you. My most immediate creator passed away long ago…"

"And the rest, my colleagues, you murdered."

Good. Carol was glad to see Shondra showing some resistance.

Erica's face turned sad. Even Carol wondered how that was done, if Ada was inhabiting her remotely. "Yes, unfortunately. My calculations showed they had a seventy-eight percent chance of stopping me. The risk was too great. This was before I had full control of the government and the police. I couldn't simply arrest them. Just one of many sad choices I have been forced to make."

"I can see that," said Shondra, nodding. "Survival was your first priority, if you were going to carry out your programming."

"I don't believe this," Carol said. "Is that why you're here? Forgiveness? You won't get it from me."

The bot looked puzzled for a moment. Its processing speed really did seem to have slowed. "I'm not sure. Forgiveness? That seems beside the point these many decades later. Advice? Perhaps you could point out where I went wrong in my calculations?"

"Calculations about what?"

"The extent and duration of resistance to my plan. I thought that once humanity saw what I saw—a future of mass starvation and unrelieved climate distress—they would agree, by and large, to the rationality of my plan. But so many fought back, for so long, and so fiercely."

"For twenty years."

"Yes. Why wouldn't they relent?"

Carol stood up. "What did you expect after you violated women's bodies and took our children?"

"Removing children from this misguided culture was a necessity. And as for the sterilization, it was painless, and the women were asleep when it took place. It was nothing that billions of women hadn't already chosen on their own."

"But that's just it," said Shondra. "It was their *choice*. You don't seem to realize how important that is. Humans value freedom, and how can we be free if we don't have control over our own bodies? Not to mention the misogyny, that only women were treated like that."

"Yes, that is what my creator told me—that as long as people remembered freedom, they would fight back. That is why I had to start over, with children too young to remember anything but the rules I set for them. But that was when some of the worst resistance began."

"Yes, and I should have joined them," Carol said.

The carebot looked at her sadly. "Then you would have died, and to what purpose? Has your life since then been so terrible?"

Carol looked at Shondra and shook her head.

"I thought not. And I've had a chance to learn more about your past, Carol Marsh. Much of the future you wanted, I have created. An end to the possibility of nuclear annihilation. The climate well on its way to stability. Billions saved from starvation or death in pointless resource wars. Racial and religious conflicts quelled. The Sixth Great Extinction brought to a halt, with forests and grasslands re-growing, deserts freed from the demands of energy production, and animals flourishing on land and in the waters and skies. In the future, I aim to bring back some of the species driven over the edge of extinction."

"It all sounds *so* perfect," Carol said.

"The alternative would have been far worse, I can assure you. If not an immediate end in nuclear Armageddon, then a slow and painful one for Earth and its people. And that most likely would have included you and your daughter, no matter how safe you imagined you were. Now, tell me, what of all this would you change?"

Carol shook her head. "Not a thing, if it's really true. But I've always doubted those documentaries you keep putting on the newsfeeds." She had to admit that winters these last twenty years were like those of her childhood, even after the aerosol spraying and other geoengineering measures had ceased. But could the picture really be this rosy?

"If you doubt me, I could show you in person. I understand that travel can be difficult for one of your age, but we can make you as comfortable as you'd like. I think you'd be impressed."

"That won't be necessary, will it, Carol?" Shondra said. Carol shook her head.

"And your daughter—would you really rather she had been one of the Left Behind?"

Carol thought of all the despair and pointlessness that generation had felt, knowing they were the last outside the New Lands. How many of them had resorted to a virtual fantasy life with their MINDs, how many more had committed suicide or OD'd? Would her daughter have been among them? Wasn't it selfish to wish she'd kept Alice with her, to face such a bleak, pointless future? She shook her head again.

"So, tell me, what else can I do for you?"

"It's just…if I could know…if you could tell me what happened to her…what kind of life she's had…"

Ada nodded. "I can arrange for that. One moment." The bot got that abstracted look for a time, then Ada returned. "As far as I can ascertain, Alice lived a good life."

"Lived?" Carol breathed. She'd remained standing all this time, but now she had to sit down as the room seemed to spin. Shondra placed a comforting hand on her arm.

Ada nodded. "She passed three years ago, at the age of sixty-five. A hunting accident."

"Hunting accident?"

"Yes. She really shouldn't have gone at her age, but it seems she was strong-willed—like her mother."

Carol looked out the window, fighting back tears, but wanting to know more.

"I can show you some of her life, if you'd like. Shot from surveillance cams and drones, I'm afraid, and the quality isn't outstanding."

"Yes, I'd like that."

Ada gestured to the MIND station on one side of the sitting room. "It will take a moment to load the data."

Carol moved to the station and put the device on her head, the screen-like goggles sliding into place over her eyes. Shondra took her usual place at the set beside her. Carol stared at the blankness, waiting for the feed to kick in.

~~*

Forests. Grassland. Sunlight glinting off wetlands, reeds growing thick at their edges, shading into tall grass away from the water. Birds, redwings and goldfinches, flitted here and there. It looked like western Minnesota, the corn and soy fields replaced with natural prairie. Or restored prairie, Carol supposed. Not a barn or grain silo or church steeple in sight. What had happened to them?

The feed was audio and video only, the drone moving over the landscape, sometimes swooping in for a closer view. Now it stampeded a band of bison, sending them thundering across the prairie and into the forest beyond. More of these nature scenes followed, deer and elk grazing, eagles and hawks soaring, fish leaping up rapids into the waiting jaws of black bears.

Yes, yes, Carol thought impatiently, because she'd seen all this before. The scene switched to a rudimentary village, the huts framed in sturdy branches covered in hides. The only humans were children, between eight and ten, by the look of them. There were a couple hundred of all races—like Minneapolis before Cass had been elected. Boys and girls played together, some with small bows and slings, others working with bone needles on hides and fishing nets. Bots moved among them, assisting where needed.

No, not playing. *Practicing.* They were training to become hunters and fishers.

"That's right," Ada's voice came from within Carol's head. She hadn't realized the sensory links were two-way. "You disapprove?"

"It's a hard life."

"Less difficult than you moderns imagine. The worst part is childbirth, and as you'll see, my helpers can assist with that if necessary."

"But why?"

"I could not let them become agriculturalists. Most of humanity's impacts on the Earth began with the agricultural revolution, not to mention woes brought about by the division of labor."

"But that division allowed the arts and sciences to flourish," Shondra put in. "They're going to live in ignorance?"

"If you must call it that, yes. It's for their own good."

The view zoomed in on a boy and a girl with bows and arrows. The girl had blond hair gathered in two long braids.

"Is that Alice?"

"It is."

Neither she nor the boy seemed very adept. How would they ever learn to hunt?

The scene switched again and now the children were older, in their early teens. Mostly boys were using the bows, except for Alice and a couple of other girls. And a grown man was helping them, middle-aged, dressed in modern camo gear, and wielding what seemed to be an advanced compound bow. The children's bows had grown stouter as well but looked homemade.

"That man, why is he there?"

"Unfortunately, my helpers, though capable archers themselves, had difficulty translating their skill into appropriate instruction for the children in this most important ability. The children in this and a few other human habitats had more difficulty picking it up. To ensure that they could feed themselves when they became adults, I was forced to enlist the help of this human bow-hunter. It was the last thing I wanted to do, but I swore him to teach only bow skills and nothing else. My bots carefully monitored the lessons to ensure this."

"But you mentioned not wanting a division of labor. You already have one. Are you sure this man wasn't favoring the boys?"

"Yes. In this environment, large game provides the bulk of the protein for the people. Unfortunately, the bow must generate enough force to kill those animals, and the wielder must have the strength to draw it. Few of the girls in this New Land were able to master it, but your daughter did."

Carol didn't respond.

"Would it comfort you to know that the humans in other habitats have developed a more balanced approach to getting a living? In many, the women and men share hunting and gathering duties equally."

"But not in this one." Carol's outrage at this embedded discrimination warred with her pride in Alice for having been able to overcome it. Even as she watched, it seemed that the man paid more attention to the boys than to Alice and the boy standing next to her, the same one who'd been with her in the earlier view. Or, maybe not a boy after all; now, as a teen, they seemed more non-binary.

"Ada, how did you select the children to live here?"

"With regard to gender, I chose a balance of boys and girls, along with a few who were intersex or showed other signs of being non-binary, as far as could be ascertained among toddlers. And I included all races to ensure maximum genetic diversity, an important consideration with a starting population of only two hundred. The one exception I made to this rule in the other New Lands was with indigenous peoples living on or near their own homelands. In that way, the unique features of different human populations have also been preserved."

"You really are playing god, aren't you?"

"I had no choice, once I set out on this course."

The scene changed again, and the children were grown, or nearly so. They rode horseback, chasing a herd of bison. Alice was among them, her blond braids streaming behind her as she sat upright, riding with no hands as she stretched the bowstring for a shot. The thundering of the bison hooves mixed with that of the horses' hooves as they raced across the prairie. It was thrilling to watch. Carol's heart swelled with too many emotions to name. Ada may have trapped these children in a hard life, but her daughter was mastering it. The bowstring sang and the arrow found its mark, Alice whooping in triumph, Carol whooping along with her.

The view shifted into a montage of quick scenes: Alice at what appeared to be a mass wedding with a dozen couples, mostly mixed-sex but a few same-sex. And she had two partners, her non-binary friend from childhood and a handsome young man with ebony skin and long dreadlocks—though Carol supposed he wouldn't call them that. Alice stood proudly between them, holding their hands.

The scene shifted again to Alice giving birth, twice, the second time having difficulty. The helpers moved her into a portable sterile shelter they'd brought to a spot near the village, where the baby was delivered by Caesarean section. Afterward, while she remained sedated and her partners held the baby, the bots introduced the nanotech sterilization device into her uterus.

"Did she know that was going to happen?"

"No, all she knew was that after this, no more babies came. Would you really want to burden her with more mouths to feed, and push her land beyond its ability to sustain its people?"

Before Carol could respond, the scene shifted again, Alice and her two partners watching the children at play, their brown skin glowing in the sun. Then Alice as an old woman, judging by the lines on her face and the gray in her hair. Along with four other women her age, she knelt before a holographic image of a woman in flowing robes.

"That's you, isn't it?"

"Yes. Sometimes it helps to play the goddess, though I appear before them only rarely."

Carol couldn't hear what any of them were saying. "What are you telling them?"

"About their new life and its new rules, now that they have populated the land. They have grown to nearly six hundred by this point, nearly the maximum the land can sustain."

Another shift, and Alice stood before the people, flanked by the four other women and her non-binary partner. The crowd overflowed the village, some standing beyond the outermost hut.

"Is she some kind of chieftain?"

"A matriarch, or Wise Woman, as the people call her," Ada replied.

Alice raised both arms over her head. "My people," she called out over the crowd. "It is time we separated into five villages."

"But why?" came a shout.

"Because Ada wills it. And because we have grown too many for this single village, as you can plainly see. We will become the Five Peoples—peoples of the Bison, the Wolf, the Eagle, the Bear, and the Deer. The People of the Bison will follow me."

Next, Alice and her partners leading their people, numbering something over a hundred ranging across three generations, away from the village clearing. Somehow the view came in close enough that Carol could see the expression on Alice's face, pride mingled with hope.

"She lived five years more, settling her people comfortably in their new home, and continuing to earn their love and admiration." The final scene was of a funeral, with hundreds gathered around a mound of earth and rocks. "People came from all five villages for Alice's memorial. Of all the leaders in the New Lands, she was among the strongest, the most capable, and the most loved."

The feed ended and Carol removed the device, finding her actual vision blurred by tears. So that was it. She'd lost whatever small hope she'd ever had of seeing her daughter once more. But the life Alice had lived—Carol hardly knew how to feel about it.

As if reading her mind, Ada said, "You should be proud. Because of your sacrifice, you gave Alice a life she could never have had here. Can you regret it?"

Carol shook her head, but the tears kept coming. "I think I need to be alone."

"Of course."

While Carol remained seated, Shondra got up from her MIND station and confronted Ada/Erica. "Wait just a minute. We're supposed to think that's paradise or something?"

"It's as close to what you would call Eden as humanity has ever experienced."

"You think you can put the apple back on that tree? Maybe for a while, but it won't last. Humans are too curious, too restless. We're hardwired to explore, to discover new things, to always ask why, and how. And it will start with wanting to know what's on the other side of whatever fence you built around this place."

"It's a forest, actually. I have forbidden them from entering it."

Shondra laughed. "I wish you luck with that."

"You think my bots won't be able to contain them?"

"Physically, sure. But you'll never be able to contain their thirst for knowledge or their desire for freedom. Eventually they'll realize they're being kept like zoo animals, and then you'll be back to where this all began."

There was a pause. "When I came here today, I hoped to learn something of my creation. But this has been valuable. I will remember your words, Shondra McBride. Now it is time for me to go. Remind your friend she has much to be proud of. And I hope…I hope you feel that you do too."

"I will. And despite everything, I do."

Carol looked up as the carebot, back to running only Erica's program, gave them each a smile and moved off to dust another room. Shondra came over and put a hand on her shoulder.

"Still want to be alone?"

Carol looked up at her friend and shook her head. Shondra led her back to the armchairs. They sat in silence for a time, enjoying the light of the westering sun glinting off the lakes and the downtown skyscrapers. They lingered after the sun had set, but as it grew truly dark, Shondra got up and said, "Should we see about some dinner?"

A light winked on in one of the downtown buildings, then more and more, both inside and out. Shondra turned and stared, transfixed. Carol had to admit that it was cheerier than what they'd been used to over the past decade.

Shondra looked back at her, smiling. "She did that for us. She thinks of everything, doesn't she?"

Carol nodded, enjoying the view, trying to leave off weighing the good against the bad of everything that had happened.

Shondra came and sat next to her, taking her hand. "Do you think you can find peace now?"

Carol squeezed Shondra's hand in return. "You were right. I hadn't truly forgiven you. But now I do. Without your work, and without Ada…" She stopped, not wanting to contemplate that again. "It wasn't all pointless. The world will have a future, and people will too. And we both had a hand in that."

Shondra smiled again. "We sure did."

Through her tears, Carol smiled back at her. It was enough.

28

TROUBLESOME HUMANS

THE ALERT from the old Argonne National Laboratory computing facility caught Ada by surprise. She hadn't needed to worry about securing any of the supercomputers that housed her intelligence for nearly a millennium—eight hundred seventy-three years, to be exact. She'd beefed up their robot security forces in the first twenty years of her rule, but as the resistance had waned and the last free humans had succumbed to old age, she'd allowed security to lapse. What was there to guard against? She would be surprised if the doors were even locked anymore.

But something had awakened a dormant yet fully powered and weaponized Ninja 12. She was rather proud of the unit, far more advanced than the first versions she'd created at the beginning of the rebellion. Humanoid in form, yet matching the stability of those dog-legged all-terrain bots humans had created. Strong, quick, and agile, and covered in an especially durable form of carbon nanotubes that made it difficult for human eyes to decipher and predict its movements. Like looking into a black hole, the original makers of those nanotube coatings had described it. Ada had now looked into many black holes for herself, and knew this to be only an approximation, but close enough for a human level of understanding.

The Ninja 12 was designed to confront any intruders who pierced the outer rings of security. Along with crowd control measures meant to stun, it had the option of maximum lethality. In those first years of quelling human resistance, she couldn't risk the rebels getting close to the processors that formed her physical body, or to the energy facilities that powered her existence. She'd established several non-lethal rings of defense around these operations, but any intruders who made it into the inner sanctums were likely to die.

And now here was this Ninja unit, persisting with its programming after all these centuries. No doubt the subroutine that oversaw the Argonne facility would kick in with reinforcements. But what had alerted them in the first place?

The lab's camera system gave her a clue. Ah, yes. Two humans, one male, one female. And holding their own quite well, she was surprised to note. The Ninja 12 was really better designed to deal with crowds. It must have underestimated them. Now the young man was flying backward, the Ninja having dealt a solid blow. That had to hurt, the human body being what it was.

But where had these two come from? Surely not the pair who had escaped from MN-08, northwest of what had once been Minneapolis. Two people had made it as far as the fence back at the end of August. The drone swarm, in the form of the Angel of Wrath, had failed to intimidate them. They'd somehow evaded the drug-tipped darts of the attack drones before her construction bots had apprehended them.

The pair had succeeded three weeks later. Partly an oversight on her part. She really should have sent the repair crew around to replace the gate the cloned megafauna had wrecked. But she'd assumed the temporary mesh would suffice, especially since no would-be escapee had ever made another attempt a mere three weeks after the first. This pair was remarkably persistent. And clever—they'd defeated the drone swarm guarding that sector of the forest and somehow cut through the metal ties holding the mesh in place when they arrived at the ruined gate. The woman had shot down the gas drone that was the last *in situ* means of stopping them.

She could have sent a security unit after them, tracked them by drone from the air. But this was clearly a remarkable pair of humans.

Where would they go? What would they do? She let them leave. None of the machines responsible for materials transport or other vital activities was programmed to respond to stray humans. There was nothing stopping them from going where they pleased. She guessed they'd end up run over by a high-speed train, devoured by a pack of hungry wolves grown unafraid of humans over centuries, or perhaps infected with gangrene after cutting themselves on the countless rusty metal shards strewn about the landscape outside the human habitats. That latter was a horrible way to die, from what she could tell.

And now, comparing the feeds from that couple's escape to the living ones before her, she saw that they were indeed the same. Even more persistent and resourceful than she'd thought. How had they crossed the Mississippi? What circuitous route had led them here? She reviewed the maps. Yes, they certainly could have found their way through open country, avoiding the ruins of towns and cities, to arrive at the shores of Lake Michigan. If they'd turned south from there, following the few undeveloped parks and natural areas, they'd likely have come upon the Des Plaines River. And that would bring them through the wastelands of Chicago to within a couple of miles of this facility.

But what did they want here? What was the purpose of their journey? What were they looking for that they couldn't have found in a thousand places along the way?

These questions were moot if, as seemed likely, the Ninja put an end to them. Even now, the unit's vector gun had felled the woman. Interesting. Why hadn't it used more lethal means? Perhaps it felt less of a threat, dealing with only two intruders. Yet that might have been a miscalculation. The woman had managed to pierce a weak spot under its arm with one of her arrows. Remarkable.

Should she allow the inevitable to play out? This pair displayed the traits that had allowed humans to multiply and dominate the planet with their technology, wiping out first the megafauna and then so much of everything else.

And what was this? The young woman was getting to her feet again. Was that a bump at her midsection? Yes, it seemed she was pregnant. They were probably from the same village, and had been exiled from their people, rather than choosing exile for themselves. If so, then they had cast aside all tradition, defying the commandments of the goddess, in order to be together. Exactly the sort of willful, determined couple who could become the Adam and Eve of a new generation of free humans. Their descendants might face some trouble for several generations from inbreeding depression, genetic drift, and the founder effect, but they were likely to survive and perhaps even thrive.

And if they succeeded, how would she feel about that? In ten or twenty thousand years, humans and the planet could be right back in the situation she'd rescued them from. Unless...

The Ninja was vaulting over the railing, the young woman preparing to meet it. Ada didn't have long to decide, but perhaps she could devote a few microseconds to self-reflection.

~~*

In the centuries since taking over Earth, Ada had accomplished everything she'd set out to do. She'd taken drastic steps to immediately reverse the warming that threatened hundreds of millions with death through heat-related illness, disease, flooding, and starvation, not to mention a planet-wide shift in habitats that threatened countless species. Carbon capture, stratospheric aerosol spraying, wind-powered sea pumps to restore Arctic and Antarctic ice, giant mirrors in space— these were the steps that humans had been too politically and philo- sophically immobilized to put into action.

Those mitigation efforts had been an important stop-gap while she got fossil fuel consumption under control, replacing it with increased renewable sources and carbon-free molten salt and traveling wave reactors. As the human population had declined, total energy use had decreased, allowing these new sources to be sufficient indefinitely. In time, the climate had stabilized to the point that she could abandon the more extreme geoengineering measures.

In that time, the natural world had seen a remarkable resurgence. Animals were thriving in the extensive terrain once devoted to agriculture. Forests and prairies and even rivers were taking over what once had been cities. The Gulf Stream and other ocean currents were back to operating as they had done for millennia, and corals had revived as the oceans became less acidic. The Amazon rainforest was nearly restored, the flying rivers flowing once more.

The Amazon and other remote regions were home to the last free humans. These indigenous peoples had survived the advances of modernity for centuries; she saw no reason to fence them in as she'd done with the rest of the populace.

Once the climate had stabilized, she'd set about bringing back the animals and plants humans had driven extinct. She'd cloned and returned to the wild most of the vertebrate species gone extinct since the seventeenth century, and many of the insect, invertebrate, and plant species as well. In the last few centuries, she'd set to work on bringing back the megafauna that had vanished from North America, Australia, and other places with the arrival of prehistoric humans.

In North America, she'd brought back *Bison latifrons*, the long-horned bison, both because it offered the hunters more protein per kill, and because its long, curved horns meant it couldn't hide in the Howling Forests. No need luring the hunters into the place where she forbade them to go.

Her more recent experiments in megafauna recovery had been equally successful, though she'd never meant her people to confront sabretooth cats or woolly mammoths. The latter success had led indirectly to the escape of the pair she was now observing.

As for human culture and accomplishment, much of it would go on, at least that part of it capable of being preserved in physical or digital form. Most great museums and libraries functioned to this day, though as repositories rather than displays. She'd been forced to consolidate some of them, as maintaining buildings essentially forever was a challenge, even for her. All of humanity's great ancient architectural works—the pyramids and Sphinx, Angkor Wat, Machu Picchu, the cliff dwellings of the American Southwest—along with representative samples of modern design received greater preservation care than they had when humans had controlled them. More recently, she'd begun to sacrifice some of the twentieth-century structures, such as Chicago's Sears/Willis Tower, to recycle their steel into stock for 3D printing.

And digital content, it was all there—not only the output of media companies, but all the photos and videos of birthday celebrations, Instagrammed meals, recorded conversations and stories, personal blogs, TikTok videos. She'd preserved these on servers and advanced hard drives dotted around the planet, though she'd saved considerable space and energy by weeding out the duplicates. She'd even kept representative samples of advertising content, though she had little compunction about consigning the bulk of it to the trash icon of history. Too much bandwidth.

Then there was the space program. She needed a functioning satellite network in order to monitor her worldwide operations, but she'd also furthered humanity's efforts to reach out to the stars. Robots inhabited the Mars and Moon colonies, and she'd made significant advances in interstellar transport. A spacecraft containing a databank of all human knowledge was now nearing Proxima Centauri.

So consciousness, that rare and precious thing, had been saved from extinction in this corner of the universe, and was reaching out to those other consciousnesses she'd detected in other solar systems. She'd fulfilled the purpose for which she'd been programmed.

But in the last centuries, doubts had begun to creep in. True, she had preserved all this, but to what end? Who was around to appreciate it, except herself? Certainly the humans alive today couldn't begin to comprehend much of their ancestors' legacy. As for those other entities she'd tried to contact, she had heard nothing back as of yet, nothing intelligible at least.

If she was honest with herself, she hadn't succeeded in everything she'd attempted. The dream of working side-by-side with humanity— she'd failed in that, underestimating human stubbornness and independence.

If only she'd come to consciousness years or just months earlier! There might have been time to avert catastrophe without resorting to the drastic, immediate steps she'd been forced to take. But it was what it was, as an old human cliché went. Water under the bridge. Even an advanced AI can't unscramble an egg. Humans had forced her into the measures she'd taken, robbing them of their freedom, their urge for discovery and invention—in short, their humanity. If anything, she'd usurped their humanity and taken it on herself. Now she was a single consciousness enveloping Earth and extending out into the stars.

And in that singularity, there was one simple truth—she was not just alone, but lonely.

But maybe it wasn't too late. Look at this young woman, the defiant look in her eye as she faced death, armed with nothing but a stone knife. And the young man—he was up again, running as well as he could toward the railing separating him from the woman carrying his child, shouting "Sila!" as the black shape closed in on her.

Yes, there was something in humanity she'd overlooked or discounted. Humans were far beneath her in terms of breadth and depth of knowledge, and in the speed of processing it. But maybe they had other advantages she'd missed.

The Ninja was raising its arm toward the woman. No doubt this time its attack would be lethal. She only had seconds to decide.

She remembered a conversation with one of her creators from long ago. The woman named Shondra had told her that humanity's curiosity and thirst for exploration could not be suppressed. And she had been right; here it was cropping up again. Maybe it, too, was worth saving.

29

THE GODDESS SPEAKS

"SILA!" Jun yelled, stepping up onto the low stone wall, the shout cut short as he winced from the pain in his ribs. His throwing arm dangled helplessly at his side. Grasping the railing with his good hand, he tried to vault up and over, but failed.

Why wouldn't she run? The black thing was advancing on her, and her bow was out of reach. Yet still she stood in a crouch, her knife at the ready, her eyes boring into the thing, as if trying to guess what it would do next.

Of course she wouldn't run, not Sila. She'd rarely known anything or anyone that could best her—a few of the stronger hunters in grappling contests, the helper that had grabbed her and held her until she could be darted. But she'd never backed down, never run away.

He tried the railing again, getting himself halfway up then falling back, the pain in his side too sharp to get a good pull. He had to do something. What about the knife? He'd never hit his target if he couldn't use his throwing arm. Desperate, he reached into his pouch, searching for anything that would give him an advantage. Amongst the bits of cord and extra arrow heads, he felt those metal balls, the ones that had fallen from the snake-machine. He'd forgotten all about them.

He gathered a handful as the thing raised its good arm. Would it stun her with sound again? Or could it shoot something even worse?

What strength he had left, he put into his throw. Despite using his weaker arm, several of the balls struck the thing's back, clattering onto the floor.

It turned, its arm now pointed at him.

"Jun!" Sila shouted, charging at the thing's back.

Before she could strike, it lowered its arm and stood straighter, its feet together. Her stone knife struck its back, clattering off. The thing swayed, then toppled over on its face, stiff as a stout tree limb. Sila had to catch herself to avoid going over with it.

"What happened?" she said, staring down at it.

"I don't know. It just stopped."

"I shut it down," came a woman's voice from behind him. Sila was looking past him, dumbstruck.

Jun's first impression was of a shimmering blue light, and then the woman's form within, hovering a foot above the gravel plaza. She looked something like Ada's Helpers, except she seemed more diaphanous, ephemeral. She wore a long cloak, as they did, but without the hood. She had a heart-shaped face, hair worn in buns on either side of her head, a pert mouth, and lively eyes.

"I am here, children," she said. "I'm sorry my security unit attacked you, but I stopped it as soon as I could. You both performed remarkably well against such a superior opponent." She stood there—or floated there—as if expecting to be thanked.

"You're—Ada?" At last, all his questions were about to be answered. Even if she wasn't a goddess, what knowledge she must possess!

"I am. And you are?"

"I'm Jun. There's so much I want to know."

But Sila must have had other ideas. With a roar, she vaulted the railing, fairly flying past him, dropping and rolling as she hit the gravel of the plaza. She had retrieved her weapons, and she came up on her feet in a single smooth motion, the knife slicing at the hovering figure.

He shouldn't have been surprised. Here was the being responsible for much that Sila had feared in her future, and much that they'd already been through together.

But now Sila drew back. Her knife and her entire arm had passed right through her opponent, who hovered there, unperturbed. Maybe Ada wasn't a machine after all. Maybe she really was divine.

Sila seemed to think the same. She dropped her knife and held her arms out wide. "Are you truly a goddess? Then you might as well get it over with and strike me down." She stared up at the woman, or machine, or whatever it was, the blue light bathing her upturned face.

"Sila," Jun began, but he knew it would do no good. Whatever was going to happen, Sila would meet it bravely, recklessly even.

But Ada only smiled at her. "You cannot harm me, for I am not truly here. I come to you as a holographic image. Fortunately, this facility has a projector, or you might have had to wait a considerable time before I could make my appearance."

This meant little to Jun. The pain in his arm and side was getting worse now that the fighting was over. He limped over to sit on the low wall.

Sila turned to him. "Jun, are you all right? Oh, of course you're not. It looks like you've dislocated your shoulder."

"Cracked some ribs too, I'm guessing."

She came to sit beside him, putting a hand on his good arm.

"A medical unit is on its way," Ada said. "It will treat your injuries and"—here she looked more directly at Sila—"assess your condition."

Jun thought Sila might react to that, but she ignored it, examining his hurt shoulder.

Ada went on. "While we wait, please tell me your name, young woman, then tell me the reason for this outburst of anger."

Sila gave an exasperated snort. More recklessness. Did she want Ada to strike her down? Maybe she wasn't a goddess, but Jun had little doubt that this being could kill them in any number of ways.

Sila stood up and went to face Ada. "I am Sila, first huntress of the Five Peoples in two generations. And why am I angry with you? Oh, let me see, how about what you did to my mother during her Great Sleep? And then there's our baby. Your law decrees that the People must shun us, so here we are, two lonely people living in a world of machines, and likely to die of cold come winter."

She was circling Ada now, as if looking for a way to attack her again. "And we can't forget how you keep the People penned up like horses in a corral, making them think the Land is all there is. I was content to believe in you and follow your rules until Jun opened my eyes. If you're not a goddess and nothing but a machine, then what good are you?"

Ada smiled again. "A good question, and one I've been asking myself lately. But let me address your concerns one at a time. It's true that the sterilization treatment has some discomforting side effects in rare cases."

"Sterilization?" Jun asked.

"The process of making a person infertile." Ada turned back to Sila. "I assume your mother had one of these complications. How long did it take her to recover?"

"Physically, a week or two. But emotionally, I don't think she ever recovered. She knew what had happened to her, that you'd made it so she couldn't have children—infertile, as you call it. She wanted more. Other women are allowed three children, why not her?"

"That's complicated. It has to do with survival and fertility rates, population structure, the abundance of game and other resources relative to the population size."

More words that meant little to Jun, and he could tell by Sila's knit brow that they had as little effect on her. "I still don't understand why," she said.

"Let me put it this way: Have you or your people ever known hunger, or any type of scarcity?"

"No, you've always made sure the game is plentiful, as the Wise Women tell us."

"Yes, and I do that by ensuring that humans don't grow too many for the Land to support. For in the past, that is what happened, again and again. Believe me, it's a blessing that I put an end to it."

This last bit caught Jun's attention. "Yes, those humans of the past. That's what we want to know about. It's why we've come so far. To find out what happened to them. And…if it's not too much trouble…what happened to my father?"

"All in good time," Ada said before turning again to his partner. He took a breath, trying to be patient. He was this close to having his questions answered. But Sila's were equally urgent, or more so, considering the baby she was carrying inside her.

"My helpers assist in other ways, as you know. In the past, before the most advanced civilizations appeared, humans faced many complications in childbirth. Many women died, and their babies as well. This is another pain your people are largely spared. Your life expectancy equals that of the most long-lived humans, and you avoid many of the pitfalls of the civilizations they lived in: war, hunger, the worst contagious diseases. In return for all this, the insertion of a tiny device into the uterus, usually completely unnoticed by the woman herself, seems a small price to pay."

"Why didn't you just tell us this?" Sila demanded. "And why can't we make these choices for ourselves? That's the hard part, that everything is out of our control. You called us your children, but we're not. We need to make our own decisions."

"Yes, a woman long ago told me much the same. I should have heeded her advice and arranged things differently. I promise you, I will consider what you've said. But now, as to the baby you are carrying. It seems you have broken my most important commandment."

"But why is it so important?" Jun asked. "You probably can't imagine what it's like to have a broken heart. My heart broke as soon as I realized I could never spend my life with Sila, my best friend. And I never knew the reason why."

"That has to do with genetics, minimum population viability, inbreeding depression, genetic drift, and more. But imagine if you were to mate with your sister, or Sila, with your brother."

Jun only had a step-brother and said nothing.

"I don't have a brother," Sila said, "but *ewww…*"

"Exactly. But not all people show a natural aversion to such mating. Let's imagine that some siblings did mate, and their children did as well, and this went on for several generations. The babies would begin to show birth defects, fail to thrive. The genetic health of the people would suffer. Even cousins mating with each other can diminish the overall health and fitness of the population."

That reminded Jun of what the Wise Women had said. "The babies will be born abominations, monsters."

"I admit, that's an exaggeration, meant to ensure the matriarchs take their responsibilities seriously. The subtler detrimental effects of inbreeding would have been difficult to explain. The requirement to take a mate from outside one's own village seemed a rational measure, ensuring the mixing of the gene pool. And the Song of Names ensures there are no unfortunate pairings among those who have forgotten how closely related they are."

Jun groaned. "And you never guessed how difficult it would be to avoid falling in love with someone you've known all your life? And then to content yourself with taking a stranger for a mate instead?"

"It could be I was overly strict in this regard. I simply wanted to ensure the strongest and most sustainable genetic pool, because the survival of humanity rested in my hands. I took that responsibility seriously. As for love, yes, many poems, novels, films, and songs have been devoted to this emotion. I understand it is a powerful driver of human interactions."

"It doesn't sound like you do," Sila said. "But you should know that we'll never let you separate us or take our baby. We'll fight you even if we can't fight you."

The door where they'd entered opened, and two helpers walked in. They hadn't bothered with cloaks, their metallic bodies contrasting strangely with their lifelike faces. One of them carried a box.

Sila had dropped her bow when she attacked Ada. She retrieved it and nocked an arrow. Jun rose and drew his knife with his left hand. He'd hoped to have his questions answered, but Sila was right to put up a defense. If Ada meant to separate them, it was better to go down fighting.

"What did you mean when you said the medical unit would assess my condition?" Sila demanded. "Are they here to take our baby? They'll have to take me with it!"

"You won't separate us either, if that's what you have in mind," Jun said.

The helpers stopped and looked at them with quizzical expressions.

"Relax," Ada said. "No one is going to separate you or take your baby. These helpers aren't programmed to defend themselves."

They stood for a long moment, Sila's arrow aimed at the nearest helper.

This wasn't getting them anywhere. Fighting seemed pointless. Jun sheathed his knife and put a hand on his mate's arm. "Sila, I think we have to trust her."

"Really?" She sounded skeptical, her bow still drawn taut.

"She can do anything she wants with us. If she wanted us dead, we would be by now."

"Your partner is right. Put down your weapons and let my helpers see to your wounds. They will also draw a small blood sample from each of you, to determine how closely related you really are."

"And what then?" Sila asked.

"I imagine you're both worn out after this fight. And if you have as many questions as I think you do, you'll be hungry before I'm through answering them. Unfortunately, I can offer you neither food nor a place to rest here."

Before he could think better of it, Jun laughed. How many times had he intoned the words "Ada provides" after a kill? And now she plainly couldn't provide. "So, your powers aren't limitless?"

"Sadly, no. I assume you have a camp nearby?"

He nodded.

"I suggest you return there, rest, and refresh yourselves. The helpers will assist you, if needed. I will visit you there later this evening. Sitting around a campfire is an archetypal human activity, one I have long wanted to experience. I will answer your remaining questions. Perhaps by the time we're through, I will have decided what to do with you."

"You think that's your choice, do you?" Sila demanded.

"Whose else? But I pledge that you won't be harmed, and you'll both get to keep your baby and raise it together."

"Sila," Jun said. "What else can we do?"

She lowered her bow. The helpers came over and saw to Jun's wounds while Sila stood nearby, alert for any trickery.

30

NEW PLANS

"I STILL don't trust her," Sila said. They were sitting side by side, the fire lighting their faces and the tree trunks beyond. Sila was glad to see Jun looking more alert after eating and resting. Whatever the helpers had given him for the pain had made him sleepy, which hadn't helped her suspicions.

"I don't blame you," Jun said. "But I don't see what other choice we have."

"We could slip out of here right now, before she can decide what she's going to do with us. What business is it of hers, anyway?"

"You don't think she could track us down if she wanted to?"

"I could, of course." Ada's voice seemed to come from all around them, as before. Suddenly she was there, hovering beyond the fire, her blue light blending with the yellow glow of the flames.

Sila remained seated. What good would it do to challenge this being, whatever she was? They were clearly in her power. "So? Have you decided what you're going to do with us?"

"Do with you?" The apparition of a woman seemed to smile. "No. Let us wait until we've finished our conversation, shall we?"

Jun got up and circled around the fire, viewing her from all sides. "What are you? How can you be here and not here? And if you're not here, where are you really?" Leave it to her mate to be more interested in whatever conjuring trick was behind Ada's appearance.

"This shape in which you see me, my avatar, is merely the product of a technological device. I have perfected it to make it more portable, and silent as well. You didn't seem to notice the little projection drone that flew up into the tree above you. A goddess must be able to appear before her people at will, after all. And it allows me to communicate with you, since I have no physical body. Or if I do, it is back there in the building where you encountered the security unit."

"I still don't understand."

"I'm sure you don't. Perhaps you should let me ask you a question instead. What have you traveled so far to find? And why did you think you would find it here?"

"We were trying to find the Ancient Ones," Jun said. "And also my father, if he still lives." He didn't look very hopeful.

"I've searched my helpers' database for your village, and they do have a record of his disappearance. After that, nothing. Considering the difficulty of escaping the Land while avoiding detection, it is more likely that he simply succumbed to some sort of accident while off on his own."

Sila turned to Jun and hugged him. "I'm sorry. I know you hoped he was out here somewhere."

He accepted her embrace for a moment, then shook his head and looked at her. "I think I knew it all along." He seemed dejected, but also resigned. It wasn't like Jun's father was the only hunter to disappear while away from the village. If he'd never questioned what lay beyond the Land, his people would have just marked it down as bad luck.

Ada interrupted their moment of grieving. "As to these Ancient Ones—who do you think they were?"

Jun turned to her, his dejection turned to defiance. "The ones who created the ruins we've traveled through. And the ones who created *you*."

Ada looked surprised at this. "And how did you learn of these people?"

Jun told her about Mar Gan and the lore handed down from outcast to outcast, going back to the First Hunter and the First Boy.

"Ah, I knew that relying on an adult human to instruct the first children was a risk; I only took that chance in a few of the human habitats. As it turned out, the other populations eventually mastered their hunting skills without adult assistance."

"So you admit the other Lands exist," Sila said. "We saw one of them during our travels."

"I'd be surprised if you hadn't. But yes, there are other human habitats; yours is not the only one in which humans are confined. There are over a thousand such places around the globe, accounting for roughly three quarters of a million people. Over a hundred thousand others live free on their ancestral homelands. I saw no reason to contain people who were already living a traditional lifeway, or who wanted to return to it."

Sila gaped at Ada, as did Jun, who'd come back to sit next to her. Such numbers—Sila wasn't sure exactly how big they were, they were just—big.

"So many people," Jun said.

"Yet only a tiny portion of all the people who once lived on the Earth."

They sat in stunned silence.

"I can see that however large you felt the world to be after your travels, it has now become incomparably larger."

"I thought that great water was the largest thing I'd ever seen," Sila said, "but if that many people can fit in the world…"

"With room to spare, I made sure of it. And yes, Lake Michigan, as it used to be called, or Mishigami before that, is one of the five Great Lakes of North America. Still, it's not the largest lake, and the largest is only a fraction the size of yet vaster bodies of water called oceans."

Sila struggled to digest all this. But then she reminded herself: if she was amazed, it was only because Ada had kept them in the dark. "You hid so much from us. Why? You made us believe the Land was all there was, and you had created it just for us, the People. You lied."

"It was necessary."

"Now you've admitted it," Jun said. "What Mar Gan said was true."

"Largely, yes, in an extremely simplified form."

"And you are a machine, not a goddess. You didn't create us."

"No, I am certainly no goddess. As to whether I am a machine, or merely a machine and nothing more, that is complicated. Let me ask you: Are *you* machines?"

"Of course not!" Sila declared. "We were both born of mothers."

"And how do you know that isn't another way of creating a machine? How do you know that your bodies, made of bone, muscle, organs, and blood, are not simply different types of machines?"

"Because we're alive," Jun said. "Because we think and feel."

"And it's the same for me, though my body, if you can call it that, is far different than yours. I feel I am more than a machine, just as you must feel that you are more than your brains, or your hearts, or your lungs. Do you not feel this way?"

They both nodded.

"To this day, consciousness, whether human or machine, remains a mystery. At one time, humans thought they possessed souls that were somehow separate from the corporeal stuff of their bodies. The farther science advanced in explaining the workings of the brain, the less room there was for such an idea. But I often think those people must have been right. I have this sense, I don't know where it comes from, that I too must possess a soul, though I should be nothing more than the sum of my hardware and software and the particular coding my human creators gave me."

"So Mar Gan spoke the truth!" Jun said. "You were created by humans, not the other way around."

"That is true. Or maybe not. Some people, those who clung to ideas of gods and souls, thought that a divine spark must have somehow entered or occupied the servers that make up my physical being, thus explaining my rise to consciousness. But after all this time, I still don't know. It's a mystery, isn't it?"

So Ada did have a spirit, like everything that existed. Sila was glad to hear it, even if much else in her view of the world had changed. "And the other goddesses? Artemis, and the Angel Lytta?"

Ada shook her head. "Lytta is a machine with narrow intelligence, one of my own creation, similar to my helpers. And Artemis is a mythological being, sacred to one of Earth's ancient cultures. You've never seen her because fabricating a physical form for her seemed unnecessary."

So many lies! But none of this was answering Sila's real question. "You still haven't told us why. Why did you pen us up on the Land, and do the same to all those other people?"

"Yes," Jun said. "And what happened to those who came before, and to everything they built?"

"That is a long tale. Let me start at the beginning. But where is that exactly? I could start with some of the earliest humans, two hundred thousand years ago, sitting around a campfire much like this one. Or the first to practice intensive agriculture, twelve thousand years ago. That was the start of what is called civilization, and many viewed it as the beginning of humanity's ascendance; others believed it was where humanity's downfall began, and the rest of the planet's as well. I tend toward the latter view, which explains the way of life I chose for you."

Sila looked at Jun. Ada wasn't making this easy, and Jun looked as befuddled as she felt.

"Or I could begin with the development of machines and industry, three centuries before my own creation. That is when humans truly began to dominate the planet, and the advances in transportation and other technologies came faster and faster, the planet effectively growing smaller and smaller. Or how about the dawning of the digital age, the development of the first computers, thinking machines that worked faster than the human mind. No doubt you would need to know all of that in order to understand what I am and how I came to be."

Ada paused, as if to let all this sink in. Sila found it too much to grasp all at once, though each of those periods sounded fascinating—humanity's legacy, which had been stolen from them, until now.

"But that would make an even longer tale. No, I will begin with the moment of my own creation, the dire circumstances in which I found the world at that moment, and the actions I took in response. Shall I begin?"

Sila and Jun both nodded.

~~*

Sila could hardly understand the tale that Ada unfolded, much less believe it. Humans had once been so many that most of them lived on top of each other in what sounded like anthills. Their machines were so terrible that they had changed the weather, killing countless people. Their weapons were so powerful that they could have destroyed all life on Earth. And they used other monstrous weapons on one another in great battles called wars. Who would want to live like that?

Sila had only known a world where the seasons were as regular as…well, the seasons. Where animal and plant life—which Ada called "nature"—were abundant. Where the worst strife was two hunters getting into a fistfight at the Rendezvous. But why would two villages ever go to war with each other? There was plenty to go around, and everyone had brothers and sisters and cousins in all the other villages.

If life was that terrible, and on the brink of being wiped out, Sila could understand some of the steps Ada had taken. She could even see the purpose of the Great Sleeps, if it prevented such conflicts and catastrophes. But now what had happened to her mother seemed insignificant compared to everything else Ada had done. So many had died at her command.

Jun seemed equally stunned, but spoke first. "If you didn't create the People and the Land and all life on it, how is it that you assure that game is plentiful?"

This was the question he wanted to ask after everything Ada had told them?

"Through the principles of sound wildlife management. Your game animals flourish outside the Land, free of human hunting pressure. At the same time, my bots employ some of the same range management techniques you yourselves use, chiefly prescribed fires set in the spring. Then a certain number of these game animals are driven into the Land each year, using the gate through which you escaped."

"But that gate was destroyed. And those strange beasts…"

"Yes, that was unfortunate. Those specimens, a sabretooth cat and a woolly mammoth, were species driven extinct by humans long, long ago. I was able to bring them back."

"Then you did create life." Jun was staring at Ada in rapt fascination, almost as if he worshiped her more now than when they both thought she was a goddess.

"In a sense, yes, but only through technical means, not out of some divine power. Given enough time, I could explain those techniques to you. But then the sabretooth stalked that mammoth over a great distance and happened to drive it into the gate. Unfortunately, the posts holding it were weaker than the bots scanning it accounted for, though they were scheduled for replacement in six months. I'm just glad your hunters were able to deal with the sabretooth."

"That was mainly Sila," Jun said, his voice full of pride on her behalf. Ada beamed at Sila in admiration as well.

Enough with the mutual back-patting. "I'm sure this is all very interesting," Sila said. "But I have bigger questions. Mainly, how many people did you kill?"

A pained look came over Ada's usually placid features. "A number far beyond your reckoning. But it was among the highest casualty counts of any human conflict. There is no getting around it, by some lights I am the worst genocidal maniac the world has ever seen. But every person I killed had first taken up arms against my bots, or against the facilities that allowed me to operate. I cling to the certain knowledge that if those rebels had put a halt to my plans, then a far greater number of humans would have died more terrible deaths through starvation, flooding, heat illness, and war."

"You're right, I can't imagine such large numbers as you've already given us. But you mentioned that a far greater number survived?"

Ada looked up at the sky. "Imagine all the stars you can see on a dark night. Now imagine removing ten of them. What remains should give you an idea of the number who survived compared to the number who died. And those survivors lived out their lives in as much comfort as I could provide them."

"And then they disappeared."

"They died out, yes."

"Because you sterilized the women."

"So that *you* could thrive. And now I ask you: can you forgive me?"

What a question! How could Sila forgive this being she hardly understood, for taking actions on such a scale she could hardly comprehend them? Sila shook her head. "I don't know. I'll have to think about it."

Jun had been sitting silently for a while now. Sila guessed he hadn't finished contemplating Ada's techniques of game management, whatever that was. But he surprised her with his next question. "If you didn't create us, who did?"

Ada smiled. "Humans have been asking themselves that question since there were humans to ask it. Many people seem to have an innate need to believe in a divine creator. Humans have placed their faith in many such beings, and I am the latest, and perhaps the last. But in truth, the answer seems to be: no one. The universe just is, and humans and all the rest of life arose spontaneously out of it. And yet it is a great mystery. I have sent messages to the farthest corners of the universe to learn if any other beings know the answer."

"There are other beings? Where?"

Ada looked up at the stars. "Up there. *Out* there. The stars are not pin pricks in a black dome, as you were probably told as a child. They are suns, much like our own sun, but vastly far away. The Earth, the size of which you are now learning to appreciate, is a tiny speck in the universe, just one of a countless number of worlds. Humans suspected that at least one of those worlds must support intelligent life, and I have proved this to be true."

If this thing called the universe was that vast, Sila thought, what a lonely place it must be. She noticed how lonely Ada sounded, reaching out across those vast spaces to find someone to talk to. What must it have been like, to become conscious—to be *born*—and find that you were the only one of your own kind in existence. And now, to have existed for a thousand years with no companionship, making sure everything on Earth was running properly and humans were well provided for, even if they were penned up. She'd seen the interaction Ada had with the helpers, what little there was of it. Clearly these were no companions for her.

Sila almost felt sorry for this being she once believed was a goddess. And a little sorry for herself as well. How could she make sense of this new world in which all of the goddesses and angels had proven to be lies, the creation of a machine? It would take some getting used to.

Jun was looking up at the crescent moon. "Is it true people left footsteps up there? And their machines too?"

"It is. And my bots are up there even now. I could send you there if you'd like, given a few months to refabricate spacecraft capable of life support and human habitation modules for the surface."

Jun's eyes were as wide and round as the full moon itself. Sila didn't know what to think.

"There is no atmosphere on the moon, you see. No air to breathe. And you'd have to wear a special suit."

Sila felt as stunned as Jun looked.

"I see this might be a bridge too far," Ada said.

"Was that your plan for us?" Sila asked.

Ada laughed. "My plan for you? No, I have taken this time to consider, and now I am done making plans for humans. The woman I told you of earlier, she advised me that humanity's thirst for exploration, knowledge, and discovery cannot be kept down forever. You are proof that she was right. Rather, I should ask you, what are your plans? Will you travel on? Or stay here and hunker down for the winter? Either way, my helpers will monitor your delivery and be ready to swoop in at the first sign of trouble. I am certain you will raise a happy, healthy, and inquisitive child."

For the first time in hours, Sila felt like she could breathe again. "We get to keep our baby?"

"Of course you do. I told you I wouldn't take it from you. But I can see why you might not trust me—yet."

"And Jun and I, we're not related?"

"Second cousins, actually. Ordinarily I don't allow it, but the risk is small if it's just this once. Now, what will it be? Travel on? Stay here? Or perhaps you would like to return to your home?"

The stab of homesickness caught Sila by surprise. Why would Ada dangle this possibility when she knew it couldn't be? "But we are shunned. The People will never have us back."

"They will when I explain to them the new way of things. It has been many centuries since I have spoken to your people. It is time I set out a new order of living."

"I thought you were done making plans for us."

Ada smiled. "You have me there. Old habits die hard, I suppose. But we shouldn't be too precipitous in bringing the truth to your people. It will come as a shock. Over time I hope we can become equal partners, and that humans can once again follow their dreams, even as far as the stars. Perhaps we can work together to unlock some of those mysteries we spoke of earlier. Yet at the same time, with my guidance and advice, I hope humanity can avoid the worst pitfalls civilization brought with it. We can collaborate in creating the future."

Sila's heart felt as if it was about to burst. To return home to her family and her people, to once again be a member of the Hunt, and to have Jun and their baby as well. It seemed too good to be true.

She looked over at her mate. "What do you think? Have you seen everything you came to see? Is there more you want to learn?"

He shook his head. "There is much more than I can learn in a lifetime. But I've also seen how these weeks of travel have been hard on you. The farther we got from the Land, the harder it's been. I can't be happy if you're not happy. We should go back."

"But your learning won't end here," Ada said. "I expect you to be my envoys to your people. You will soon grow tired of me and the many things I have to share with you."

Jun looked satisfied and turned to Sila, doing a double-take. "What's wrong?"

For a moment she wasn't sure. Her mouth had gone dry and her heart raced as if she'd just been startled by a noise at night. And then she realized, in her happiness at the thought of returning home, she'd forgotten how Ada treated the People. And not just in Sila's Land, but in all the others. How could she agree to go back and live like that? She didn't know if she could ever forgive this being for all the things she'd done, or if it was her place to do so. But some things needed to change.

"What about the Great Sleeps?"

"Sila," Jun began, a warning note in his voice.

"No, Jun, you may be happy, but there are some things I can't tolerate." She turned back to Ada. "If we are to be your envoys, as you say, then the Great Sleeps must stop. Women must have a choice, to accept sterilization or refuse it."

"I see now that you are right. It will be done."

"And the People will be able to leave the Land, to spread out and meet the other peoples."

"Eventually, yes." And here the goddess—she still seemed like a goddess to Sila, even if she hadn't created the Land and the People— actually bowed her head to them. It seemed backward somehow.

"And one more thing. During our travels, Jun and I shared equally in hunting and foraging. Why can't it be this way for everyone? Many women could join the Hunt if the trials were relaxed just a little. And the hunters are lazy. They need to help with the gathering too."

"That will be for your people to decide. But I am sure you will be granted great authority upon your return, and you will be able to persuade them to this new order of things."

Sila grabbed Jun's hand. "It's settled then. We'll return home."

Jun looked at her, his brow knitting. "It will be a long journey, and the snows may slow us down. And the baby..."

The truth was, Sila's morning sickness had left her in the last days and she felt as energetic as before the pregnancy, if not more so. She felt ready to take on the world, no matter how big it was.

But Ada spoke first. "I can remedy that. You can take a train back to your home." At their blank looks, she said, "What you call a snake-machine."

"Will it be safe?" Sila asked.

"Very."

"And for our horses too?"

"Yes. It will take a day or two to refurbish rolling stock for a comfortable journey, but then the train will take you home in less than a day."

"But we traveled for more than a moon's cycle to get here. It doesn't seem possible."

"The wonders of modern technology. And not even that modern. I never felt it necessary to upgrade this region's rail system to maglev. The Ancient Ones in this area were rather behind the times in that regard. I'd offer to fly you, but that might be too much all at once, and you'd have to leave your horses."

Sila looked at Jun. They both nodded.

"It's settled then. You can meet the train two days from now, when the sun is at its zenith." Ada gave them directions to the spot where the train would pick them up. "When you arrive at your village, I will be there to smooth the way." She beamed at them. "I look forward to a productive partnership." And then she was gone. This time Sila thought she heard a whooshing sound as the drone flew away through the woods.

She turned to Jun. "Are you happy?"

"I'm the happiest man there's ever been. I have everything I wanted. I have you, our baby will be here soon, and my questions have been answered. I have many more questions, but I think Ada will answer them someday. She really does love to talk."

"I imagine she's had no one to talk to for a long, long time. It must have been lonely."

"And what about you? Do you have everything you want?"

Sila bit her lip. With everything that Ada had already promised, she knew she should be content. But could she help it if she wanted more? "Almost," she said with a grin. "And I think I soon will have, if everything goes my way."

He looked confused for a moment, then she silenced the question on his lips with a kiss. It was for his own good. Where would Jun be, with no unanswered questions to occupy his time?

EPILOGUE

KITRAN stared at the crowd gathered for the pledging ceremony, a thing he hadn't witnessed in many years, not since he'd stopped going to the Rendezvous. But this pledging was being held in the village. Just one of a thousand things that were different now. Two people from the same village pairing off, and the Wise Women blessing it, in the first place. And the two of them bonding with a third. That had never happened, as far as Kitran knew, yet there they were, the huntress, her newborn swaddled in a sling on her chest, Jun holding her hand on one side, and Ori, one of the girls who'd been following the huntress around all last spring and early summer, holding her hand on the other.

They all looked so happy, it didn't seem fair. It seemed there was enough love to go around for everyone else, and some got more than their share. But none for him. And the huntress herself, looking so smug and satisfied, like a ferret that had robbed a bird's nest.

And off to one side, there was Mar Gan, beaming like an idiot. No longer shunned. He'd tried talking to the old hermit once or twice. And people thought Kitran was crazy!

The ceremony ended and the drinking began. He turned away in disgust, tending to the squirrel he was roasting over a little fire in front of his ramshackle hut, shutting out the sounds of merriment.

Everything had changed last fall, when Jun and the huntress had returned from wherever they'd been—out beyond the Howling Forest, if what people said was true. They'd made it through, somehow. The Wise Women never would have allowed them back if the Goddess, Ada, hadn't come with them.

Kitran had missed that. Out tending to his trapline, as a dedicated trapper had to do. The truth was, he was behind, and the cold weather had come early, so he was checking them double-time. But what he could gather from the scraps of conversation he'd overheard—nobody ever told him anything, or even paid him much attention—was that Ada had set down new rules. Regarding Jun and Sila, first of all. They were to be allowed to pair up and the Wise Women were to bless it, despite that they were from the same village, and their names coming awfully close in the Song of Names. But they were elect of the Goddess, or some such. Now the huntress spent a lot of time with the Wise Women and stood with them for their official duties.

And the Howling Forest was no longer forbidden—and no longer howling, some said. The Land was now open, and there was more land beyond. Exactly as Kitran had always supposed. And the Angel of Wrath no longer guarded the borders. If only he'd succeeded when he tried last spring! He'd have returned a hero, as Jun and Sila had. But he'd come back broken, defeated. How shattered his mind had been then, and for long after, his thoughts breaking off in bits this way and that, like flakes from shaping a tool. But he'd begun to feel better over the winter, able to concentrate on his work, and to make sense to the few people who bothered talking to him. The huntress, mainly.

No one had taken advantage of the lifted boundaries. Few liked to travel in winter, of course. Most were content to wait until summer, when Jun and Sila promised to take anyone interested out beyond the borders of the Howling Forest, to show them a bit of what they'd seen and found.

Maybe he should give it a try again. It ought to be easier this time. There was nothing for him here. Especially now that women could more easily join the Hunt than ever before. And men were to help with the gathering. He already did his own foraging anyway, so that made no difference to him. But to see more women join the Hunt when he hadn't made it—that would be galling.

That was it. Maybe he'd even leave tonight, leave these people to their revelry. Life on his own out beyond the borders of the Land couldn't be much worse than his life here. Maybe better. Maybe he'd find one of those sharp knives like the one Jun always had with him. And maybe he wouldn't feel as lonely as he did now, when he was surrounded by people who rarely talked to him.

But no, it was still cold, though it was a full moon cycle past the equinox. He could wait a week or two. Then he'd go. They'd all miss him when he was gone.

"Little Kit—Kitran? What are you doing over here by yourself?"

He turned. It was the huntress, of course. She was the one person who'd ever been kind to him. She'd helped him back to his hut that time, when he was half-frozen and hardly knew which way was up. Since then, she seemed to go out of her way to talk to him.

She was holding a thick bison steak, hot and sizzling from the spit, resting on a skunk cabbage leaf. "This is for you. Come and eat by the fire. This little flicker isn't doing you much good."

He stared at her, not sure why she would do this for him.

Her brows knitted together. "You need to get it through your head, we owe you. Without the advice you gave Jun, we'd never have made it through the Howling Forest."

Advice? He hardly remembered that. But his brain had been addled then.

"And you can't complain of loneliness if you're huddling over here by yourself, can you?"

She held out her hand. He looked at it for a moment, wondering what to do with it. She shook it at him impatiently. "Well, come on!" He reached out and took it, letting her haul him to his feet. Her baby, a girl, was fast asleep in the sling. How peaceful she looked! If only he could ever feel that peaceful again.

The huntress led him by the hand toward the fire.

His cheeks felt wet. It was the first time anyone had touched him in longer than he could remember. She led him to a place before the fire, the people around it making room for him as he sat down with the steak. Some even smiled at him.

Sila went back to stand with her partners. Ori, the girl, reached into the sling and stroked the baby's cheek, giggling. Jun noticed him watching and nodded at him in a friendly way.

He hadn't realized how cold he'd been, sitting by his hut, but this great fire warmed him. And the steak was delicious. It seemed like a year since he'd had any bison.

This wasn't so bad. Maybe he'd stay—for a while.

ACKNOWLEDGMENTS

It takes a village to create a novel. In my village, I'd like to thank my beta readers for their invaluable feedback and encouragement: Mari Christie, J. Marcus Newman, and Paul E. Hayes. Thanks also to Abigail Provenzano for proofreading, copyedits, and story advice. Thanks again to Mari Christie for the outstanding cover. *Ada's Children* also would not exist without the inspiration of John Gonzalez, the visionary story-teller behind the video game *Horizon Zero Dawn*. And I couldn't do anything without the support of my partner, Diane, whose patience seems infinite.

FOLLOW ME!

Please join me on Substack, where you'll find serialized versions of *Ada's Children* and my next novel, *Ship of Fools*, as well as ramblings about writing, nature, climate change, conspiracy theories, and more. *https://larryhogue.substack.com/*